KU-411-728

WILD HUNT

BY
LORI DEVOTI

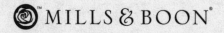
MILLS & BOON

DID YOU PURCHASE THIS BOOK WITHOUT A COVER?

If you did, you should be aware it is **stolen property** as it was reported *unsold and destroyed* by a retailer. Neither the author nor the publisher has received any payment for this book.

All the characters in this book have no existence outside the imagination of the author, and have no relation whatsoever to anyone bearing the same name or names. They are not even distantly inspired by any individual known or unknown to the author, and all the incidents are pure invention.

All Rights Reserved including the right of reproduction in whole or in part in any form. This edition is published by arrangement with Harlequin Enterprises II B.V./S.à.r.l. The text of this publication or any part thereof may not be reproduced or transmitted in any form or by any means, electronic or mechanical, including photocopying, recording, storage in an information retrieval system, or otherwise, without the written permission of the publisher.

This book is sold subject to the condition that it shall not, by way of trade or otherwise, be lent, resold, hired out or otherwise circulated without the prior consent of the publisher in any form of binding or cover other than that in which it is published and without a similar condition including this condition being imposed on the subsequent purchaser.

® and ™ are trademarks owned and used by the trademark owner and/or its licensee. Trademarks marked with ® are registered with the United Kingdom Patent Office and/or the Office for Harmonisation in the Internal Market and in other countries.

First published in Great Britain 2010
Harlequin Mills & Boon Limited,
Eton House, 18-24 Paradise Road, Richmond, Surrey TW9 1SR

© Lori Devoti 2008

ISBN: 978 0 263 88202 5

46-0210

Harlequin Mills & Boon policy is to use papers that are natural, renewable and recyclable products and made from wood grown in sustainable forests. The logging and manufacturing processes conform to the legal environmental regulations of the country of origin.

Printed and bound in Spain
by Litografia Rosés S.A., Barcelona

Lori Devoti grew up in southern Missouri and attended college at the University of Missouri-Columbia, where she earned a bachelor of journalism. However, she made it clear to anyone who asked that she was not a writer; she worked for the dark side – advertising. Now, twenty years later, she's proud to declare herself a writer, and visits her own dark side by writing paranormals for Mills & Boon® Intrigue Nocturne™.

Lori lives in Wisconsin with her husband, daughter, son, an extremely patient shepherd mix and the world's pushiest Siberian husky. To learn more about what Lori is working on now, visit her website at www.loridevoti. com.

SCOTTISH BORDERS LIBRARY SERVICES	
007827674	
Bertrams	20/01/2010
	£3.19

To my husband for introducing me to the books of Isaac Asimov, going along with me when I said, "Let's move to Montana," and, far from least…for telling me, "You should write a book." Twenty-one years and I'd do it all over again in a heartbeat.

And as always, special thanks to Tara Gavin,
Sean Mackiewicz and Holly Root.
You are truly the best!

SCOTTISH BORDERS COUNCIL

LIBRARY &

INFORMATION SERVICES

Prologue

"**W**here is she?" Jora Brynhild, leader of the Valkyries, strode through the halls of Valhalla, her feathered cape slapping against her legs.

"She was in her room—"

Jora pushed past the Valkyrie who'd been charged with keeping an eye on Jora's sister—to stop her from doing something foolhardy. Rune stones covered the small bedside table. A note lay propped against a pillow.

A fist gripping her heart, Jora snatched up the piece of vellum and turned so the light was to her back, illuminating her sister's ornate script.

I love the Valkyries, but I love my daughters more.
The ErlKing is coming.
Halda

Jora crushed the letter in her hand. Her sister was the first half-Norn Valkyrie. With the Norn talent for seeing the future, Halda had become a key tool in the Valkyries' battle against the ErlKing.

Halda's note left no doubt in Jora's mind that the Erl-King was on his way to take what Halda, what all the Valkyries, valued more than anything—Geysa and Runa, Jora's nieces.

"Gather the others. We fly immediately."

Halda's guard hurried from the room. Jora listened to her yells, to the sounds of weapons being grabbed and horses readied. She started to follow, but paused to calm her racing heart and regain the iron control the Valkyries expected of her.

She wouldn't let her sister sacrifice herself. If the ErlKing was targeting Geysa and Runa, she would stop the otherworldly hunter from getting his prey—somehow. It was her job. She was leader of the Valkyries.

She closed her eyes and fought a wave of doubt. Had the choices she made so far been the right ones? It had been her responsibility to stop the ErlKing and his pack of vile hell-hounds from stealing the spirits of the dead, spirits meant for Valhalla. And, with Halda's help, the Valkyries had been able to cut off most of his efforts, known where the ErlKing would appear early enough to get there first. But their success had come at a cost. Halda'd had a vision days earlier, this one showing the ErlKing—not stealing spirits but Halda herself.

Jora had sought to save her sister by confining her, but she hadn't thought to call back her nieces from their visit with their Norn relatives.

And now it appeared Halda'd had a second vision. Halda's daughters were the hunt's new targets.

Jora stared down at the crushed paper in her hand. If anything happened to the girls, or her sister, it would be her fault.

She had to stop him.

The wind howled around Halda, whipping hair across her face. She shoved it from her eyes, ignored the pinpricks of pain where it had snapped against her cold skin.

The smell of damp leaves and dirt engulfed her. The woods. The human woods. She'd never been here. The Valkyries didn't venture into the human world with the regularity of the Norns, and Halda's mother hadn't allowed her to visit her Norn relatives.

How Halda wished she'd placed the same restrictions on her daughters.

With stiff fingers she tugged at the leather ties of her feathered cloak, let the cape fall to the ground. She wouldn't need it any longer. She'd leave it for Jora to find, for her eldest daughter to inherit. After a second's thought, she tugged at the chain around her neck, felt the metal give. She pressed a kiss to the tiny charm attached there, then placed chain and charm gently atop the cloak. Rising back to a stand, she glanced around.

It was dark, like always when the hunt arrived. The ErlKing was here, hunting her children. She'd stop him— from that. The runes had told the tale. He would lose what was most precious to him.

An equal exchange for what the Valkyries would lose tonight.

No choice, no escape.

Halda pulled free the blade she'd stored in her boot, wrapped her fingers around the hide-covered handle and closed her eyes. She would turn the hunt back to her, then use the weapon.

The ErlKing's pack wouldn't survive this night.

But then, neither would she.

Chapter 1

The peal of a horn pierced into Venge Leidolf—stopping the breath he was about to take, freezing every movement but the beat of his heart. He felt himself being swept away, his human body still standing in the human world, but his hellhound spirit traveling…following the horn's call.

He landed somewhere dark. A biting wind howled around him and shoved against his fur. He padded forward. The scent of prey, sweat and blood filled him—a heady potion that urged him to run again, faster, until his feet left the ground and he flew through the clouds. Other hounds pressed against him, all hungry and driven to find whoever or whatever left the irresistible trail of adrenaline and fear they followed.

The noise stopped and the vision faded with it…releasing Venge. His gaze darted around the human-made street, searching for whomever…whatever manned the instrument, but the streets were empty. Venge pulled in a breath and waited. Waited for the call to sound again…for the intoxicating mix of pleasure and pain to wrap around him, twist through his very soul. Waited because he had nothing else to do, nowhere else to go.

When it came, he was ready. This time the call was softer—less demand, more offer, a promise. Venge's heart beat faster; his nostrils flared. *Come, run, hunt, be free…* the horn whispered. The call licked at Venge, stoked his desire to give in, to follow. And with nothing to hold him, no reason to care whether he lived or died…he didn't resist; he shimmered.

Venge shook his head as the last few tingles of his shimmer faded. His muscles tensed and he tried to pinpoint where the peal of the horn had led him.

It was daylight. The sun beat against the back of his neck, but the air was cool, crisp and clean. Not that different from the air in the land of the elves where he'd spent the last few months.

Rocks rolled under his feet and he glanced down, realizing he was standing in the middle of a gravel road. Flanking both sides of the rough street were dilapidated, weathered buildings. Many of them barely managing to stay upright. Beyond the street and buildings stood a never-ending forest of tall pines.

He breathed in deeply, let his lungs fill with the scent of the evergreens. The invigorating mountain air lured him, causing him to take another breath. He'd never been this close to the wild. His early life was spent locked in a cage, or contained some other way. And since his escape, he'd been too busy searching for a way to increase his strength, traveling the nine worlds looking for a tool or training that would enable him to defeat his father.

The sound of water flowing over a streambed drew his attention away from his thoughts. He turned, planning on finding the source, but another sound interrupted his action.

The doors to one of the buildings he'd assumed were abandoned flew open and three men—hellhounds, he knew instinctively—tumbled out onto the dirt. Country music and yelling voices spilled after them.

His gaze shot to the front windows. Grime covered them so completely that any movement or sign of life within was blocked. As he watched, someone rubbed a hand over the grungy surface and peered out at the men still rolling around in the street.

His curiosity piqued, he took a step toward the building. The other hellhounds, caught up in their struggle, surged backward, knocking against Venge. One of them, a younger male with a clipped beard and an earring, grabbed Venge by the front of his shirt.

"Might as well head back home. There's already about ten too many for the hunt." The other hellhound tightened his grip on Venge's shirt and waited for a response.

Venge didn't bother to supply one.

Apparently taking Venge's silence as weakness, the other male's lips slid over his teeth, forming a grin. Shooting a sideways glance at his companions, he pulled his head back then jerked forward until his forehead collided with Venge's skull.

The crack of bone on bone echoed down the street.

A move hard to ignore—even for Venge.

Venge's lip worked upward into a snarl. He mimicked his attacker's posture by curling his fingers into the other male's shirt and pulling him closer—until Venge could smell the stale stench of beer on the hellhound's breath and see the tiny red lines that zigzagged across the whites of his eyes.

"Why don't I help you out by eliminating a few? But who?" Venge gave the insolent male a tiny shake as he glanced around. Looking back at the hellhound in his grip, he continued. "Oh, I know. I think I'll start with you." His eyes narrowing, Venge jerked the male toward him, letting his skull again whack against Venge's, but this time his opponent fell backward, only Venge's grip on his shirt keeping him from crumpling onto the dust.

Venge held him upright for another few seconds, long enough to murmur against his ear, "If you're going to take on an opponent, it's best to know you can beat them. They might just kill you otherwise. Or—" he glanced around "—discard you in the dirt, just for the fun of seeing you squirm." With that, he let the hellhound slip from his hands, until he was facedown on the gravel road. Without a backward glance, he stepped over his body and left the male to face whatever fate awaited him.

The other hellhounds let Venge pass, their muscles taut and their eyes assessing. He'd passed a test—not a planned one, but one if there were other hellhounds around he'd have to pass again and again. He'd grown up in the kennels. He knew better than most how to fight to survive. You either proved your dominance or got crushed into the dirt.

Only one hound had ever been successful in making Venge eat dirt—and it wouldn't happen again. Not while there was a breath left in Venge's body.

His eyes focused on the building in front of him, he strode forward.

The familiar smell of decades of alcohol spilled onto battered wood and the sound of bottles sliding across tabletops as patrons turned to size up the newest intruder assaulted Venge as he entered. He let their glances flow over him, his eyes returning their stares until, one by one, they dropped their own back to their drinks.

Bar patrons, he was as used to dealing with them as he was with handling his own rage. But…his gaze slid over the tables. These patrons were different. The normal scent of sadness and desperation was missing. Instead the place teemed with aggression, eagerness for something. For what the horn had promised, he guessed. And, even more unusual, the bar was filled with hellhounds.

Despite his best efforts to avoid such an event, Venge found himself surrounded by his own kind.

His brows lowering as he tried to figure out what all this meant, he strode to the bar. A woman possessing hair streaked with silver and a steely gaze stood behind it.

"You new?" she asked.

Not bothering to answer, Venge crossed his arms over his chest and studied her. One brow cocked, she met his scrutiny with a stare of her own.

"You drinking?" she added.

Not being able to peg the female unsettled Venge. He'd traveled to four of the nine worlds in the last five years and had come to know most of the inhabitants on sight. But this woman… He frowned. Despite the fact that she was behind the bar, a place he had come to associate with garm, she lacked the edge of wildness and scent of pine all garm possessed, and despite the fact the place was filled with hellhounds, she wasn't one of his kind, either. So, what was she? What other type of being would choose to serve a bar filled with hellhounds?

"If you're new, you'll need a place to stay. Best talk to Geysa." She jerked her head toward a door in the back.

"She's in the kitchen now, but she'll be out." With that, she turned her back on him and strode to the other end of the bar where the hellhounds he'd seen fighting outside had gathered.

A place to stay? Venge twisted his mouth to the side. He still didn't know why he was here—or even where *here* was. It was like some strange dream. Somehow he'd fallen down the rabbit hole and found himself in a twisted version of the human world's Old West. He wouldn't be shocked if the door the bartender had indicated flew open and the sheriff, six-guns blazing, barreled inside.

Instead the door edged open, then bumped wider as another woman carrying a tray laden with plates pushed against it with a curvaceous, denim-clad hip.

As he looked at her, Venge became aware of the earth spinning on its axis, but slowly. Every movement the woman made seemed emphasized, slowed down, just for his enjoyment. She tossed her head, flipping her waist-long hair out of her eyes and away from the steaming plates. A few stubborn strands of the flame-colored locks refused to move, instead choosing to cling to her lips. She frowned and pushed her tongue out of her mouth, trying to shove the recalcitrant strands away, but it was a wasted effort. The strands hung there, somehow drawing attention to the perfect bow of her upper lip and the impossible fullness of her lower.

With a sigh, she muttered something to herself and began maneuvering her way through the tables. Hellhound after hellhound stopped what he was doing and followed her with his gaze.

A surge in adrenaline and desire hit Venge like a boulder to the gut. She was almost next to him before he realized both were coming from him.

She brushed by him, barely giving him a glance, but he

caught her scent—honey and spring. He inhaled, felt his nostrils flare, his eyes dilate.

He'd never wanted anyone or anything as badly as he wanted this woman. His feet shuffled forward, following her without his mind giving the movement a conscious thought. As he did, a hellhound at a nearby table surged to his feet, then another until all but a few were knocking over chairs and tables in an attempt to follow the red-haired siren.

"Geysa!" the woman from behind the bar yelled.

Geysa paused, her gray eyes flickering as she watched the males shove their way toward her. Her lips rounded into a perfect O, and the world picked up speed. The demanding desire Venge had felt just seconds earlier disappeared. He stumbled to a halt, a frown creasing his forehead as he blinked at the waitress. Still attractive, with red hair that danced around her oval face, full mouth and a body that even clothed in loose jeans and a worn T-shirt left no doubt of her gender. But that was all—just another attractive female. Not the irresistible, have-to-have object of desire she had been seconds earlier.

Her gaze wandered the crowd again, worry causing tiny lines to form at the edges of her mouth. When she reached Venge, she stopped. He could see her inhale sharply, her eyes bright, as if waiting for some response.

His frown deepened. He'd been trapped, almost unable to think of anything but this woman, and now nothing…at least nothing he couldn't control. He purposely let his gaze roam her body, let her see him do it—just to show how unaffected he was.

To his surprise, instead of insulted, she looked relieved, at least until she disappeared from sight, a group of hellhounds knocking her over as they continued to brawl around her.

Without stopping to wonder at his actions, Venge leaped over the table that had fallen in front of him and kicked the top two hellhounds off the pile of bodies and onto the floor. He was struggling with a third, a male with the flat face of a boxer, when the sound of an arrow piercing the air sang overhead. Heat singed the side of his face. He shoved the boxer out of his way, wrapped his hand around Geysa's arm and jerked them both away from the fray.

Sticking out of the nearest tabletop was a flaming arrow. Venge spun the waitress away and toward the door.

The bartender dropped a bow, then, holding a four-foot-long sword, leaped onto the bar top. With an angry whack, she slammed the weapon into the bar, then stood there, her hand resting on the hilt.

"Let her go," she demanded.

It took Venge to the count of three to realize the bartender was speaking to him. He glanced to where his fingers pressed against the ivory skin of Geysa's arm. He had no reason to hold the waitress, hadn't pulled her from the other hellhounds with that intention, but for some reason, no matter that his brain said to release her, his fingers were unable to comply.

"I said—" The bartender's voice took on a new edge, like the shriek of an angry hawk.

"Yeah, she said to let her go." The boxer scuttled to his feet and, chest pushed out, sauntered toward Venge. "She's mine."

Venge tilted his head to look at Geysa. "Really?" he asked.

A huff of air escaped her lips and she met his look, but her expression revealed none of her inner thoughts.

Irritation flickered to life inside him. If she wanted the flat-faced cur, he should hand her over, leave her to her fate.

His eyes narrowed; he stared at her. Was she so naive to think she could survive an encounter with the other hound?

She was tall for a woman, with impressive muscle tone, if the bicep he gripped was any indicator, but there was no way she'd be able to survive an assault by a hellhound riled to bloodlust. And the flat-faced boxer was close to such a state—Venge could smell it on him.

Venge's lips thinned, his index finger sweeping softly over the arm he held just to reassure himself he still had control.

At his small movement, Geysa tensed.

So, she wasn't as oblivious to what was happening as she would have him think. He smiled, then cocked his head toward the other male.

"I don't think so." Then, still smiling, he shoved his body in front of Geysa and grabbed the boxer around the throat. His fingers digging into the other male's skin, Venge pushed him backward until the male was pressed next to the still crackling arrow. The smell of singed hair followed.

"Heard the phrase 'finders keepers'?" he asked.

Chapter 2

The boxer stared back at Venge, his eyes bulging and filled with hate. Venge squeezed his hand a little tighter around the other male's neck. The boxer's eyes flashed red—the first sign he was on the cusp of shifting to his canine form—and he managed a snarl.

Venge snarled back.

"Enough." Geysa jerked the arrow out of the tabletop and snapped it between her hands, extinguishing the flame in the same move. "In case neither of you noticed, I'm not interested."

The other hellhound was seconds from changing. Venge could feel the shift coming; aggression rolled off him like smoke off a dampened fire. For Venge to drop his guard now would mean death for someone. He had survived too much to die in a bar brawl over an unappreciative female.

Ignoring Geysa, he concentrated on letting his own

humanity slip—not past his control, but enough the boxer would realize Venge wasn't averse to playing the game, no matter where it took them.

"I said, enough."

The sharp point of the arrow pricked Venge's neck. Geysa stood to his side, her feet wide, her eyes intent. "I'll kill you if I have to."

Unable to believe what she was doing, Venge froze.

"I mean it," she added, pushing the metal tip firmly against his neck.

The boxer's head jerked to the side, surprise jolting him out of his rage.

With a murmured curse, Venge twisted, flinging the boxer to the side, then momentarily free of one threat, he turned on the other. His arm wrapped around Geysa's waist and jerked her body against his.

Staring into her rounded eyes, he replied, "You better."

It took a second, but she recovered to press the arrow against the vein in his throat until he could smell the musty scent of his own blood.

His lips twisted into a humorless smile. "How long have you been waiting on hellhounds? *How* have you survived?"

Her jaw clenched, but she made no reply.

"Like this." The edge of a much longer blade slid against the side of his neck, opening his skin. The pain was dull, almost imperceptible in Venge's adrenaline-ridden state, but again he didn't have to see the blade to know his blood now stained its length. The woman from behind the bar spoke from behind him. "I've heard hellhounds are hard to kill, but I'm thinking even a forandre would have a hard time reattaching his head."

Venge waited, stared down at Geysa, tried to get a whiff of her emotion or some sense that she realized how much danger she had put herself in. She glared back at him, but not with fear—more annoyance, like he was nothing more than a passing irritation.

With a growl, he pulled her tighter.

The blade at his neck jerked, a sharp rap against his opened skin. This time he felt it. A muscle in his jaw twitched.

His captive arched a brow. She was mocking him; he could feel that, too.

"I said—" the woman behind him began, but Venge didn't give her a chance to continue. With a frustrated curse, he shoved the waitress away from him and strode from the bar.

Jora Brynhild, leader of the Valkyries and Geysa's aunt, slammed her fist onto the bar top. "What were you doing?"

Geysa dropped the beer mug and metal plate into the sink and turned to clear another table. Jora's fingers wrapping around Geysa's bicep, in the same place the hellhound had grabbed her earlier, stopped her. Geysa's lips thinned. She turned on her aunt and let the sweet demeanor she'd been forced to portray for the past few days fall away. "I'm tired of playing the helpless barmaid to these…" Unable to come up with anything more insulting than what they were, she jerked her arm free of her aunt's hold and continued. "Hellhounds. Why is it necessary?"

Jora sighed, but her expression remained tense. "It's an honor being trusted with this mission. I didn't have to choose you *or* your sister, but I did because I know what the hunt and its hounds have taken from you." The fingers of her aunt's free hand found the two tiny gold shields that hung from Geysa's throat.

"I knew you would work harder than anyone to find the

horn." She dropped the charms and loosened her hold on Geysa's arm, the touch as close to a caress as Geysa had ever received from the older Valkyrie. "Don't prove me wrong."

Geysa bit her lip to keep her frustration from showing. "I won't. You know that, but why can't I just be myself? Runa isn't playing a role."

"Your sister isn't a Valkyrie, either. We need the hell-hounds to trust us—at least some of us. Until we find the horn, you have to be less Valkyrie and more Norn."

Geysa huffed out a disbelieving breath. More Norn? The statement itself was ludicrous. The Norn were the keepers of the fates, delivering a destiny to a child at birth. Geysa and Runa shared a mother, the only half-Norn, half-Valkyrie to ever exist, but that was it. Runa was all Norn, from her fortune-telling to her *comme ci, comme ça* out-look—and Geysa…wasn't. Wasn't Norn or much of a Valkyrie, either, for that matter. She'd never shown much skill in either arena…she just was.

She glanced at her aunt. Jora wanted the horn found more than anyone, except Geysa and her sister, and Geysa didn't want to disappoint her, not when she was finally showing a little faith in Geysa. Trusting her with something of importance.

Plus, while she might not like her aunt's plan, it was the smart one. As much as Geysa would like to use the dagger she kept tucked in her boot to chop off the next hand that wandered across her ass, she knew it would only slow their quest.

The horn was here and someone was using it—the con-tinued arrival of new hellhounds told them that. Unfortu-nately, only the hounds could hear its call, making the Valkyries all the more dependent on the bloodthirsty beasts to locate the missing relic.

She shook her head to remove the disturbing thoughts and asked, "Where is Runa?"

Her aunt dropped her hand from Geysa's bicep, but her gray eyes, so like Geysa's, remained assessing. "At the bath-house. She wanted the night off to read fortunes. She thought maybe if she could read the fates of a few hellhounds, she could locate the ones destined to run in the hunt."

Geysa's chin snapped upward. "She thinks the hunt will return?"

Jora frowned. "She hasn't said that, but…yes, I get that feeling."

Geysa swallowed the bile that surged into her throat. The Norn were secretive, even with everything that was at stake. Telling fortunes was one thing; Runa never revealed more than possibilities, and vague ones at that. On a person-by-person basis, Geysa wasn't even sure if Runa *could* detect more—but on a grand scale? Something as big as the return of the ErlKing and the Wild Hunt? Surely the Norn could sense that. Something twisted deep in Geysa's stomach.

"Geysa." Her aunt's voice pulled her back from her reverie. "Are you with me?"

Her teeth sinking into her lower lip, Geysa nodded.

Relief flickered through Jora's eyes. "Good. I was think-ing. We haven't made much progress. I think it's time we change tactics—be direct."

"Direct?" Suddenly exhausted, Geysa leaned against the sink.

Her aunt didn't seem to notice. "Instead of just working here, trying to listen in for leads, we need to target one or two hellhounds more closely, build their trust and use them to ferret out the horn."

Suspicion lowered Geysa's brows. "One or two?"

Jora nodded. "Runa will find the hellhounds most likely to be involved in the hunt, and you'll befriend them."

A harsh laugh exploded from Geysa's mouth. "The hounds I've met aren't looking for a friend." Her mind flicked back to her encounter earlier with the red-haired hellhound. She'd messed up, forgotten to shield herself. Valkyries were created to attract men fallen in battle, to make their transition from warrior to resident of Valhalla a smooth one. It was something they did with finesse, but it wasn't until the Valkyries arrived in this deserted human town that they had learned how their presence affected hellhounds.

The Valkyries were forced to keep themselves shielded at all times or risk a scene like the one that had occurred earlier—hellhounds filled with lust brawling and unable to control their basest of urges.

Just another example hellhounds were little more than the beasts she'd heard tales of since childhood.

"You can handle them. Just keep your shields up from now on." Delivering Geysa a piercing look, Jora grabbed a rag out of the sink and turned back to the bar.

Suppressing her remaining thoughts on the topic, Geysa returned to the dining area and shoved the dishes from the last table onto a battered tray. After dumping them into the sink, she headed to the door.

Her aunt's voice stopped her before she could turn the knob. "Did you get a chance to talk to the one who arrived today?"

Geysa paused next to the cracked glass windows that made up the front of the bar. With her bare hand, she rubbed away a large circle of grime and peered into the dark streets. The red-haired hellhound. What was his story? There was something different about him. Most of the hellhounds arrived demanding information on the hunt, bragging that they were sure to be chosen by the ErlKing, challenging anyone and everyone to secure a space for themselves in the hunt. But this new male—

"Geysa?" Her aunt startled Geysa from her thoughts again. Geysa pressed a hand to her brow. She must be tired; she'd certainly never had a problem with her thoughts wandering so badly before.

Without turning, she replied, "No, why?"

"There's something about him…a wildness…" Jora let her words trail away. "I think I'll ask Runa to start with him. Tomorrow, find him and get him to the bathhouse for a reading. If my senses are right, he may be the key we've been hoping for."

Geysa twisted her lips to the side. Jora was Geysa's mother's half sister. She hadn't a drop of Norn blood nor their fortune-telling ability. But Geysa suspected her Valkyrie aunt was right. The new arrival held himself differently, straighter, as if he possessed a hard determination the others didn't.

Something deep inside Geysa told her his arrival signaled a change.

But a change in or against their favor?

It was growing dark and the temperature was dropping faster than the sun. In the deepening shadows, leaning against the log wall of what appeared to be a deserted blacksmith shop or perhaps a stable, Venge pondered why he was still here.

Originally, the peal of the horn had lured him, without his conscious mind even entering into the decision. But now? He could leave, or thought he could. He hadn't noticed any feeling that he was trapped in this place. Of course, if he did leave, the horn might just call him back—but he'd be prepared next time, perhaps that would be enough to resist.

So, why didn't he try? He tilted his head against the rough wood. Curiosity? That certainly played a role. Someone had a horn with the power to lure hellhounds to this place, and a large congregation of his kind had already answered. Would more? Would his father?

Venge was stronger now, but was he strong enough to take down his father if he did show? Especially if he appeared with his witch wife?

Venge would have liked to think so, but he doubted it. He stared into the darkness, the old anger bubbling inside him.

He wasn't ready, so why stay? Better to stick with his plans—search out and defeat every despicable creature the nine worlds had to offer, collect every tool and bit of knowledge he could use to his advantage until he knew his father would prove no threat.

His last trip had been profitable—others might be more so.

Remembering his latest prize, Venge unhooked the burlap sack he'd knotted onto his belt earlier, and slipped his hand inside. His fingers curled along the bottom of the bag, searching for the delicate wire he'd placed there before leaving the land of the elves. Barely heavier than a strand of the waitress's fiery locks, the wire coiled around his finger like a live snake hugging a tree. He pulled it free and admired the silver glow of magic in the dim light.

His other hand pressed against the chain at his neck. The wire, named Hugge by the dwarves, had been hard to separate from the elves who had plundered it a millennium ago, but Venge had managed, not without a few new scars. He valued each as a lesson learned.

The wire, seeming to draw what little light there was to itself, winked at him. This tiny strand had, according to the elves he'd taken it from, the power to separate him from at least one piece of his past, one very visible piece.

He ran the pad of his finger over the silver chain again. He had worn this chain since birth. It was the only visible link to his past—to what he had endured because of his father, at his father's hand. With one quick slip of the wire beneath its links, one quiet tug, he could shed the collar, leave it behind in the dirt beneath his feet.

He'd heard his father's wife and her sister had freed him from the symbol of Lusse's ownership. Venge deserved as much, didn't he?

His eyes narrowing, Venge held the wire up to his face, stared at it for a second. Then, clenching his jaw, he shoved his hand back into the sack and slid the coiled wire off his finger. After retying the bag, he thrust the top back through the loop of his belt.

Not yet. Not until he was truly free from his past. He wanted to remember what had happened to him, wanted to make sure his memories didn't dim.

The immediate decision made, he dropped his hand from the chain and stared into the darkness again—until the tension relaxed from his body and his mind began to wander over the events of the evening—back to the bar and the waitress.

The feel of smooth skin covering a hard, toned bicep. The memory brought the hint of a smile to his lips. Stubborn and stupid…or just naive? Or was the whole thing some complicated act? For what purpose?

He frowned. He could move on, probably should move on, but something about this place intrigued him. Something was happening here. Something he didn't understand. Something dangerous.

And Venge found danger irresistible.

He smiled, his hand again drifting to the sack at his side. He might not be able to free himself from the past yet, but that didn't mean he was averse to investigating a few new possibilities.

Besides, this place was filled with intriguing puzzles. An image danced into his mind—red hair brushing over bare white shoulders.

He could afford a few days trying to figure them out. There was no telling what rewards he might find here.

Geysa picked her way along the rutted path, the beam of her flashlight dancing along the ground in front of her. Towns of the human world's Old West were supposed to have wide boardwalks to accommodate the women in long dresses that had sashayed their lengths. But this place— she kicked a clod of dirt out of her way—must have been designed with burros, not people in mind.

As she stepped over a deserted tire that was blocking the path, something skittered across the metal roof of the building next to her. She froze. Just a rat, or a squirrel, she told herself as a shiver shook her shoulders. She pressed her free fingers over her arm and willed the hand holding the flashlight to quit shaking.

Praise the gods, Jora hadn't been around to see that embarrassing display. Valhalla didn't have wildlife. Valhalla didn't have anything—not really. Just warriors deluded by the magic of the hall into thinking what surrounded them was real, that the battles they still fought hourly were important, the food nutritious and the ale intoxicating. But none of it, good or bad, really existed. It was all just a sham, to keep the shades who used to be men content.

Geysa shook her head. Her trip to this town was one of her

first experiences with so much reality. Funny, but it was the little things that threw her. Hellhounds, no problems—but a rat? Geysa muttered a curse at the insanity of her weakness.

The thought of hellhounds drew Geysa back to her current mission—finding the red-haired male Jora seemed determined Geysa "befriend." Another hellhound had told Geysa he'd seen a newcomer near the old livery.

Part of Geysa's duties was keeping tabs on the hell-hounds, which meant knowing where they spent their time whether awake or asleep. To accomplish that, she'd been working as a hostess of sorts, hooking each new arrival up with a bed. Mattresses and some furnishings had been brought in from Valhalla insuring the males didn't find better accommodations on their own.

But in the confusion, this one had slipped away before Geysa could steer him toward a place where she could keep tabs on him. And after her conversation with Jora, she wasn't content to wait until tomorrow. She needed to know what the hound was up to now.

The livery was nothing more than a small rectangular building constructed of rough-hewn logs. The doors hung from hinges long ago rusted to the point of inoperability. The building was so far gone, the Valkyries had quickly marked it off their list of usable real estate.

Geysa paused, her palm resting lightly on top of an old wagon wheel that partially blocked the entrance. He wouldn't have gone in there…would he? She pointed the beam of her light at the ground to keep from startling whatever might be inside, and carefully leaned closer. It was quiet, the deep kind of quiet only found in a crypt or other long-forgotten space. Unease flitted over her, but she shook off the feeling. *Nothing here.* She forced out a breath.

Knowing Geysa's discomfort with the human world's

wild creatures, Runa had warned her a family of skunks had taken up residence in the building.

Among her other talents, if the Norn was in physical contact with some part of a creature, she had the ability to speak with animals. Since they had come to the town, Geysa had seen Runa working on the skill, gathering fallen feathers or bits of antler, then calling the animals to her side. It was an impressive talent, but not one Geysa would have encouraged.

Thankful she didn't have to introduce herself to the creatures tonight, she turned to leave. As she did, the faint sound of toenails scratching against wood halted her steps. She waited; the sound didn't repeat. Mumbling a curse against all things that skittered through the night, she took a step, knocking against the wagon wheel as she did.

The heavy wheel rolled forward, into a stack of deserted beer cans. Geysa jumped at the sound, then laughed as she realized how idiotic the entire scenario was. She was a Valkyrie. Her ancestors had ridden into the fiercest of battles and plucked warriors off the fields midswing of their swords, and here she was jumping at the skittering of an overactive rat and the clanging of a forgotten pile of beer cans.

She pinpointed one of the cans with her flashlight, pulled back her foot and sent it sailing off the porch and into the side of the building next door. It landed with a rewarding clank.

There. Whatever had been skulking around in the dark was probably scurrying for safety. Satisfied, she turned to leave.

The rusty hinges she'd thought inoperable squealed behind her. Her body moved before her brain registered what was happening—before she heard the low growl of an animal set to kill or saw the telltale flash of the red eyes of a hellhound with prey in its view. She spun, bending her legs as she did to retrieve her dagger.

The ridges of the bone handle were familiar, reassuring, but the sight that greeted her still made her blood run cold. A ginger-colored hellhound, his eyes burning crimson and his lips pulled back to reveal two-inch-long fangs, stood facing her. His hair was disheveled, bits of straw sticking out in places. He stood, feet braced shoulder-width apart, his head low and his hackles raised. Ready for attack. He was still, still as death, but a low, warning growl rumbled from his chest.

A band tightened around Geysa's heart in response.

Was this the last thing her mother saw? Did she have a chance to fight or were there too many, attacking too suddenly?

Anger churned to life inside Geysa. Her mother was the last victim of the Wild Hunt before it was shut down, before the ErlKing disappeared. Geysa had hated the monsters all her life because of it, but somehow she'd managed to set that aside the last few days. Fooled herself into forgetting at least to some degree that the men who harassed her in the bar were those monsters. But now seeing one in his true form, seeing the demon that took her mother…

Rage guiding her hand, she threw the knife.

Fear. Sorrow. Rage. The scents assailed Venge. His lip rose in response. The basest part of his hellhound nature thrust forward, demanded to be set free.

A light shone into his eyes, blinding him, but he could still smell the emotions, knew where they were coming from, where to attack. The light dropped. He inhaled. Another scent leaked through the heady emotions, one he knew…honey, fresh grass, spring.

The waitress, Geysa.

He lowered his lip, struggling to pull back the demon

that stormed inside him, but as he did, as he battled to ignore the compelling scents that clouded around her, his eyes adjusted to the darkness. He saw her bend, pull a blade from her boot and fling it toward him.

In the space of one heartbeat, he leaped, shimmered as he flew. The blade still hit, slicing into his side instead of piercing his heart.

Cursing the weakness that made him hesitate, he rematerialized and Changed in one breath. With a thud, he collided with his target, knocked her off the porch and onto the rocky overgrown path beside it.

Naked and bleeding, he stared down at her. As he looked into her oval face, smelled her anger and felt her breasts rub against his bare chest, the control he'd gained while in dog form slipped again. The compulsion was back—the same uncontrollable urge to be near her that he'd felt back at the bar.

Heat surged through his veins, pooled in places he longed to press against her, into her. Deep in his throat he felt a growl form.

Geysa lay on the ground, her breath knocked out of her and her mind snapping with anger. Hound, kill, revenge, were the only thoughts she could manage.

She pressed her palms against the body pinning her to the rocky earth, tried to regain her freedom so she could continue the fight.

"Lay still." A voice, heavy and breathy, growled into her ear.

Suddenly she was aware of the weight pressing against her, of the hot skin under her palms, the firm muscles beneath that. She stilled, her heart still pounding, urging her to move on the hellhound, even as her mind and body reacted…softened…to the feel and smell of male so close.

"Better," the voice grunted, but its owner didn't move back. Instead he inched closer. A hand brushed against her neck, warm breath tickled her skin.

Her mind raced as she cataloged what had happened, was happening. The dog…the hellhound…now a man.

Everything clicked. She tried to bend her knee, to pull her leg up and grab her dagger, but the male on top of her draped a leg across hers, pinning her down.

"Too late. You've already tossed that little surprise." He grunted again, this time with an edge of pain, then raised up on his forearms. She saw his face—the new hellhound, the one Jora had told her to befriend. His hand drifted down the side of her face, her neck. He closed his eyes and inhaled, holding the breath as if breaking it down into parts…memorizing it.

Her gaze darted to his bare chest—solid and broad with a sprinkling of reddish-gold hairs. Her palms itched. She wanted to run her hands over the firm muscles, to explore, to see how that hair felt beneath her palms. Geysa's heart beat faster at the thought and at the realization of exactly how close she and he were—and how little clothing separated them.

He moaned, his eyes flying open. Barely harnessed lust poured through his eyes. Her body reacted, her nipples hardening and her hands reaching for him, to touch him, to see if his skin held the same burning heat as his gaze. Inches from her palms making contact, she remembered who he was, what she was, and the lie of what was passing between them. There was no desire for her, not really. It was just another Valkyrie sleight of hand—another hellhound reacting to the luring ability with which she had been born. And, she muttered mentally, she didn't want him, either…couldn't. He was a hellhound, one of the

Valkyries' few enemies and everything she had ever hated, just bundled into an attractive male package.

He leaned down again; his gaze fluttered over her body. Goose bumps formed on her skin, but she licked her dry lips and concentrated on building her shields. Once she felt them slide into place, she raised her eyes, studied his face, and forced a casual expression on her own. "I was looking for you," she said.

Confusion flitted across his face and a breath shuddered from his body. Then he shook his head and gazed down at her; the intensity she had seen before was gone, replaced by something lighter but perhaps as dangerous…curiosity.

"Really?" He cocked a brow, then tugged free a strand of hair that had found its way into her mouth. He wrapped the lock around his finger with slow deliberation, then added, "Interesting greeting."

His thumb caressed the lock, rubbing over its length like he stroked fine silk. Geysa shivered, her shields hiding the emotions roiling inside her, but not her all too physical reaction.

He frowned. "Are you cold?"

"No." She shook her head. "But…" She nodded to his body covering hers. "I could be more comfortable."

"Really?" he said again, his lips tilting into a dangerous smile. "I couldn't."

Chapter 3

Venge stared at the enigmatic woman beneath him. Just as they had done earlier at the bar, her emotions had suddenly clicked off. Her personal scent still curled around him, tugged at him, but the irresistible aroma of her emotion was gone.

It couldn't be. No one had that much control. She had to feel something.

He let his body drop closer, let his lips brush against her ear, down the line of her jaw. His tongue drifted out of his mouth, just a flicker against her skin, enough to give him a taste both sweet and salty. It made him want more.

She stiffened, her hand reaching down—for the dagger she'd already thrown, he guessed. But despite her obvious desire to be free of him, he couldn't pick up even a hint of her emotions. It was strange…impossible.

"Who are you?" he asked, even though he had already guessed her name.

Her lips thinned. "Geysa."

"Geysa." The name rolled off his tongue, the last syllable stretching into a whisper, a promise….

"Are you going to get up?" Her words were terse, impatient, but something else—anxiety?—flitted across her face.

His eyes narrowed. *Damn whatever was stopping him from reading her.* He wanted her emotions, felt cheated and handicapped at his inability to sense them.

Irritated, he shoved himself to a sit even though his instincts protested the move away from her warmth. "How are you doing it?" he asked.

She pushed herself to a stand, cast a quick glance over her shoulder at him, then hopped onto the porch. Her eyes cast down, she searched the darkness.

Muttering a curse, he stood and leaped onto the wood beside her, landing in a crouch. The knife had fallen where he'd shimmered, halfway between the door and the end of the porch where she'd stood as she had tossed the blade. He scooped up the dagger, holding it by the handle, the blade pointing upward and hidden behind his forearm. He stood, the blade well hidden.

She had recovered the flashlight and flipped it on. The beam wavered. With a curse, she smacked it against her leg, apparently knocking something into place. With the beam again glowing brightly, she let out a breath and began running the light over the wood beneath their feet.

He flipped the dagger in his hand and held it up. "Looking for this?"

The beam jerked, coming to a halt as it glistened off the blade. An unmistakable streak of dull red colored the tip.

"I hit—" She bit off the sentence, the light darting again, this time to Venge's form. The beam seemed fixed on his chest as if she was afraid to let it drop lower, afraid of what she would see. He smiled at the thought, considered using her discomfort with his nudity to torment her more, but suppressed the urge, instead answering her question.

"Me? Yes, you did." He pulled back his arm and twisted his body to reveal the seeping gash where the dagger had sliced through his skin.

She pulled in a breath, but said nothing. With the light shining in his face, and the damper on her emotions, he was left wondering at her reaction. Shocked at what she'd done? Regretful? Or only disappointed she'd come so close and missed?

Irritation returning, he stood, throwing the dagger as he moved. With a thunk, the blade sunk into the log wall, inches from her head.

She didn't turn her head or even blink—just reached up blindly and jerked the knife free from the log.

Even more annoyed, he waited.

"I was looking for you," she said.

She still held the knife. Would she throw it again?

He let an impatient puff of air escape his lips. "So you said." He paused, but she didn't speak. "If you're going to use that, might as well do it now." He nodded to the knife.

She tapped the blade's edge against her leg. "I'm sorry about that." Her gaze dropped to the wound in his side.

His body reacted, hardened. He wished she'd look lower, see how he responded to her.

"Are you? For some reason, I don't believe you." He stepped over a broken board in the porch floor and crossed his arms over his chest. "Not that I blame you…but next time, throw faster."

Surprise darted through her eyes and her mouth opened, then closed.

When she made no further response, he turned his back

on her. Without the ability to read her emotions, it was a stupid move, but at that moment he didn't care. He wasn't much for games. If she wanted to kill him, she should go ahead and try. Others had.

When he looked back she still held the knife, but slowly she slid into a crouch and slipped the blade into her boot. After standing back up, she opened and closed her fists, licked her lips, then raised her eyes to his. "My mother was killed by a hellhound."

He barked a laugh, a cold sound completely lacking in humor. "What a coincidence. So was mine."

Geysa stared at the man she'd tried to kill minutes earlier. Something twisted in her stomach. She'd told him about her mother. She didn't talk about her mother—only the Valkyries and Runa knew the story. And when she decided to share, who did she pick? One of the very beasts responsible for her mother's death.

Then his words registered. "A hellhound killed your mother?" she repeated. "But…you are…"

He stood unmoving, except for the clenching of his jaw. "Loving, aren't we? My kind, I mean. It was my father. He raped her, then left her for dead. The witch who owned them both kept her alive long enough to give birth to me. I'd say I was lucky, but that would just be a damn lie." Without warning he turned and strode back inside the livery.

Venge didn't wait to see if Geysa followed. Didn't care. Nostrils flaring, he crossed the room and squatted next to a musty mattress he'd discovered earlier and his clothes, which were folded neatly beside it. The mountain night had turned cold, and while Venge was used to much worse conditions, he had known he'd be both warmer and stronger in his canine form. So, he'd Changed.

Geysa's boots tapped along the floor behind him. "Were you sleeping here?"

Venge picked up his jeans and shook them out. He should ignore her, but… "I've slept in worse places." He stood and began pulling on his pants in short angry moves.

Geysa took a step backward, knocking against a pail of old iron tools as she did. She whirled, her glance shooting to the bucket then the rest of the room.

"Nervous?" he asked.

"Never," she replied.

"Really?" He cocked a brow. "You hide it well, but somehow I doubt you. Actually…" He took a step forward. "I'd think you were—" he tapped his index finger against his temple "—touched if you weren't." While his words were light, he kept his expression grim. He wanted a reaction from her. Any reaction.

Her gaze darted to the side and she folded her fingers into her hands. "Anyway…" She let out a breath. "You don't have to stay here. We have rooms, nice ones. No one knows what's happening with the hunt. You might as well be comfortable while you wait."

Venge tilted his head to the side. "'The hunt'?"

Her head snapped toward him. "Isn't that why you're here? Didn't you answer the call of the horn?"

Buying time to contemplate what she was saying, Venge stepped behind her and picked up the bucket of tools she'd bumped into. As he did, his arm brushed against hers and her scent wafted over him.

"You smell like spring, and honey." The words fell from his lips and he regretted them instantly. They sounded soft, vulnerable. Something that was beaten out of Venge years ago. He spun, the metal rods in the pail clanging so loudly he almost missed her reply.

"We all do."

Surprised she'd given something to him that might reveal what she was, he set the bucket down. "We all who?"

She shook her head, seeming to knock herself out the soft mood that had settled over them. "Nothing. We were talking about you."

He let his gaze drop to the pail beside him. "No, we were talking about 'the hunt.' What hunt?" He plucked an iron rod from the twenty or so shoved into the bucket. It felt heavy in his hand. He smacked it against his open palm, measuring its weight.

"The hunt. *The hunt*," she repeated. "The reason all these hellhounds have come here. You have to know what I'm talking about."

He glanced up, realization almost causing him to drop the tool he held. "The Wild Hunt? The horn that I heard, that was from the Wild Hunt?"

She ran a hand through her hair. "Yes. Someone is using the ErlKing's horn."

"Impossible. The horn has been missing for centuries."

"Yeah, well, someone's found it," she shot back.

He twisted his mouth to the side. "What can they do with it?"

She frowned. "What do you mean? What they are doing. Call up the Wild Hunt. Harness the power of a pack of hellhounds and send them after any being in the nine worlds…destroy them." She folded her arms over her chest and gripped her forearms until the skin bulged white around her fingertips.

"So…" He touched the end of the iron rod to his cheek. "Whoever controls the horn, controls the hunt?"

Her lips parted and for a second he thought she wasn't
going to reply. Then, "That's the story."

He smiled. He'd just found the key to his problem.
Alone he might not be able to kill his father, but with a *pack*
of hellhounds behind him?

Even the legendary Risk and his twin witch wife
wouldn't be able to fend off the Wild Hunt.

"So, that's why you're here?" Geysa's voice pulled him
from his thoughts.

It is now. "I travel a lot." He bent to slip the rod back
into the bucket.

"But you heard the call? That's why you came here,
right?" There was an edge to her words, anxiety. *But damn
it, still no scent.*

His face angled toward the bucket, he watched her with
half-closed eyes. *She wanted something.* Normally he'd say
that was reason to put distance between them, but she certainly knew more than Venge about the hunt and the horn
that controlled it. It might pay to let her get closer *and* to
let her think she was the one in control.

He looked up. "Yes. I heard the call. Why?"

A gleam flickered through her eyes. "No reason."

Glancing down again to hide his smile, he rested his
hand on the bucket.

"So, you want that room?" She moved from one foot to
the other, as if in a hurry to leave.

The mattress was musty, and the livery full of pests, but
normally he would prefer that to going somewhere that
offered no privacy—which he suspected her lodging
wouldn't. But, to find the horn, sacrifices would have to
be made.

He glanced up at the gray-eyed beauty.

And to kill his father, he was willing to sacrifice anything.

* * *

Geysa slowed her steps to match those of the man—
hellhound—beside her. He'd heard the horn, and he'd
agreed to go with her. So far, Jora's plan was working. Now
Geysa had to get him to Runa to see if she confirmed Jora's
suspicions—that this hellhound was, despite his apparent
ignorance of the horn right now, going to be instrumental
in the Wild Hunt's unfolding story.

After a silent trip down the deserted street, she came to
a halt in front of the bathhouse.

The hellhound arched a brow. "Baths?" he said, his gaze
wandering up to the words painted across the front of the
old false-fronted building.

Geysa shrugged. "We didn't name it." Light leaked out
from under the front door. It was late, but Runa would be
up. Geysa's sister would have sensed their impending
arrival. After pulling in a deep breath, Geysa moved to
open the door.

The hellhound's hand on hers stopped her. "'We'?" he
asked.

Geysa froze.

His palm was warm against her skin. For the first time
Geysa realized the night had turned cold. Licking her lips,
she tried to twist the brass knob.

"You talk like you're part of a group."

Geysa sucked in a breath. None of the other hellhounds
had questioned the presence of the Valkyries, who they
were or what they wanted. The males all simply accepted
that the women were here to serve them—a state of mind
Geysa had come to expect during her centuries serving
fallen warriors.

She laughed and fiddled with the flashlight she still
held. The light flicked on and off, a silent SOS she hoped

one of the other Valkyries would notice. "Isn't everyone? You're a hellhound and I'm a…"

His hand tightened almost imperceptibly on hers.

"A woman."

"Woman?" He removed his hand from hers and leaned back. "As in female or human? You don't strike me as human. I've only heard of a couple who mingled in our worlds."

Relieved that he was no longer touching her, Geysa shook her head. "No, almost all the humans left this town right after the first hellhounds arrived. There were only a few, and from what I hear they were kind of eccentric." She smiled, hoping the conversational tone of her voice would throw him off his earlier track. "At least the one that's left is. He hangs out at the bar some. He wasn't there tonight, though, not that you would have noticed him. He just sits in the corner wrapped in an old Indian blanket."

"So you are—"

The door to the bathhouse jerked open. Geysa's sister, Runa, stood in the doorway, the yellow glow of a kerosene lamp behind her shining through her thin cotton blouse, outlining her lithe form. Her black hair flowed freely around her face, adding a darkness to her ethereal image. A stray cat Runa had taken in wove between her legs.

"Geysa, I thought I heard voices." Runa bent to stroke the cat, then murmured into its ear. The animal scampered off into the night. Runa straightened, then signaled for Geysa and the hellhound to enter. Geysa stepped up into the building, slipping her hand over her sister's as she passed and giving it a thankful squeeze.

Runa made no sign of the exchange. "So, you have another guest?" She motioned with her head for them to step farther inside. In the center of the room sat a round wooden table. Runa's fortune-telling tools—runes and cards—lay scattered across its scarred top.

"Yes…" Geysa gestured to the hellhound. "This is—" She stopped, realizing she didn't know his name. It seemed odd, as though they'd already been through too much for such a basic piece of information to be missing. The oversight made her wonder how many other things the male had been able to hide from her without her suspecting.

He stood back from them; his hands slipped into the front pockets of his jeans. "Venge…Leidolf." His voice hardened as he said the last.

"Venge." Runa glided forward, her bare feet seeming to barely touch the ground. She held out a hand, an obvious invitation for the hellhound to slip his into hers, but Venge didn't move. An awkward silence fell around them; Venge seemed completely unaffected by the quiet.

Geysa stepped forward. "Jora thought you might be able to find Venge a room." With her face turned from Venge, she widened her eyes at her sister, hoping she would pick up on the signal.

Runa cast an enticing glance at Venge, her gray eyes taking on a catlike allure. "Of course. That's why I'm here." She pursed her lips then stalked around him, her gaze gliding over his body. Once back to the position beside Geysa, she tilted her head and said, "We have one room left here."

Geysa's shoulders stiffened. Runa had been adamant about not sharing the bathhouse with any of the previous hellhounds. Why would she offer now?

Venge's jaw jutted to the side. He turned and began to examine the room. When he reached the runes, he stopped.

"Would you like to hear your fortune?" Runa asked. Her hand skimmed his arm, not quite making contact with his skin. His attention snapped from the table to the Norn beside him.

And that was the only way Geysa could think of her sister right then, as a Norn. There was no doubt Runa was in full Norn mode, beguiling, trying to lure Venge into doing…what? Get a reading?

Geysa bit the inside of her cheek, forced herself to remain quiet. Whatever was happening, Runa had more information than Geysa and their goal was the same. To jump in could ruin whatever plan her sister was working, but still… Geysa's stare fell to where Runa's hand hovered inches from Venge's.

Venge flipped over one stone rune.

Runa let out a tiny "Oh" of sound, her hand flattening onto the table's top.

Venge picked up the stone and ran his thumb over the small arrow design incised on its length. He stood there, saying nothing…long enough that Geysa thought he wouldn't reply, but then, his gaze still on the rune, he responded. "I don't believe in the future, just the past, and—" he glanced at Geysa "—the present. Anything else may never exist." He set the rune down and flipped it back over. His finger pushed the carved side down against the table.

"Interesting," Runa murmured; her gaze clung to the rune he'd held. Her lips parted, she glanced up. "But the room? Do you want that?"

Venge tapped his finger against the back of the stone. "Yes, I think I do." He lifted his hands from the table and turned to face Geysa and her sister. "As long as I can afford the price, that is."

"Oh, there's no cost. We—" Remembering his questions earlier, Geysa stopped.

"We would never ask anyone to pay more than they're able." Her sister took a flickering candle from a nearby table, then slid into place beside Venge, her arm slipping through his. "I'm sure we can come to some kind of agreement, but I'll let you and Geysa work that out. She's much more business-oriented than I." With that, Geysa's sister began subtly tugging him toward the stairs.

Geysa narrowed her eyes. Runa was pulling out all the stops tonight—pouring the siren thing on heavy, perhaps too heavy.

Halfway to the steps, Venge stopped and pulled Runa's fingers from his arm. "I'm sure I'll be able to find my way."

After plucking the candle from Runa's fingers, he looked back at Geysa. "I'll be at the bar for breakfast. You never answered my question. Perhaps by then you'll be able to think up a believable lie." With that, he spun on his heel and stalked up the stairs.

Chapter 4

"What question was that?" Once Venge had disappeared up the stairs, Runa tilted her head back toward Geysa.

Geysa pursed her lips, annoyance with her sister's act gnawing at her. "He's…curious, about us. I evaded his questions, successfully I thought."

"Hmm." Runa plucked the rune Venge had held earlier up from the tabletop. "A warrior."

Geysa frowned. "Aren't they all?"

A smile curved Runa's lips. "No, the rune. He chose the warrior."

Geysa glanced at the rectangular piece of stone in her sister's hand. How choosing one sliver of rock over another said anything about the person doing the choosing had never made sense to Geysa, but she'd witnessed Runa's accuracy with the tools too many times to doubt that it did.

"What does it mean?" she asked.

"He has…issues." Runa flicked her eyelashes up and peered at Geysa, a mischievous light in her eyes.

All of Geysa's anger melted away. This was the Runa she loved—the sister she had shared pranks with as a child and bantered with as a teen, not the Norn she didn't understand and, if truth be told, at times avoided.

She grinned back. "Don't they all?"

The two shared the moment of levity, neither seeming to want to be the first to break the light mood they hadn't experienced since the horn had disappeared from Valhalla.

Runa pulled in a breath and set the rune down. "His are bigger than most, though. And while he thinks he knows what he wants, what he needs, he has a battle within himself to wage before he can even begin to understand what he *really* needs."

Geysa stared at the small stone, no bigger than the first joint of her thumb. "That tells you all that?"

Runa sighed. "Yes. But what it doesn't tell me is his role in the hunt."

"He has one, though." Geysa's words came out a statement rather than a question.

Runa's eyebrows shot upward. "You know that?"

Geysa trailed her hand over the top of the table. Her fingers bumped against one of the runes lying there. She started to flip it over, but stopped herself. "No, of course not. I just…feel it, you know?"

Runa's regard turned assessing. "I do, but I didn't know you did."

Geysa shoved her hand into the pocket of her jeans. "No, don't be ridiculous. There's just something about him that's different. Besides, Jora felt it, too."

"Did she? Is that why you brought him here?"

Relieved the attention had turned from her, Geysa nodded. "She wanted you to give him a reading—see if he might be important. She thinks it's time we get closer to one of the hellhounds, use them to find the horn."

"She trusts them?"

Geysa stared at her sister, unable to believe she'd even suggest such a thing. "Of course not. But none of us can hear the horn. Our only hope to find it is to work with someone who can."

"So she wants my opinion on this one?" Runa arched a brow toward the stairs where Venge had disappeared.

Geysa nodded.

"Tell her…" Runa stared at the rune Venge had chosen, her finger tapping lightly on the table beside it. Suddenly she glanced back up. "Tell her to follow him. I think he's the perfect choice."

"What about his…issues?" Geysa asked.

Runa's teeth worried at her lip. At Geysa's question she looked up, uncertainty in her eyes, but with a shake of her head she seemed to shove the emotion aside and a new smile lit her features. "Didn't we already establish they all have those?"

With a laugh, Geysa agreed. A few minutes later, after a brief time chatting about how things were going at the bar and among the other Valkyries in the town, Geysa gave her sister's hand a quick squeeze and walked to the door. Her fingertips on the knob, she turned to wave, but Runa had already sat at the table, her eyes closed and the runes lined up in front of her.

The sister she missed had already faded again—replaced by the Norn. Dropping her hand, Geysa twisted the knob and left.

It was hard enough missing her mother, but missing her

sister, especially with her still physically near…somehow that was even more difficult.

Venge placed the candle on a small table near the bed and glanced around the simple bedroom he'd chosen for his own. He'd actually found five rooms in the bathhouse's upstairs, only one with signs of occupancy. Based on the decidedly feminine scent that lingered there, he had guessed Geysa or her sister claimed that one.

He frowned—the sister. Geysa's scent was fresh, filled his mind with images of new earth, bees lighting on the first flower of spring, and those same flowers pushing their way stubbornly through the last bits of winter snow. The scent in the room he'd visited was spice and mystery, more sexual. Strangely, it held little appeal.

He shook the thought from his head and concentrated on learning the room he had chosen. It was small, like all the rooms here, with space for little more than a single bed and the table where he'd placed the candle. But this room boasted what the others didn't—a window overlooking the main street of the town.

He crossed to the window and pulled back the thin curtains. The streets were dark. Obviously—he glanced at the wax dripping from the candle near the bed onto the table beneath it—while the bar had electricity, not all the dwellings did. Based on what Geysa had said, he suspected only a few of the buildings had been occupied before the hellhounds arrived, or perhaps some of the humans didn't mind a rustic existence without electricity, or—he glanced at the pitcher and bowl sitting on the table—running water.

A sound outside caught his attention. He jerked his head toward the window. The round beam of a flashlight appeared on the dirt below.

Geysa leaving.

He leaned closer, his breath forming a circle of fog on the glass.

The beam moved farther into the street. Behind it he could make out the curvaceous form of the waitress. The muscles of his chest tightened, his body prickling with arousal at the sight of her, even yards away and totally unaware of his perusal.

He frowned, pulling back slightly. She intrigued him, that was all. And she was hiding something—such as why she and the other females were here and what type of beings they were. Innocent people didn't keep secrets. Not that Venge had much experience dealing with innocents.

No, he was much more comfortable working with those coming at the world with somewhat shady motivations.

He smiled, relaxing some.

The beam was moving at a steady pace back toward the bar. Obviously the building she must call home. He stood there, unable to leave until the light disappeared inside the bar. Within seconds, a bigger light shone from the windows, and through a clean patch where someone had rubbed away the grime, he could see Geysa's form as she strode deeper into the room, then out of view.

Annoyed at his need to watch her every step, he started to turn, to get to his bed, when a movement halfway down the street caught his eye. Someone was there, watching. Him or Geysa?

It didn't matter. Without giving it any more thought, he shimmered.

Venge materialized between two buildings. Shrubs, long untended, grabbed at his arms, thorns tearing into his skin.

Intent on discovering who stood hidden in the shadows just feet away, he ignored the pain.

The rustle of clothing, huff of rough breathing and faint clink of metal against metal told Venge he'd seen correctly. Someone lurked nearby. But where?

He edged toward the end of the building until he could spy around the corner. In human form, he didn't have the near-perfect night vision he had as a canine, but still it was sufficient to determine nothing except an old wooden barrel filled with lumber waited in the darkness. He didn't move, didn't step forward to investigate. Something was wrong. He couldn't see anyone, but… He inhaled. Nothing. At least nothing indicating a living being, just the sharp scent of rusty metal and old wood. Exactly what he'd expect around a deserted building.

A curse formed in his mind. Never before had he had reason to doubt his senses, but since coming to this town, he'd encountered two in mere hours.

A wind whistled through the street, rattling an empty beer can along the ground and brushing a branch of the shrub against Venge's arm. He wrapped his hand around the thorny plant and squeezed. The pain pierced his doubt, assuring him at least some of his senses were still working. He just needed to choose which to trust. Decide which were most easily fooled.

He closed his eyes. The sounds of the night came to him first—small animals skittering across the ground, tree branches scratching the tin roof of the building beside him, and breathing…it was still there. The smells—the earth, the rusty metal and the plain, cold scent of night—they were all there, but there was more…faint, but familiar.

Just as he thought he had the odor identified, it slithered away, out of his mind. He gritted his teeth and tried again, this time checking for something else, something mundane senses would pass by, something most hellhounds wouldn't notice. But Venge had spent time with the elves, learning talents all beings had, but most never put to use.

Relaxing his fingers, he willed all his muscles to loosen and, just for a second, he lost himself, let his mind drift. That's when he felt a prickle in the air, like tiny, ice-cold needles nipping into his skin, as real and obvious as the building beside him—magic.

Someone was nearby, but they were hiding, confusing Venge with magic. A growl formed in his throat, escaping into the night before he had a chance to stop it. Something moved to his left—near where he'd seen the barrel and lumber. His eyes flew open and he started to shimmer, but before the first tingles could begin, he felt another force— magic. Raw this time. Unmistakable and extremely mundane, at least to a shape-shifter, a forandre.

Whoever had stood hidden nearby had shimmered, too.

With a curse, he jumped into the street, his arms held out ready to fight, but there was nothing, no one. And this time he knew whatever—whoever—had been hiding was gone.

Sigurd pulled the cloak's hood from his head, his eyes automatically scanning the interior of the small cabin he'd been inhabiting for the past weeks. It was empty save a few pieces of furniture and a woodstove left by the previous owner.

With an exhausted curse, he grabbed a stained coffee mug and tapped the wooden keg of ale he'd stolen from the Valkyries' bar the night before.

After swallowing a mouthful of the wheatie brew, he allowed himself to relax.

He'd been sloppy tonight and almost been caught because of it. He glanced at the cloak he'd tossed across the back of a chair. He'd trusted the elf magic woven into the cloth and forgotten to use his own hellhound senses. He set the empty mug on the table with a clunk.

He'd been too intent on following the Valkyrie and completely missed that the latest hellhound was no normal hound easily beguiled by her and her Norn sister. Another sign of his laziness. How could he not have recognized the pup, the hound he'd tried to humiliate, kill so many times?

He stared into space for a moment, memories of how steadfastly Venge had refused surrender or defeat—how willing he had been to face death first, how much he was like his father, Risk, the ex-alpha of Lusse's pack. The hellhound that at one time Sigurd would have done anything to destroy, but whom Sigurd had learned not only to respect, but like.

Five years ago Sigurd had made a promise—to see Venge freed from Lusse's clutches. He'd kept it, but now, knowing Venge was so close to the danger of the Wild Hunt, he couldn't help but feel his promise hadn't yet been fully met.

The younger hound, like Sigurd, still wore the witch's mark of ownership… Sigurd wrapped his fingers around the heavy silver chain at his neck. Even dispersed, the pack was still the pack, and the job of alpha now Sigurd's.

He owed it to all of them to protect them from further bondage, especially bondage as inescapable as what the Wild Hunt would hold. But Venge… He'd made a personal promise involving Venge.

He dropped his hand from the chain and picked up his empty mug. The heavy china was cold against his skin.

Tomorrow he'd resume his mission—to find and destroy the horn before it could be used against the hellhounds, but first he'd do whatever it took to get Venge as far away from here as possible.

* * *

Venge entered the bar the next morning watchful and wary. He'd walked the short distance from the bathhouse, purposely passing by the building he'd visited last night. In the morning light, it was easy to see the space in front of the boarded-up building was empty—no barrel full of lumber, nothing Venge could have mistaken for such.

Which meant either someone had removed the items or—and Venge was having a hard time believing this— he'd mistaken whoever he'd sensed there for the inanimate objects. But that was impossible, wasn't it?

His mind still occupied with the puzzle, he didn't notice the boxer from the day before until the hellhound had ground to a halt in front of him, blocking his path.

"You still here?"

Venge leveled a steady stare at the forandre, then made a move to step past him. The boxer blocked him again— this time placing a square hand on Venge's shoulder. "What's with the jewelry?" he asked, his gaze flicking to the chain at Venge's throat. "Your owner let you out for a run, and you forget your way back?"

Something deep in Venge's psyche began to crack.

"I've heard there are hellhounds that like life on a leash. You one of them?" The boxer gave Venge's shoulder a shove. "You have a sweet little bed to curl up in and a basketful of squeaky toys, too?" He laughed, glancing at the other occupants of the bar as he did so.

Venge kept his attention on the boxer, ignoring the nervous laughter that greeted the forandre's taunts. He just waited, watching as the boxer, encouraged by the reaction—weak though it was—grew bolder, careless.

The other hellhound turned sideways and attempted to catch Geysa's gaze as she slid a tray under her arm, a concerned line between her brows. Venge took advantage of the boxer's inattention by slamming his forearm into his windpipe. A surprised gurgle escaped the boxer's throat as his hands flew to his neck.

Not waiting for him to recover, Venge grabbed him by the hair and kicked him in the back of the knee. The shorter hound fell forward, only Venge's fingers in his hair keeping him from hitting the ground.

Venge leaned forward until his lips were against the other male's ear. "You're a slow learner, aren't you?"

The boxer started to raise his arms to fight, Venge assumed, but before Venge could deliver another blow, the bartender strode forward, the blade of her sword pointed at the downed hellhound's throat. "Don't," she said.

The boxer jerked under Venge's hand. Venge pulled the other male's head back farther, exposing more of his throat.

"And, you—" The sword rose until it pointed at Venge. "You seem to bring trouble with you."

His concentration still focused on the boxer, Venge didn't bother with a reply.

"Now, enough. No more fighting. At least until after breakfast." The bartender lowered her blade, but only slightly.

Venge shook his head inwardly at these women's lack of understanding of the hellhounds they served. The boxer had challenged him twice. Venge couldn't walk away from that. The boxer knew that, as well, and expected a response.

But it didn't have to be here. Shooting a blazing glance at the bartender and Geysa, who now stood behind her, he shimmered, taking the other hellhound with him.

The pair of forandre materialized in the center of the rutted main street. Within seconds, the hellhounds they had left in the bar appeared around them, forming a circle.

Venge shoved the boxer away from him. "Forandre rules?" he asked.

Performing a backward somersault, the boxer landed on his feet. "Of course," he replied, but his eyes were already glowing. It would take little prodding on Venge's part to get him to slip into bloodlust, to shift to his hellhound form. And when he did, it would be a death sentence. The hellhounds surrounding them would tear him to bits.

Forandre rules: fight in your weakest form. To Change was forbidden, and if a hound slipped, lost control of the beast inside him, the other hellhounds would team up and punish him with death.

The two began to circle. Dust rose around them in a cloud. "There a reason you've targeted me?" Venge asked, more to keep the other hound's mind occupied than because he cared to hear his response.

To his surprise, the boxer answered, "I didn't target you. I just beat you to the attack. Did you think I'd let you choose the battlefield and time?"

His words made no sense, but Venge didn't have time to analyze them. The hellhound began to move, his fists held high, protecting his face. He feinted forward. Seeing his ploy, Venge slid easily to the left, out of the other hellhound's grasp as he made a quick move to his right.

Venge grinned. The boxer had experience, but nothing to match what Venge had endured while part of Lusse's pack.

A curse exploded from the other forandre's lips; his eyes glimmered. He stepped forward again, striking with a closed fist as he did. This time he was faster, his fist making contact with Venge's face before Venge could twist away.

Blood spurted from Venge's mouth. The hit was hard—too hard. His gaze on the boxer, Venge licked at the blood that clung to the side of his mouth.

The boxer grinned and opened his hand slightly, letting something silver shine through his semiclosed fingers.

"Ah, I see you brought a toy." Venge spat onto the dirt, a mixture of blood and saliva. Venge had no fear of the hellhound's tricks—although it was obvious he'd come to the bar prepared. He had planned for a battle. All because of their disagreement over the waitress? Or was the boxer hungry for any fight and Venge merely convenient? What about his comments regarding Venge targeting him?

There was no sense to be made of any of it. Of course, most hellhound fights weren't driven by logic. And at the moment, the reason for the attacks didn't matter—tools or no tools, logical or not—Venge had a hellhound to defeat and dominance to prove.

"Just so you know." Venge yanked off his shirt, revealing he had no tricks of his own hidden against his skin. The other hound shook his head, denying Venge's unspoken challenge to do the same, then tightened his grip around whatever he held in his hand and again began to circle.

Venge laughed. So be it. He'd never had the luxury of a fair fight—why start now? Lowering his shoulders, he followed the boxer's lead.

A murmur worked its way through the onlookers. Then, without explanation, two strips of iron—what appeared to be two-foot-long pieces of railroad track—landed in the dirt beside Venge.

The crowd was growing bored.

The boxer paused, his gaze shooting to the iron bars, but Venge got there first. Slowly, calmly, he picked up one then the other, swung them both up to rest on his shoulder like a massive bat. "You want one?"

With a growl, the boxer lowered his head and charged. Venge tossed one bar to the side, then waited until the boxer was within reach. Sucking in a breath, he slammed the rail downward like a sledgehammer. The strip of metal smashed across the back of the boxer's head and neck. There was a crack. The impact reverberated up through the metal and along Venge's arms. For a second he thought the other hellhound wouldn't fall, that somehow he had managed to withstand the blow, but the thought was fleeting. The boxer froze, his face tilting upward, disbelief sketched in his eyes. Then, with a thud, he landed in the dust. Dirt rose where he fell, clogging the air, making it hard to see or breathe.

Venge ignored the cloud of dust and strode to the fallen forandre. Then, like his father had once done to him, he placed his foot on the other hound's face and ground it deeper into the soil.

He'd won. He'd established his dominance. Others might challenge him, but none would do so without warning.

Wiping a bit of blood off his face with the back of his hand, he dropped the bar on top of the fallen hellhound, retrieved his shirt and strode through the parted crowd.

He got as far as the bar's porch before he heard it—the crystal peal of a horn. The sound rippled over his skin, teasing, elevating his already surging adrenaline, until he could almost hear his own blood humming through his veins.

Chapter 5

"Where did they go?" Geysa's stare shot around the empty bar that just seconds before had been filled with demanding hellhounds.

The sounds of fighting outside answered her question. She rushed to the window. Venge and Carr, the male he'd scuffled with the previous night, stood in the center of the street, a ring of hellhounds surrounding them.

Carr landed a punch to Venge's jaw. Venge's body tilted under the impact, but he stayed upright. He ran his hand over his mouth, glanced down at his open palm, then back up at Carr.

A band tightened around Geysa's heart. "What should we do?" she asked Jora, who had strolled up beside her, her sword shoved through the leather loop at her waist.

Jora cocked a brow. "Watch? Enjoy the sight of them destroying each other?"

Biting her lip, Geysa turned back to the fight. A group of hellhounds near the bar pulled two pieces of the deserted railway line out of the ground and tossed them into the circle.

Jora smiled. "Making things interesting."

Geysa itched for the feel of her dagger in her palm. She took a step toward the door.

Jora frowned. "Don't."

Unsure, Geysa waited. The crowd closed in tighter, blocking her view. She glanced at the door.

Jora shook her head. "It's not our fight, and why do you care?"

"I don't…I just… You said to befriend him, and helping him—"

Jora's hand slapped against the hilt of her sword. "Saved by a woman? Don't be stupid. That would only cost us. Besides…" She nodded toward the scene outside. "Looks like he won."

Geysa lifted her eyes. The gathering of hellhounds parted and Venge strode through them, not bothering to look left or right. Behind him, facedown in the dirt, lay Carr, unmoving.

"I think he can take care of himself." Jora patted her sword, then turned toward the bar. As she did, Venge froze, his head tilting to one side. Then, with no other warning, the air around him turned to waves and within seconds he was gone. As a group, the others followed.

"Jora. The horn!" Geysa yelled.

Venge materialized next to a creek; water roared through it so loudly he could hear nothing else for a second. He glanced around, searching for the horn and whoever possessed it. About fifty yards to his right stood the town—the creek ran behind it. To his left, past the creek, there was nothing but towering pines, and no sign whatsoever of any being capable of blowing the horn. But he already knew he couldn't trust his senses in this strange place.

He focused, blocking the sound of water rushing over rocks, and closed his eyes. The horn sounded again…it was close, but not near the ground where he expected it. The silvery peal resonated from above the trees.

He opened his eyes to search the skyline, but as he did, the air around him shifted. The twenty or so hellhounds he had left at the bar solidified around him. The sounds of their feet shuffling and their voices yelling drowned out the horn again.

He grabbed the closest hellhound—the male with the earring he'd encountered when he'd first landed in the town—by the shirt and jerked him forward until their noses almost brushed.

"Did you find it? Has it started?" the other hound asked, his eyes darting side to side.

Venge clenched his fingers tighter in the other male's shirt and shook. "What are you doing here?"

Surprise rounded the hound's eyes. "We followed the horn…and…" He glanced at Venge's hand wrapped in his shirt. Then, his gaze dropping, he added, "And you, of course."

The horn. Of course the other hellhounds would follow the call. Stupid of Venge to forget. But, the rest. Why had the hellhound added that? Venge tightened his grip. "Why follow *me?*" he asked.

The male frowned, confusion showing in his face. "You beat Carr. You're the alpha now."

Venge stared back at him, disbelief making him mute.

The other hellhound dropped his gaze again. This time Venge couldn't mistake the gesture for anything aside from what it was—a clear sign of submission.

With a curse, Venge tossed the younger male onto the ground. The alpha? He'd wanted to prove his dominance, not take a place among the hounds. His father had been the alpha. Venge was not his father. All he wanted was the horn—to control the pack. He did not want to be *part* of the pack.

Still cursing, he shook out his arms and stared at the males around him. They stood silent, watching. Being alpha wasn't a simple thing. Alphas were watched, constantly, and challenged. Now every new hellhound who arrived would search him out, try to take his position from him—a position he neither wanted nor could give up, not without admitting someone else was stronger, faster, harder to kill.

So, he'd be watched, challenged nonstop and, technically, he'd be responsible for settling others' problems. And, unless he had the horn, he still wouldn't truly control them—couldn't trust them.

He could never trust another hellhound. No, he needed the horn and time alone to find it.

His task was now harder…unless he got some help.

As the thought was forming in his brain, one of the hellhounds called, "The women, they're coming."

"I see them." Geysa pointed to the creek that ran behind the bar. "Should we call the others?" she asked.

Jora, her sword slapping against her leg, came to a halt beside her. "Not yet. We don't want to spook them. We need to know the horn is here first."

"So what do we—"

Geysa's question was cut short by a bucket being shoved in her hands. "I think we need water—spring water."

"But—"

Jora shoved Geysa toward the path. "Just get close and

see what they're doing. Signal if you need me." Her aunt spun, disappearing around the side of the building.

As Geysa approached, the men fell silent. Venge stepped away from the crowd, his hands on his hips. "You looking for something?" he asked.

She glanced from him to the others. She'd never seen them gathered like this before. This was definitely different.

"Did I interrupt something?" She smiled, trying one of Runa's tricks and letting her gaze drift across the hellhound closest to her. The male stiffened, stared at Venge. The redheaded hellhound made no change in his stance, but the other hounds began shifting in place, moving from one foot to the other.

With a curse, Venge darted a look to the bar and, one by one, the other males shimmered.

Geysa looked around, not believing what she had seen. "What happened?"

"Nothing." Venge turned his back on her, his face tipping up as he searched the sky. Her gaze followed his.

"Is there something up there?" she asked.

He dropped his gaze, his shoulders stiffening. After a second, he turned around. "Just a hawk. Did you hear its cry?"

"No…" Geysa glanced back at the sky. She'd seen no hawks around—and she would have noticed.

Venge gave her a cryptic stare. "Must have missed him." Then he turned and started walking back up the steep hill toward the town.

"Wait."

At her call, he turned. Geysa bumped the bucket she carried against her leg. She had no experience dealing with men in this way. She was trained to either lure them toward

Valhalla—with the power she now had to keep hidden behind her shields—or battle them as an equal. This talking and teasing was beyond her.

He frowned. "There's no water at the bar?"

She stared back at him blankly, before realizing he was looking at the bucket still knocking against her knee. "Water. Yes, I came for water."

He quirked an eyebrow, but didn't comment.

Pursing her lips, she squared her shoulders and began picking her way over the time-rounded stones that lined the creek bed. The water rushed over the rocks at an intimidating speed. The sound was so loud she could hear nothing else. Disgusted that she'd failed so miserably and would have nothing to show for her efforts other than a bucket of dirty water, she bent at the waist and plunked the bucket into the stream.

As the full force of the creek rushed against the bottom of the pail, the bucket jerked forward, pulling Geysa with it. She felt herself begin to topple, saw the water pouring past and the hard rocks that lined the bottom of the stream, could feel tiny droplets of water splashing against her skin. Then, just as she had closed her eyes and resolved herself to a cold, painful collision with the creek, an arm shot around her waist and pulled her out of danger.

She stood panting, her eyes still closed, a firm body pressed against her backside.

"Your water." The bucket dropped on the ground beside her. Icy liquid splashed onto her feet, over the tops of the hiking boots she wore and onto her bare legs. She jumped, pressing herself more firmly against the man behind her.

His arm, still wrapped around her waist, tightened.

"Thanks," she muttered. She fought off a shiver—from the cold splash of water or the inviting feel of Venge's warm chest against her back and the even more inviting feel of his pelvis cupped against her backside, she didn't know.

"Anytime," he murmured. His head dropped lower. She could feel his breath through her hair, against her neck. He was smelling her, inhaling her again. It was as unnerving this time as last.

She squirmed against him. Why did she find that enticing?

His hand splayed over her stomach, pressing her more firmly against his body. He inhaled again.

A fog of pure desire settled around her.

"Who is all of *us?*" he asked.

"Who?"

"Your smell. Yesterday you said all of you had it," he replied.

She frowned, an annoying sliver of reality cutting through the fog. She started to pull away; his arm tightened, keeping her close.

"They don't," he murmured again. His lips brushed the top of her shoulder, which had somehow been bared.

A tingle danced through her and she tilted her head to the side, giving him freer access to her skin.

"No one smells this—" he made a small circle with his nose against her neck "—good."

The sun beat on them, warming the side of her face as she tilted it. The roar of the water, while still loud, no longer seemed threatening; it seemed more encouraging, like the murmurs of a crowd telling her to stay, enjoy.

And smell, he'd mentioned smell…. She inhaled. Grass, dirt, nature. Things missing in the golden halls of Valhalla. Then finally the almost hot pressure of his body against hers. Another thing missing in Valhalla. Yes, the place was filled with virile warriors…or men who had once been virile warriors, but now they were nothing more than spirits. No strong arms to wrap around her, no chest corded with muscle to press against. She hadn't realized how much she could revel in the most basic feel of another person's body touching hers.

She almost groaned with pure pleasure. She started to turn, not away this time, but toward him. She wanted more.

Venge felt Geysa begin to turn in his arms. He wanted her to, wanted to feel her breasts pressed against him, to see her face tilted up to his. But he still couldn't read her, couldn't smell her emotions. The way her body trembled in his arms told him she wanted to be closer, too, that she was as aroused as he was, but…

Damn it. Much as he reveled in the fresh spring scent of her, he still couldn't smell her emotions. Without that ability, how could he know what she was feeling? How could he trust what she was doing? She could as easily be spinning in his arms to press her dagger against his throat as to press her lips against his.

With a curse, he pushed her away. She staggered, almost falling as he did so. He curled his fingers into his palms, stopping himself from catching her again. Her leg bumped against the bucket he'd set beside her; more water slopped over the side. She glanced down, frowned as if confused by its appearance.

That's when he got it. She was lying to him. She didn't need the water. She'd come to the creek to spy, to trick him, and she'd almost been successful.

"Why are you here?" he asked, his arms folding over his chest. This time he was determined to hear an answer, even if it killed him…or more likely her.

* * *

Geysa teetered on her feet, the sudden separation of her body from Venge's catching her off guard. Frigid water sloshing onto her leg helped bring her back to where she was and what was happening.

Just an arm's length away, Venge stared at her, anger simmering in his eyes, but thankfully minus the red she'd seen when a hellhound was about to lose control. She wrapped her arms around her body and stared back at him, waiting.

"Why are you here?" he repeated.

"I…" She glanced at the bucket.

"Don't bother," he rasped out. "The truth. Why are you *here?*" He motioned with one hand—around them, behind them, back toward the town.

"I…" she started again, but she could tell by the glimmer in his eyes he wasn't going to buy the lie forming on her lips. He'd seen through her somehow. "I'm looking for the horn," she said, her chin rising and her gaze holding his.

He pulled back slightly, surprise replacing anger for a second, then quickly moving to suspicion. "Why?"

"To stop the hunt." She dropped her arms away from her chest and balled her fists at her sides. "I told you my mother was killed by the hunt. I don't want that to happen to anyone else."

He tilted his head. "And the others?"

"Family."

"Big family," he replied, but without emotion. Geysa couldn't tell if he was questioning her response or just commenting. She made do with a nod.

He twisted his lips, his head turning back toward the town as if considering another question.

Geysa cut him off. "Will you help?"

He jerked his head back to face her. "Help?"

"Help me find the horn."

His brows lowered. "You want help, from me, to stop the hunt?"

Geysa licked her lips. Why had she asked him that? As soon as the words had left her mouth, she'd wished she could suck them back in. He was a hellhound. They were in this town because they wanted to join the hunt, not stop it. She started to take back her request, then realized there was no way to do so…better to forge ahead.

"You haven't decided to join the hunt, have you?" She kept her voice firm, as though the idea were idiotic.

He stared at her for a second, not a single glimmer of doubt in his eyes.

She cursed mentally. That's what she got for letting her emotions run away with her. He was going to turn her down, and now she couldn't even trick him into letting her follow him under the guise of attraction. She froze for a second, her mind flitting back to how she had felt with his body pressed against hers.

"No, I haven't." The words were firm, solid.

Geysa glanced up, startled again. "You haven't?"

"I haven't—" he took a step forward until he stood right in front of her, close enough she could feel the heat of his body "—decided to join the hunt. But the question is, say I help you, what's in it for me?"

The sun beat against Geysa's back. The heat from Venge's body warmed her front. But as she stood there, staring into his hazel eyes, a shiver of pure anticipation danced over her skin.

Unable to maintain the closeness, she glanced away, over his shoulder, back toward the bar. Jora stood in the shadows, her hand resting on the hilt of her sword. Geysa's resolve was strengthened just by knowing her family was close, she turned back to him.

"What do you want?" she asked.

He smiled and the shiver started again, this time bringing with it the urge to lean closer to him, to feel his breath against her skin again.

"What do I want?" he murmured. He reached out, wrapping his hand in her hair slowly, one loop then another, until she couldn't move without pulling him with her. "What do you think I want?" he asked.

What did he want? What did all the males she'd ever encountered want? "Power," she muttered.

His thumb, which had been caressing the length of hair trapping his hand, paused midstroke. "Power." He nodded, then, as if reinforcing the thought, repeated the word. "Yes, power. That is what I want." He pulled his hand free, letting her hair flow down her shoulder, over her breast. "Can you give it to me?" he asked, but there was something off in his expression, as though he were testing her.

He probably doubted she could deliver. "Depends on what kind of power you want. I can't make you a god, or teach you to fly, but I can get you riches or weapons, or both."

"Weapons?" His eyebrow cocked. "What kind?"

What kind? All kinds. Valhalla was filled with weapons from every battle ever fought throughout the nine worlds and time.

Pulling in a breath, she flicked her hair over her shoulder; its reassuring weight fell against her back. "Any kind you want," she responded, her expression steady as she looked back at him, expecting him to be considering her offer. Instead, his gaze had moved to the base of her neck where her and her mother's shield charms dangled.

He ran a finger under the tiny piece of gold. "You always

wear this." It was a comment, not requiring a response, but even if it had, she'd have had no reply. Her breath had caught in her throat.

He twisted his finger, letting the sunlight catch on the charms, then dropped them, his finger still lying against her skin.

"Power is good, but I think I want more."

"More?" The word came out little more than a whisper.

"Yes, more." He leaned in, then curled his finger back around the chain at her neck and used it to tug her that much closer. Afraid the tiny links would break, she let herself be pulled until his lips hovered above hers. "A kiss. One simple kiss to seal our bargain. That's fair, don't you think?"

Then, without waiting for her response, he lowered his face and captured her mouth with his.

Chapter 6

Venge pulled Geysa closer. Her lips parted beneath his.

One simple kiss, that's what he had said, but as soon as her lips opened, as soon as she tilted her head and her body softened against his, he knew that was a lie. There was nothing simple about this kiss and he wanted more, much more.

His tongue slid into her mouth. She tasted like she smelled, like honey—sweet and addictive. He ran his fingers along her scalp. Her hair draped over his arm, heavy, luxuriant, like strands of gold.

Her fingers pressed against his chest, shyly. After a lifetime of having nothing, of just surviving, the sheer richness of everything about her felt almost decadent. Like something he didn't deserve.

With a frown, he pushed her away.

Again she stood blinking at him, her gray eyes wide, her pupils dilated.

"So, we have a deal?" he asked. He let his gaze rest on her only for a moment, then glanced away, hiding the desire he knew lurked in his eyes.

She didn't reply and he looked back. Her fingers rested lightly against her lips and she was staring at him, as if trying to figure out what piece was missing from a puzzle.

"So, you need this?" He gestured to the bucket behind her.

She blinked again, then shook herself as if waking from sleep. "No…yes." She let out a breath. "It doesn't matter."

Glad to have something to occupy his hands, Venge stepped past her and picked up the bucket. The water slopped against the side. He gripped the handle tighter and fought the urge to tip the pail over his head and let the water rain over his body—could almost feel the cold liquid sluicing over his chest and thighs…knocking him out of whatever deluded state made him think even for a second that he could be with someone like Geysa.

"So, the deal…you agree?" Glancing down, she pressed her palms against her thighs.

He nodded. "But you'll have to tell me what exactly you need from me."

She looked up. "Your ears. We can't hear the horn. We have no way of knowing when it's being blown unless a new hellhound arrives or if a big group disappears at once." A line formed between her brows. "Why did all of you come here?" She glanced around as if the horn might be lying on the ground nearby, deserted and forgotten.

"Someone made a mistake."

She frowned and he could see she was going to push the issue further. He stopped her with a frown of his own. "So, you want me to play bird dog? Point when I hear the horn?"

"Well, not point…" Geysa twisted her lips to the side.

Why did he make this sound so insulting? "It's just the horn is pitched for hellhounds, not… We can't hear it." Afraid she was beginning to sound petulant, she squared her shoulders. "I said we'd pay you."

"'We' again? The whole family's in on this then?"

Did that matter? "Yes." She looked back toward the town. Jora had disappeared. With her face directed back toward Venge, Geysa continued. "Any weapon you can imagine, we can get for you, and, if you need it, training to use it."

"*Any* weapon? Something that can kill a hellhound?"

"Why would you—" The shuttering of his eyes told her not to ask. "I'm sure," she finished.

"Then…" He stood to the side and gestured up the path. "I guess we have a deal."

Sigurd settled into his customary corner of the bar, the cape wrapped securely around him. Venge had defeated the alpha—disturbing, and not part of Sigurd's plan. When Sigurd had approached Carr and told him a new hellhound with aspirations of becoming alpha had arrived in the town, he'd known Carr, the reigning alpha, wouldn't be able to hold his own against Venge. That was why he'd suggested and supplied the weapon.

Unfortunately, Venge had grown even harder to defeat since his days in Lusse's kennels, and the weapon had done nothing more than annoy him. Perhaps even increased his desire to beat Carr.

Sigurd's misjudgment might cost him. Carr was, as alphas went, weak. There was a possibility the ErlKing hadn't shown up yet to claim the horn and choose from the gathered hellhounds because of Carr's weakness. The alpha of the hunt had to be among the strongest—if not the strongest.

And after five years on his own, Venge fit that bill. Now that Venge was alpha and the other hellhounds had chosen to follow him, the ErlKing's arrival couldn't be far away.

Time was running short. Sigurd had to find a way to convince Venge to leave before the ErlKing arrived.

Sigurd reached in his pocket and fingered the cylinder that was hidden there. There had to be another hellhound willing to take on Venge. Sigurd would find him, and this time the weapon he supplied would be a lot harder for Venge to ignore.

Geysa entered the bar. Venge walked a few feet behind her, still carrying the pail filled with water. While Geysa paused to let her eyes adjust to the dimmer light, he strode past, setting the bucket on top of the bar right in front of Jora.

"You ask for this?" he asked.

Geysa's aunt arched a brow. "I don't recall."

He leaned forward, the muscles of his back clearly visible through his T-shirt. "Bad habit, not knowing what you've asked for. Beings get hurt that way."

"I'll keep that in mind." Jora wrapped her hand around the pail's handle and swung the bucket onto the floor. With it out of the way, and after Venge had turned to scan the occupants of the bar, Jora shot a questioning look at Geysa.

Geysa answered with a short nod. Things were set.

Later that night, after leaving Geysa and her aunt at the bar, Venge stood at the window in his bathhouse room, again looking out into the street.

He'd agreed to help the females even though he didn't trust them and knew they were keeping some secret about themselves. They'd never admitted what type of beings they were, what powers they had. But the lack of knowledge didn't worry Venge too much. There wasn't much that posed a threat to a hellhound.

Although… Venge thought of Geysa, her eyes wide after their kiss, his own reaction. He closed his eyes, his hands forming fists. She made him want things, things he didn't even believe existed—acceptance, love, trust.

Gritting his jaw, he shoved the idealistic thoughts out of his head. He was helping her, or saying he was because it was the smart thing to do. Pretending to play along with whatever game she'd chosen ensured he'd know what she was doing. She might even prove helpful in his own hunt. The gods knew the hellhound hearing she seemed to value hadn't done him any good so far.

It was going to take more than being the first to arrive when the horn was sounded. He had to see the horn…get to it.

Maybe Geysa would help him do that somehow.

Worst-case scenario, there were the weapons she had promised. If he couldn't get the horn, perhaps one of those would give him enough power to destroy his father.

He stared blankly into the darkness outside his window. Just like the previous evening, he sensed movement, someone lurking. He tensed, ready to shimmer, but the motion ceased; whoever had been there was gone.

He stood there a few seconds longer, his gaze searching the street, adjusting to the dark. He was almost ready to give up when the flap of wings yanked his attention to an area not far from the bathhouse. A mouse sat beside a pile of rocks, chewing intently on something wedged between his paws. Venge waited, expecting an owl to surge down and snatch the obviously dense rodent away, but to his surprise, the flapping noise quickly faded into the darkness and the mouse continued his dinner unconcerned. Feeling somehow cheated, he turned to his bed.

He'd just pulled back the covers when the peal of the horn sounded again.

Geysa awoke with a start. A hand was pressed over her mouth; a chest hovered over her own. A very real, very corporeal man was in bed with her. Without pausing to think more, she shoved her hand under her pillow and wrapped her fingers around the knife she kept there. Unable to see more than a rough shape, she slashed the knife sideways. The feel of its tip hitting the resistance of muscle told her the blade had found its target, but before she could more than register the thought, the resistance was gone and the knife clattered onto the wood floor beside her bed.

She sat upright, rolling across the mattress in the same movement, toward the bedside table and the throwing ax she had left propped against its leg.

"Geysa," a masculine voice, rough with some emotion she couldn't peg, murmured.

Her palm touching the inlaid handle of the ax, she glanced up. Eyes, simmering red, stared back at her. Hellhound. A band tightened around her chest. She edged backward until she was crouching on the balls of her feet, her arm free to throw.

"What are you doing here?" she asked.

"The horn. It sounded." The eyes glimmered for a minute, then darkness, as if he'd closed his eyes or passed his hand over them.

Her heart still hammering in her chest, she lifted the ax. Her mind was so intent on defending herself, it took a few seconds for his words to sink in. "The horn?" she repeated.

The ax weighed heavy in her hand, but she made no move to lift the weapon higher.

"I came to get you, but…" His eyes—Venge's, she was sure of it now—flickered again, his words staccato, as though he was struggling to get them past his lips. "What are you?" he asked. "I want to…"

She needed to see him, to calm her racing heart. With her free hand, she jerked the chain that dangled from the bedside lamp, casting the room in a warm yellow glow.

Then, before she realized what he had planned, he was kneeling beside her, one hand running down her back, his other lifting her hair. "…be close to you. I can't seem to be close enough." She felt his breath on her cheek, heard him murmur something near her ear in elvin or some other language of the nine worlds she couldn't identify at that moment. Then his lips touched hers and her fingers went limp, the ax falling onto the floor with a thump.

His lips were warm and firm. Her own opened beneath his; her hands grabbed his sides. Firm muscle met her touch. She groaned in pleasure as her fingers traced the lines of his abdomen. His tongue slipped inside her mouth, began exploring. She pushed closer, her body calling to be pressed against him, to feel the solidity of his chest, the heat of his body and the pounding of his heart. She wanted to touch every inch of him, to *be* touched, to feel for once in her life truly alive.

His hand moved to her shoulder and the loose cotton nightgown she wore slipped, baring her skin. His fingers were rough with calluses, earned in battle, she knew, fighting to survive like all the men she'd known before— but different, so different.

He pulled his mouth from hers and began pressing tiny

kisses to the side of her neck, down to her shoulder. She arched her back, her breasts pushing forward.

"Why? What?" he murmured, and she felt him pause, his forehead dropping to her shoulder. Then he looked up into her face. His eyes were no longer red, but even if they had been, she doubted it would have stopped her. She ran her hand over his chin, rejoicing in the prick of each bit of stubble she encountered. So real…

"Why can't I resist you?" he whispered, then lowered his head again, his lips just brushing against hers before she realized what was happening—what she had done.

Jerking her head back, out of his reach, she snapped her shields into place, an arrow piercing her heart as she saw him flinch as if struck, then shake his head as he came slowly out from under the power her Valkyrie half held over him.

She dropped her gaze, unable to face him after what she had done to him, made him do.

"Geysa?" He blinked and placed his fingers under her chin, tipping her face up.

She pulled her face away and stood, tripping over the fallen ax as she did. She caught her lip between her teeth to stop the curses she wanted to yell at herself and shoved the weapon back under the table with her foot. In angry strides she crossed to the trunk that sat at the end of her bed and the dirty clothes she'd tossed there when she had undressed earlier. As she jerked on her pants, she could feel Venge walking up behind her.

"What happened?" he asked, suspicion beginning to edge into his voice.

"You surprised me. I didn't mean…" Her shirt halfway over her head, she remembered the knife, the feel of the blade slicing into muscle. She jerked the shirt down and spun.

Her attention raced to his shoulder. The black T-shirt he
wore clung to his skin, a grapefruit-size spot even darker than
the material clearly showing her blade had found its mark.
Without thinking, she closed the distance between them.

"I hurt you." Her fingers danced around the wound,
unsure whether to pull the material free or leave it as it was.

He barely glanced at the spot. "You… I can smell you."
He inhaled, his chest expanding beneath her touch.

Geysa's fingers trembled as she tugged lightly at the
material of his shirt. Death and gore were things she was
all too familiar with, but the men who called Valhalla home
hadn't survived their wounds. She had no idea how to treat
a living, bleeding man. And she had caused not only this
wound, but another only a few nights earlier.

"You smell like fear…but not…" Venge's fingers
brushed along the line of her jaw, coming to a stop at the
point of her chin. He tilted her face until she was staring
into his eyes. He frowned. "I've never…" He leaned
forward and again captured her lips with his.

Geysa tried to resist. She pushed against his chest, but
even as she did she knew the effort was useless. She could
no more resist the pressure of his lips and the feel of his
fingers kneading her back, than she could deny what she'd
done, was apparently still doing—that he was acting this
way not because he chose to, but because of the horrible
hold her Valkyrie powers had on his kind.

She'd entrapped him, and damn it, she wasn't strong
enough to walk away.

Venge pulled his lips from Geysa's, his mind still scram-
bling to interpret what he'd just experienced. First the in-
satiable need to be with her, to follow her wherever she
went. Then the sudden cutting off of that sensation, leaving

him shaken and unsteady. And finally, just as he was beginning to sort all that out, he'd caught, for the first time, a whiff of her emotions and what he'd smelled hit him harder than any physical blow he'd ever taken.

She was afraid, but not *of* him. She was afraid for him.

Never in his life had Venge felt anyone experience fear *for* him.

He inhaled again, checking. Still there, softened now by the desire clouding around her, but still obvious enough that he knew he hadn't been mistaken.

He ran his hand over her back, lingering when his fingers found bare skin. Her pants rode low on her backside, baring the swell of her hips. Her skin was soft, like the skin of a peach. He kissed her again, small kisses, tugging her lower lip into his mouth then releasing it.

She relaxed against him, air leaving her lungs in a whoosh and her palms flattening against his chest—as if some last piece of resistance had fallen away. With a sigh, she ran one hand up his chest and around his neck, her fingers playing with the hair that fell over his nape.

He walked his fingers up her spine, tracing each bone with the pad of his fingers. She moaned and rubbed herself against him. The feel of her sex pressing against his urged him to move faster, quit playing, but he waited, enjoying the smell and feel of her and the soft warmth of her body tucked against his.

She tilted back her head, her hair falling down her back, her back arching and her breasts rubbing against his chest. Unable to resist the invitation, he shoved her shirt up and stared at the apricot-tinted tips of her breasts. They curved upward, tempting him to taste them.

He bent down and captured first one nipple then the other in his mouth. She jerked, her fingers digging into his shoulders. A sizzle of pain shot from his wound, but he ignored it—more than willing to endure any hurt rather than stop what they had started.

As she squirmed, he found the zipper to her pants and slowly worked it downward. She moved again, her hips urging the material lower. Impatient, he lifted her against him and pulled the jeans from her legs. Dressed only in the T-shirt that he'd pushed up only seconds earlier, she wrapped her long legs around his waist and stared down at him.

Her eyes glimmered. "I'm sorry," she whispered. Before he could question her response, she arched backward again and yanked the shirt over her head. Nude, she wrapped her hands around his face and pressed her lips to his.

The material of Venge's jeans rubbed against Geysa's sex, his erection pulsing beneath the thick denim. She could feel it there, so close, grew damp just thinking about it. She wanted him inside her so badly she could have screamed, but still some tiny part of her brain yelled at her for using him, deceiving him. She should stop, free him, tell him what she was and what power she had over him.

His hand ran down her back, over her buttocks, his fingers slipping inside her as he did so. She sucked in a breath and shoved herself down farther, praying he wouldn't stop. Even as the thought formed, she heard the hum of his zipper releasing and felt his erection spring forward. Like her, he wore nothing under his jeans. She lowered herself again, until the head of his penis brushed against her folds.

"I'm sorry," she murmured again, then tilted her hips forward.

His lips against her neck, he turned and pressed her back against the wall. "Don't be sorry," he whispered. "Be sure."

Her eyes finding his, she replied, "I'm sure." And

despite knowing what he was, what the other Valkyries would think, she was.

With a smile, he pulled back and plunged inside her.

Geysa squeezed her eyes shut, the sensation of him inside her, stretching her, pulling in and out, all the stimulation her mind could process at this moment. Then he began kissing her again and she responded, her tongue slipping into his mouth, finding his, sparring.

She clung to him, arms and legs wrapped around him, her entire body engaged in maintaining the rhythm he had set. One of his hands moved to her breast, palming her. His thumb found her nipple and rotated, teased.

Her head lolled to the side, resting on his shoulder, and she realized she was doing nothing but take, doing nothing for him. Small breaths escaping her lips, she nuzzled against his neck, nipping then licking his skin. He smelled of fire and man, tasted like smoke and salt.

Deep inside her a fire built. She panted, trying to prolong the moment, but even as she did, Venge's pace increased, his body growing heated. Faster and faster they went, and she joined him in the race, her blood pounding, her heart beating so fast she thought it might explode.

Then, just as she thought she couldn't take any more, her body began to shake, her muscles to contract. Beneath her hands, Venge shook, too, and he pressed her more tightly against the wall, his lips finding hers one last time as he exploded inside her.

Venge let his forehead rest against the wall beside Geysa. His heart was still pounding, his brain still spinning with the scent and feel of the woman wrapped around him. Sorry. She was sorry. For letting herself go? For having sex with a hellhound? With him?

A wire wound around his heart, tightening until he wanted to slam his fist against the wall and knock a hole in the plaster. But he didn't. Why should he? He was used to rejection—expected it.

The thought still burning in his mind, he pulled back, slipped from her body and let her feet find their way to the floor.

She leaned against the wall with her head bowed and her fingers pressing into the tops of her bare thighs. Shame. He could see it in how she slumped, could smell it oozing from within her.

He spun, anger making his motion sudden, then strode to where her clothes lay in a pile. He stooped to pick them up, his fingers curling into the cloth so tightly he could hear the material stretching, the threads close to breaking.

What was it about this female? How could he have misread her earlier emotions so severely?

He threw the clothes at her feet, the metal snap on her jeans banging against the floor. "Get dressed. We've wasted enough time. The horn is probably gone, but maybe we can find some clue." The words sounded abrupt and sudden in the silence of the room, but he didn't care...not about her or anything.

She glanced up. Her eyes were wet with tears and her sorrow hit him like a fist to his gut.

He pulled back then stepped forward in one movement, his hand stretched toward her. She shook her head, mumbling to herself, and started pulling on the clothes. Her shoulders shaking with a suppressed emotion that, unknown to her, he could smell—hurt. He had hurt her, not physically, but deeper.

Venge's fingers curled into his palms, his arm falling to

his side. He knew all too well the type of hurt she was experiencing. Rejection.

He hadn't…but he had, by turning from her, acting as if he didn't care. He had rejected her, but not until she'd shown her shame at being with him. She deserved his rejection. He'd given her pleasure, shared something with her…he'd thought. And she…she was ashamed. He glanced at her again, expecting the cold curtain of apathy he'd come to depend on to fall into place, to protect him.

But this time, it didn't. All he saw was her pain, and he had a new hellhound to hate…himself.

Chapter 7

Venge and Geysa stood on the edge of an old logging road. Trees towered overhead. To their right, the semi-even surface of the road gave way abruptly to mountain. Venge pushed his boot against a large rock and watched it plunge over the side.

"Here? The horn was here?" Geysa asked, glancing around. Back at her room, she had pulled on her clothes and Venge had shimmered them both to the side of the mountain, neither of them saying a word about what had passed between them just minutes earlier.

His eyes focused on where the rock had come to a rest thirty feet below, Venge didn't reply. The horn had been here. He could feel it in his blood as it hummed through his veins.

He shoved his hands into his pockets, and looked at her. "It was here."

Geysa stared back, doubt in her eyes. "How can you be so sure? It isn't here now—is it?" She glanced down the hill to the spot where the rock had settled. Without waiting for his response, she took a step forward. He grabbed her arm and pulled her back.

"It isn't here now, but it was. I can feel it."

"Feel it?" Her eyes wide, she looked up at him.

He could hear her breath and smell his own scent still wrapped around her. He wanted to pull her close again, re-capture the moment in her room when he had thought she cared for him…feared for him. Instead he dropped her arm as if it might sear his skin. Once he knew he was under control, he answered. "It isn't just that hellhounds can hear the horn. It has power over us, calls to us. It's almost like we're bound to it in some way." His hand drifted to the chain around his neck. What irony that hellhounds, one of the strongest and most feared of the nine worlds' beings, were also the ones so often bound to serve another—forced to do someone else's bidding.

"But you resisted…earlier…when you came to get me."

He laughed, a short, dry sound. "I have experience re-sisting."

"Oh." She turned away from him. Her back straight, she stared up the road. "Can you resist everything?"

He studied the way her shirt, pushed by a light breeze, clung to her back, the way her long hair danced forward into her face. "Not everything," he replied.

"Oh," she repeated, her shoulders slumping. "I'm sorry."

He frowned. Why did she keep saying that? "Not your fault. Maybe I'm not trying hard enough. Maybe…" He let the words fade off, finishing the sentence in his head. Maybe he didn't want to.

* * *

He knew. Guilt crawled over Geysa, enclosing her like a moth in a cocoon. She bit her lip and began walking up the steep incline of the road.

"Where are you going?" he called, his voice husky.

Her gaze cast onto the dirt in front of her, she shrugged. "We're here. Might as well look for some clue." And she needed distance…from him, from her guilt. The sound of his feet crunching over the gravel followed her.

He came up beside her. "Pretty big area."

She kept walking, trying to add distance between them, but a few feet wasn't enough. The only thing that would end the building confusion inside her was to get completely away from this town and Venge—a hellhound.

She murmured the word under her breath. She'd had sex with a hellhound. The Valkyries would despise her if they found out. Geysa had told Venge she was sure. And she had been at that moment. But now…reality was crashing around her. A part of her didn't regret the act…only the lie of using her powers to make him want her as much as she wanted him. But another part knew what she had done would be seen as unforgivable by the Valkyries. They wouldn't understand what had driven her…she didn't understand herself.

Her steps had slowed with her thoughts, and Venge now stood beside her. She scanned the ground, trying to ignore him, trying to concentrate on what had brought them to this mountainside—the horn. If she could find the horn, get away from this town, then maybe everything would fall back into place. Maybe she could go back to seeing hellhounds as nothing more than the beasts that stole souls for the ErlKing, as the monsters who killed her mother.

Maybe she could forget Venge.

Holding on to the thought, she concentrated on finding something…anything.

Then she saw it—a single feather. Her stomach clenched as she bent to pick it up. With the shaft pinched between two fingers, she pulled the feather through her free hand. The edge tickled her palm, taunted her. "The sound. You said it came from up high?" she asked.

Gravel grinding under his feet, Venge turned to face her. He glanced from the feather to her face, then frowned. "That's from a bird."

She waited.

"A bird couldn't carry the horn, or if it could, it couldn't sound the call." He plucked the feather from her hand. "What type of bird do you think it's from?"

"A falcon." She stared at the black-and-white plume he twirled between his fingers. "A gyrfalcon."

"A hunter," he replied. He ran his finger gently over the top of the feather.

"The best of all the falcons," she agreed. She held out her hand, willing him to return the item.

He glanced from her outstretched palm to her face, a line forming between his brows. *Give it to me,* she urged mentally, but she kept her shields up. She'd already forced him to her will once; she wouldn't allow herself to do it again—not for a feather that surely meant nothing. Not for anything, she corrected.

He tapped the plume's tip against his palm, then, his mouth firm, gently laid it across her palm. Her fingers snapped closed. She slipped the feather inside her shirt, made sure it was hidden, then smiled, her lips tight. "Nothing here. Next time we'll have to move faster."

His attention was focused on the neck of her shirt where

she had tucked away the feather, but at her words, he glanced up. "Yes, faster. No more…sidetracks."

She could feel blood rushing to her cheeks, but she hid it by spinning on her heel and moving back down the mountainside. "I need to get back. It's almost time for the bar to open. Jora will be looking for me."

He caught her within a pace and grabbed her by the arm. "You made a good point."

Distracted by the feel of the feather pricking into her skin, she blinked. "I did?"

"About the time. When we made our agreement we assumed we'd be together when the horn was sounded."

"Before, it was during the day," she replied, pressing her hand against the feather. Falcons hunted in the daytime.

"Yes," he replied.

"And the call came from the treetops," she said more to herself than to him. "But this time it was at night."

"Yes." He stared at her, obviously expecting her to continue, but she couldn't because, honestly, she had no idea what any of this meant. She was grasping for an explanation that didn't exist. Falcons hunted during the day, but Venge was right, a falcon couldn't use the horn. She was grasping for meaning where there was none.

But there was one being that could use the horn, had had access to it, hunted both day and night, and at times wore a cloak covered in feathers—feathers just like the one nestled against Geysa's breast. A Valkyrie.

Venge narrowed his eyes. Something was going on in Geysa's mind, something she had no intention of sharing with him. The feather… He glanced to where it rested between her breasts. After she'd found the feather she had acted differently.

The item meant something to her.

Tilting his lips into a smile, he looked back at her face. "If the calls come at night, how will I alert you in time?"

She jerked, as if startled from her thoughts, then frowned. "Like today, except…"

Except next time she wouldn't invite him inside her body, let him press her against a wall, let him forget even for a while that he was alone. His gaze roamed from her eyes to the curve of her lips, then her breasts. Her chest moved up and down with each breath.

"I'll—we'll get there in time," she finished, her tongue darting out to moisten her lips.

He jerked his eyes away from the flash of pink tongue and concentrated on not getting distracted. "Maybe, but why risk it?"

"We don't have a choice."

"But we do." He stepped forward; he couldn't help himself. His hand rose, itching to touch her, to brush back the hair that had blown onto her face.

She turned, moving away, and he let his hand drop.

He folded his arms over his chest. "I could move into the bar, or you could move into the bathhouse. We need to be closer if you want this to work."

"Do we?" Her hand drifted back to where she carried the feather. "Maybe. I'll think about it." She held her hand out toward him. "For now, let's get back. Like I said, Jora will be looking for me."

His teeth grinding together, he took her hand and shimmered them back to the town.

Geysa slid behind the bar. Her aunt shot a sideways glance from her to Venge who had entered a few minutes earlier and promptly stalked to a table in the back. The other hellhounds had lowered their eyes to their respective plates and drinks as he passed.

They were treating him differently than they had treated him before—differently than they treated any other hellhound. Geysa mulled over the change in their behavior for a few seconds before turning her back to all of them. Confident none, including Venge—especially Venge—could see her lips move or overhear her words, she addressed her aunt.

"When we find the horn, do we have a plan?"

Jora's gaze darted to the hellhounds chowing down their breakfasts, then back at Geysa. "Why, did you learn something?"

Geysa forced herself to keep her hand at her side, away from her shirt where the feather was still tucked between her breasts. "No, not yet, but we hadn't discussed it and I thought…" A hellhound entered the bar. Geysa nodded in acknowledgment, then turned back to Jora. "Did you bring your cloak?"

Jora frowned. "My cloak?"

Geysa picked up a tray and slid it under her arm. "Your cloak. Did you bring it or leave it in Valhalla?"

"I brought it, of course. You know how important—" Jora cocked her head, understanding flowing into her eyes. "Is this about Runa?"

Geysa straightened, her sudden action causing the feather to poke the sensitive skin on the underside of her breast. "I didn't mention Runa."

"No, but…" Jora placed a hand on Geysa's arm and steered her toward the wall, farther away from the audience of hellhounds. "You know it's tradition for the oldest daughter to inherit a Valkyrie's cloak. It was just a twist of the fates that in my sister's case her eldest child didn't inherit the Valkyrie skills to go along with it. Have you asked Runa to give up the cloak, give it to you?"

"Give me her cloak?" Geysa stared at her aunt. She thought Geysa was jealous Runa had received their mother's falcon cloak when their mother died. The cloaks allowed Valkyries to fly over battlefields and carry off the warriors deemed worthy of Valhalla. Runa was a Norn. She had no use for such an item…at least, Geysa hadn't thought she had before today.

"When it's time, I can earn my own," Geysa replied, struggling to think of a way to steer the topic back where she needed it.

"I know you can." Jora gave Geysa's arm a squeeze. "Gyr-falcons are rare, but not unheard of. You'll earn a cloak."

She said it with confidence, but Geysa knew her words were only that—words. As a second daughter, Geysa was dependent on taking whatever bird chose her. The odds of being selected by a gyrfalcon were slim, but despite her aunt's beliefs, the unlikelihood that a gyrfalcon would find her worthy didn't concern Geysa. Her lack of a cloak or what that cloak might turn out to be wasn't something she gave much thought. However, if it helped to let her aunt think she did, she'd use that misconception to learn what she really needed to know.

"Are any of the other Valkyries here gyrfalcons?" she asked, adding a tinge of longing to her tone.

Jora turned away, her voice lowering as she fumbled with a stack of dirty cups. "No. Actually, I only know of one outside of our family and she's been missing for years. The call of the wind was too much for her. She left one day and never came back."

A little-known risk of being a Valkyrie. Some mourned

for the days when Valkyries spent most of their lives flying over battlefields, swooping down in their feathered capes and taking the spirits of the fallen warriors. Today, the battles were fewer on the nine worlds and the majority of a Valkyrie's time was spent serving the warriors in Valhalla.

Occasionally, a Valkyrie took her cape and left, giving herself over to the wind. Some said they shifted permanently into bird form, but there was no record of this truly happening. Of course, the believers claimed that shifting was the last stage of a Valkyrie losing herself, that once she shifted, she was gone—losing her secret along with herself.

But Geysa didn't believe such tales. If a Valkyrie was using the horn, Geysa fully expected to find her with no feathers beyond those on her cloak.

"So, she could be here?" Geysa asked, her mind grasping the idea like a lifeline.

Jora dropped one of the cups, ignoring the clatter as it split in two on the floor. "What's going on?" she asked.

Realizing her aunt's naturally suspicious nature was stirring, Geysa tapped the tray under her arm and said, "I'd better get to that hellhound. He's looking restless."

Jora shot a glance to the bar's most recent arrival. Her brows lowered as she watched the bald hellhound bend at the waist and rest his forearms on a chair back, his gaze wandering over the other occupants of the bar, but showing no signs of impatience.

Ignoring the skeptical look on her aunt's face, Geysa strode away.

Venge watched Geysa and her aunt's conversation with interest. He strained to hear their words, but even his hellhound hearing was tested by the noise inside the room. He only managed to make out a few words…enough to know they were discussing some kind of cloak, but little more. The topic seemed innocent enough, but he'd seen the way Geysa had strode toward her aunt, her heels digging into the wood as she walked. There had been a reason for the conversation, a reason he suspected involved the feather she had found on the mountainside.

He was still considering this when she left the bar with the same determined stride, this time intent on leaving something or someone—her aunt, he guessed—behind. Geysa crossed the first six feet of floor in seconds, then stopped, glancing around as if deciding on a target. Her gaze lit upon a hellhound who had entered the bar not long after Geysa and Venge returned from the mountain.

The male, young, with a shaved head and a neck tattoo, had been studying the other hellhounds since his arrival. His body language screamed his purpose. He was new and he was looking for a fight. Venge had decided to ignore him, but as Geysa ground to halt beside him, her gray eyes tilted with a smile. The hellhound turned, his glance caressing Geysa's body with a heavy touch.

A growl formed deep in Venge's chest and his fingers gripped the edge of the table in front of him until a chunk of the old wood broke off in his hand. Without giving it conscious thought, he moved to his feet and traveled the few paces that stood between him and the pair.

His back to Geysa, Venge placed his palm flat on the table and separated Geysa from the intruder with his body. "I think you're looking for me," he said, his gaze grabbing the other male's and challenging him to look away.

A flash of something resembling victory appeared in the hellhound's eyes. "A welcoming committee. How convenient."

"No committee, just me." Venge held up his hand and the other hellhounds in the room shimmered away.

With the arrogance only untested youth can contain, the new arrival smiled, glanced around at the empty chairs then tilted his head and looked past Venge at Geysa. "How's that for service? He sent them all away, tails between their legs." He turned his gaze back on Venge, but his next words were directed at Geysa. "So, how about you? He have a claim on you?"

Venge couldn't see Geysa's expression, but he felt her move; a start of surprise, he suspected. Not waiting for her response, he leaned to the right, again grabbing the other hellhound's gaze. "I have claim on everything."

The tattooed hellhound dropped his regard to the chain at Venge's neck and smiled, revealing even white teeth. "I was looking for you, but I wasn't told…" he stepped to his right so he could again see Geysa past Venge "…what all this place offered."

The growl passed Venge's chest and then his lips. He grabbed the tattooed hellhound by the front of his shirt and shoved him backward, until he was pinned against the bar.

"If you were looking for me, you found me. Now what?"

"This, I guess." The male slipped his hand behind him and pulled something from the small of his back. Before Venge could move, a white-hot pain shot through his side. The smell of blood engulfed them, but caught up in a new wave of rage, Venge hardly noticed. He dropped his hand, grabbed the other male's wrist and squeezed until he heard the metallic clank of a weapon hitting the floor.

His anger growing, he kept squeezing, even as he felt his shirt, damp with blood, cling to his skin. The hellhound he held began to bend at the knees. He twitched to the right, his left hand rising as he did. Venge grabbed the middle finger of the other male's hand and twisted backward until he heard the pop of a broken bone.

"Your neck can be next," Venge said, his voice low. The pain in his side began to morph, to snake under his skin. He ignored it.

"Not here, it can't." Jora, the bartender, slammed her ever-present sword into the bar beside them, the steel edge of the blade slicing into the wood. "I've warned you before, hellhound." Her gray gaze pinned Venge; he could feel it, but kept his own on the hellhound who had admired Geysa then shoved a blade beneath Venge's ribs.

The pain in Venge's side began to slither then change, as if something with tiny talons was moving beneath his skin. He resisted the need to drop the male he held and claw at the wound.

"What's happening?" Geysa stepped closer. "What is that?" Her voice dropped as she knelt behind him. The butterfly-light touch of her fingers followed. Venge gritted his teeth against the resulting new throb of pain, and gripped the hellhound he held tighter.

"Leave it," he ground out, but he knew this injury wasn't a simple one. The tiny talons dug into muscle as if some living thing was burrowing inside him, crawling like a spiked spider up his side, toward his heart.

She mumbled a curse in response. "Jora, come here," she called.

The bartender cocked an eyebrow, then vaulted over the bar, landing lightly on her feet next to Geysa. Bending next to Venge, she muttered, "The gods' fire. I haven't seen one of those in centuries."

The hellhound in Venge's grip moved, angling his head to see what the two women were discussing. Whatever had taken up residence under Venge's skin continued to inch upward, like a rock climber sticking in one spike then another as it pulled itself along. Just to take his mind off the pain, Venge grabbed another of the hellhound's fingers and jerked.

"Me or the alpha?" he asked.

The females beside him whispered, but intent on settling one problem before he moved on to another, he blocked out their words.

The tattooed hellhound stared back, his eyes belligerent.

Geysa stood. "Forget him. We have to get this out of you."

Venge acknowledged her statement by shifting his grip to the male's third finger. "Running out of time. Maybe this one I'll tear off," he said, the growing pain making his voice rough. "Forandre heal, but we don't usually grow back parts." He pulled until he heard the first crack of bone. Then, the other male's finger still grasped in his hand, he asked again, "Me or the alpha? Who were you looking for?"

The hellhound bared his teeth.

Venge bent his finger a micrometer more. "Last chance," he said.

Behind him, Geysa or her aunt pressed another finger to his wound. Instinctively he jerked away from the pain, pulling the hellhounds finger as he did.

At the other male's growl, Venge forced his lips into a grin. "Oops," he said. The male scowled back.

"Alpha or—" Venge started.

"Both," the other hound spit out. "I wanted to defeat the alpha, and someone told me how to find you."

"Who?"

His knees buckling beneath him, the tattooed hellhound shrugged. "Couldn't say. Hood. Stood in the shadows. I got the feeling he wanted you taken down, but didn't think he could do it himself." He stared at Venge through eyes darkened with anguish, but kept his head high—defiant. Venge respected that.

"And you thought you could?"

The male tilted his chin upward. "Of course." His reply was matter-of-fact. It wasn't in a hellhound's nature to doubt his success at battle. It's one of the things that made them so dangerous, to others and themselves.

Venge laughed and shoved the hound away. "You still think so?"

His broken fingers hanging limply from one hand, the hellhound balled the other into a fist. "I may be hurt, but I'll heal. How about you, alpha?" His glance moved to Venge's side.

Venge could feel whatever the hound had loosed on him continuing its climb, but he refused to look, refused to admit the crawling torment was anything more than a petty annoyance. He'd overcome worse.

"If you're so sure. Stick around." He took a step forward. Something jerked in his side. Whatever the other hound had pushed into him was anchored to something. Venge could move no farther without causing even more damage to his already torn-up side. The knowledge angered him as much as the pain. He used both to feed his rage, to let the other hellhound know how far he was willing to go.

The other male held Venge's stare for a second, his lips thinning.

A hand, cool and feminine, touched Venge's arm. Geysa. Having her so close, while the other hound still posed a threat, caused Venge to slip a little further. Heat simmered into his eyes. His blood pumped heavy but fast through his veins. A snarl curled his lip and he could feel the tension in his body as it prepared to change. Human and wounded, he was dangerous. Canine and wounded, he'd tear the other hellhound to pieces.

And the other male could see it. His gaze darted from Venge to Geysa, then back. "I can wait. Shouldn't be too long." Without another word, the hellhound shimmered and disappeared.

"Jora," Geysa called, her fingers digging into Venge's arm.

Still fighting to ignore whatever was clawing a path between his muscle and skin, Venge clenched his jaw and started to stride away—somewhere he could investigate this invasion in private.

Geysa stepped in front of him, stopping his exit. "Sit down. Jora says he used a quill blade on you."

The name meant nothing to Venge. But he had torn more than one weapon from his body. His attention still on Geysa, he moved his hand to the blade's entry point. He found a squirming cable of metal protruding from his side. Hiding his shock, he wrapped his fingers around the thick piece of moving wire and prepared to jerk it from his body.

Geysa jumped forward. "Stop. It's Svartalfaran." She waited, her eyes searching his. "It works under your skin, destroying tissue as it goes. If it isn't removed carefully, it can be deadly."

"It is deadly." Jora stepped next to Geysa, her gaze cool as she studied Venge's face.

"Svartalfaran," he muttered, twisting to see where the weapon had pierced his side. As he had thought, a twisted metal cable protruded from under his ribs and ran down the length of his leg. Resting on the floor was the handle, a small metal cylinder no bigger than his fist. "Hand it to me," he said.

Geysa hesitated, but then bent to retrieve the pewter-colored object. As she stood, the cable disappeared back into the handle. She stopped when only a foot of slack was left.

The other end of the wire twisted under Venge's skin, inching farther away from its original entrance point. He could see the bulge of it moving, like a mole burrowing beneath the ground.

"What's it made of?" he asked. As the bulge moved higher, leaving his side and crawling up his chest, a cold sweat beaded onto his body.

"I'm not sure. The Svartalfar are secretive—especially of their metalwork." Jora again, her voice dispassionate.

Locking his knees to stay upright, Venge nodded. He knew she spoke the truth. Svartalfars were almost as talented with metal as dwarves, but much less boisterous, and they didn't tend to make goods for trade. Anything of Svartalfaran origin was made for a Svartalfar's use, most likely against a typical Svartalfar enemy. In other words, not a forandre. The thought generated an idea.

"I can escape it," he said.

Skepticism with a flicker of interest shone from Jora's eyes.

"Are you sure?" There was a tremble in Geysa's voice. Worry? Again he wished he could sense her emotions. She turned to her aunt. "What will happen if he can't?"

"I've known a number of warriors who've tried," Jora replied. A look Venge couldn't interpret passed between the two. When their gazes returned to him, Jora's eyes still held cool indifference, but Geysa's were round with…horror? Shock? Venge couldn't tell, and at the moment was too distracted by the object crawling inside him to care.

Geysa lowered her attention to the cylinder cradled in her hand. "What if we left it in?"

Ignoring Geysa's question, Jora turned to Venge. "If

you're going to do something, you might want to do it now." Then she crossed her arms over her chest and waited. Leaving no doubt that she had no interest in whether he succeeded or failed, just wanted to get on with the show.

Venge glanced at Geysa. He thought he could escape this thing boring inside him, but in case he couldn't, he wanted to...what?

Nothing. He wanted nothing.

Steeling his mind to cut through the fog of agony surrounding him, he nodded to the cylinder she held. "Hold on to it. If it's only touching me, it may not work."

Geysa wrapped her fingers around the cylinder and nodded.

Gritting his teeth, Venge shimmered.

Chapter 8

As Venge disappeared in a glisten of light, a soft whirring noise sounded and the cylinder in Geysa's hand vibrated slightly. She glanced down. The strange metal object felt cold and foreign. As she watched, the metal wire that had been lodged in Venge's body sped back into the handle. With a click it came to a stop, leaving nothing but a two-inch-long bloody tip visible.

"It's out," she murmured. She looked at her aunt. "Does that mean he's safe?" Her voice cracked slightly, just enough that she heard the emotion she was trying to hide. She couldn't deny how desperately she wanted Venge to be okay, at least not to herself.

Jora opened her mouth to reply, but before she could voice the words, the space next to Geysa began to shimmer again. She stepped back, clutching the cylinder tight in her fist.

In the space of two heartbeats, Venge stood still bleeding

but solid beside her. She took a step forward, her first instinct to throw herself against him, but a questioning glance from her aunt stopped her.

"You're okay," she said. Her heart beat so loudly it seemed to echo in her ears.

He stepped forward, his palm outstretched, asking silently for the cylinder. "I'll live."

While she wanted to rush forward, to press her body against his just to reassure herself he spoke the truth, there was no emotion in his reply…as if none of this mattered… She stared at his open palm for a second, reality crashing around her. She cared…really cared…about a hellhound. The realization held her trapped for a moment, then cold anger flowed over her.

How had she screwed up so thoroughly?

"How'd you do it?" Jora grabbed a towel off the top of the bar and tossed it to Venge.

He pressed the cloth to his side. Blood quickly seeped through the white towel, forming a deep red stain. Trying to be as nonchalant as Venge and her aunt, Geysa grabbed a second towel and moved to Venge's side. He pulled the first away and held out a hand for the second, but she ignored him, instead pressing the cloth against his wound herself, pressing hard enough he jerked. Realizing her emotions were showing, she gentled her touch. And despite her disgust with herself, a silent wish that she had some power for healing formed in her head. Frowning, she pressed the towel tight against the tear in Venge's side and tried to keep her expression passive.

His gaze dropped to her, and for a second she thought he might touch her, but instead he placed his hand on the cloth she held. "It's fine." His voice was firm.

Her fingers curling into her palms, she nodded and stepped back.

Glancing at her aunt, he said, "I shimmered."

"Obviously," Jora replied.

Venge studied her for a second, then continued. "Svartalfars don't have much reason to deal with forandre. Why build a weapon to kill them? Once I thought about it, it made sense. Besides, shimmering wasn't going to make my situation worse."

"Probably," Geysa murmured. Then louder, asked, "If forandre don't go to Svartalfaheim, where did the hellhound who used this thing—" Geysa gave the quill blade she still held a tiny shake "—get it?"

"That's a good question." Venge paused, balling up the newly stained towel and tossing it onto a table. "You said your 'family' had access to weapons, didn't you?"

Geysa could only stare at him, her mouth opening a bit in disbelief.

"You told him that?" Jora looked at Geysa.

"She offered me a deal. You in on that, too?" Venge pulled out a chair, turned it around backward and sat.

The anger Geysa had been directing at herself changed, turning full force on Venge.

"What kind of deal?" Jora asked, her glance shifting from Geysa to Venge and back again.

Venge cocked a brow and watched Geysa.

"Nothing. He's delusional. You know I would never trust a hellhound." Geysa walked to the bar and slammed the cylinder down.

Neither Venge nor Jora moved. They just stood watching her, waiting.

She shook her head. Neither trusted her, and right now she didn't give a damn.

"I need to talk to Runa." Brushing past her aunt and ignoring Venge, she left the bar.

* * *

Almost blind with anger, Geysa stepped off the porch and collided with the old human male who had stubbornly stayed in the town after the Valkyries and hellhounds had taken over. He had never given his name, but Geysa had taken to calling him Audun.

Today, like all days, he was wrapped in a moth-eaten wool blanket, only his face and legs visible. He walked crouched over, his gaze on his feet. When Geysa plowed into him, he wobbled and she rushed forward, pressing a hand against his back to steady him. She was momentarily distracted by the unexpected feel of muscle under the wool, but as a coughing fit caught the old man in its hold, concern raced over her, knocking aside the anger that had sent her storming from the bar.

"Here." She guided him to the side of the building where he could lean and catch his breath. "The bar isn't open right now. Were you coming for breakfast?"

He nodded, obviously weak. She hadn't seen the old man around in the past day. Had he not been eating?

"I'll walk you back home." She started to place her hand on his arm to guide him down the street, but he shook her off, struggling to straighten his body and follow her under his own steam.

Knowing her pity would only insult him, she stepped back and slowed her pace to match his shuffling steps. She had left the bar because she was angry and needed to get away from both Jora and Venge, but she also needed to talk to Runa about the feather. A conversation best had without an audience. She darted a glance at the man shuffling along beside her. He stumbled, almost falling onto the dirt.

She frowned. *He needed to eat.*

As he righted himself, Geysa came to a decision. She

could get Audun something to eat and *then* pin Runa in a corner. The old man would be no threat to their privacy. He could barely stand upright and Geysa doubted he was aware of even half of what went on around him. Which was probably a better explanation than stubbornness or bravery as to why he stayed in the town once it was invaded by hell-hounds, but either way, she respected him for clinging to life as tenaciously as he did.

And there was something basic and honest in how he lived…sparse, asking for nothing, no matter how great his need.

With her world turning upside down around her, Geysa needed a little of that honesty right now.

When Geysa left, Venge blocked out the sound of her retreating footsteps. She was angry. He could see it in the flash of her eyes and hear it in the snap of her heels as they dug their way across the floor. His intention hadn't been to anger her, but he couldn't ignore the fact that she had admitted to having access to an arsenal of exotic weapons. He couldn't let her think he trusted her, and he didn't. Trust was something foreign to Venge. Something he didn't believe he could ever experience.

He stood and walked to the bar. After picking up the quill blade, he turned and faced Jora. "So, is this yours?"

The older woman arched one brow, an amused look on her face. "It doesn't matter the breed, males are all alike."

Venge frowned, not liking her tone or expression. He flicked his wrist, causing the tip of the blade to quiver. "This probably works fine on your kind—whatever that may be."

"Probably, but you won't use it."

Venge's frown deepened. He took a step forward. "You don't know hellhounds very well, do you?"

Jora laughed. "Better than my surprisingly naive niece. Did she tell you hellhounds killed her mother, my sister?"

Venge didn't reply. The blade grew warm in his hand, heavy.

Jora tilted her face, studied him. "I'm beginning to wonder exactly how naive she is. Naive enough to forget what hellhounds are...what they were bred for? Beasts created with the hunt in mind...that kill just to hear the snap of their victims' spines, to feed on their fear and pain." She spit out the last word and her disgust hit Venge full force.

He narrowed his eyes.

She hadn't said anything he hadn't said himself—didn't believe to be true. But she wasn't a hellhound, didn't understand the torment of their lives. She had no right to judge them.

He held out the blade. The tip brushed against her chest, over the material that covered her heart. One quick jab and she'd be dead. There'd be no waiting for the quill to work its way deeper...no recovering from a wound like that. The strike would be direct and fatal.

She held his gaze; her gray eyes so like Geysa's filled with a knowledge deep and ancient—and pain, an old pain that even Venge couldn't understand.

Something clenched in his gut. And with a muttered curse, he spun, slammed the blade back onto the bar's top and strode from the building.

Runa was at her table, cards overturned in front of her. When Geysa and Audun walked in, she swept them off into her lap.

Geysa angled her brow in question. Runa wasn't usually so secretive, probably because she realized her cards and stones meant nothing to Geysa.

"Slow day," Runa said, stacking the cards into a pile.

"Not for me." Geysa motioned to Audun. "Do you have something he could eat? Then we need to talk." She placed her hand on the feather still hidden beneath her shirt, reassuring herself it was still there even though she could feel its soft edge brushing against her skin.

"Sure." Runa gave Geysa an assessing look, then pushed herself to a stand and wandered into the kitchen.

A few minutes later she was back, a steaming plate in her hand. She draped a cloth over the top of the table and slid the plate onto it. "Here. Stew. Vegetarian. I'm afraid I don't do meat."

As the old man shuffled forward, Geysa pointed her sister back toward the kitchen.

Runa plucked a dirty pan off the woodstove and dropped it into the dry sink. Geysa jumped at the clatter. Apparently unaware of the noise, Runa poured water out of another pan and began scrubbing the pot.

"So, you were doing a reading?" Geysa asked.

Runa nodded.

"You don't do that often—read your own cards."

Runa shoved a strand of hair from her face.

"Any reason?" A queasy feeling was sneaking up on Geysa. Something wasn't right. The feather felt unnaturally heavy pressing against her skin.

"That I don't usually read my own cards or that I did today?" Runa dropped the dishrag into the pan, her back still to Geysa. Then without warning, she spun. "I just did. Norns do that sometimes. Just like Valkyries wait on men sometimes."

Geysa's brows lowered. She gestured toward the main room where they had left Audun. "He was hungry. We don't ask you to work in the bar."

Runa strode to the doorway between the kitchen and the main room. Geysa had left the door ajar so she could check on Audun if needed. After peering out, Runa looked back at Geysa. "I just don't like men in my house."

"But you invited Venge to stay here. Why?" A flicker of anger began to grow inside Geysa.

"He's different."

Geysa folded her arms over her chest.

"You told me you wanted to watch the hellhounds destined to be in the hunt."

Geysa froze. "And Venge is?"

Runa looked back at the sink.

"Is he?" Geysa asked.

"I can't tell. One stone isn't enough. But there's something about him. Something different from the others. I just thought he merited watching."

"And that's all?"

Runa looked up, surprise in her eyes. "Of course, what else?"

"Nothing." Geysa pushed open the door a bit more and peered out at Audun. The old man had finished his meal and was now slumped back in the chair. A soft snore rumbled from his lips.

Confident he wasn't listening, she turned back to her sister. "Have you learned anything about the horn?"

"Wouldn't I have told you if I had?" Runa pulled a towel out of a drawer and began drying the stew pot.

"So, you haven't targeted a hellhound and followed him to where it was sounded?"

"Follow a hellhound? I thought that was your assignment."

Geysa frowned. She had an uneasy feeling her sister was playing some Norn trick with her, evading questions and leading Geysa astray. Despite her doubts, she answered. "I was, but…"

"But what?" Runa turned, interest shining bright in her eyes.

"Nothing." Geysa shook her head, forcing herself not to get sidetracked. "You haven't been where the horn has sounded? Perhaps wearing Mother's cape?"

Runa folded the towel and laid it on the table. "How would I know? I do wear Mother's cape every now and then. It makes me feel…" Her fingers dug into the white cloth of the towel. "Makes her feel closer." She glanced up, tears glimmering in her eyes. "She was more like you than me—more Valkyrie than Norn. In her cape, I get to feel a little of what the two of you shared." She pressed her hand flat over the towel, her fingers turning white. "You don't mind, do you?"

Geysa yanked her gaze back to Runa's face. "Mind what?"

"That I…you know…got Mother's cape."

"Have you been talking to Jora?" Irritation made Geysa's voice sharp. Seeing the confusion on Runa's face, she softened her tone. "No, I don't mind. I got her shield." She pinched the tiny medallion between her fingers. The feel of the gold warmed by her body's heat reassured her that, no, she was not jealous. First Jora, now Runa accusing her of it, had started to make her doubt her own mind. "That's enough. The only thing left I want are her killers stopped."

"Killer, you mean." Runa's eyes snapped, her previous sorrow disappearing instantly.

"No, killers…the hellhounds, the hunt…all of it. What do you mean?"

"The ErlKing. He is the hunt. The hounds are just one of his tools, no more responsible for what happens in the hunt than the stallion he rides or the horn for that matter."

Runa took a step forward, her fists balling at her sides. "If you want to avenge Mother, you need to concentrate on the ErlKing."

Something about Runa's stance, the gleam in her eye, made Geysa take a step backward. She bumped into the semi-open door, pushing it loudly against the wall. Audun made a sputtering noise, then sat up, rubbing his eyes.

Her gaze again on Runa, Geysa took another step back into the main room. "I'd better get Audun to his house, or the bar, wherever he wants to go. Thanks for letting me bring him here."

Runa made a flapping motion with her hand. "Just don't do it again."

With a nod, Geysa walked to Audun and waited for him to stand. Once erect, he paused for a second, his attention wandering to where Runa stood in the doorway of the kitchen. "Thank you for the meal," he muttered.

Without responding, Runa turned and walked back into the kitchen. Geysa stared after her sister, her hand automatically going to her breasts and the feather tucked between them. Runa had admitted to nothing, but she hadn't really denied anything, either—then her adamant hatred of the ErlKing. Hatred that apparently overshadowed any feelings she had toward the hellhounds or the hunt as a whole. Geysa'd had no idea her sister felt this way. They had never discussed her mother's death—not really.

All this time Runa had been blaming the ErlKing, while Geysa's hatred had been focused on the hounds. The realization stopped Geysa for a second. Was Runa right? Were the hellhounds no more than a tool? No more responsible than the horn?

Audun wobbled on his feet, snapping Geysa out of her thoughts. Jumping forward, she laid a steadying hand on his elbow. He quickly righted himself and began shuffling toward the door.

Geysa waited a second, her glance moving over the cards her sister had left on top of the table. How she wished she could deal a few cards and come up with some answers.

Sigurd kept his stride slow and shuffling. The young Valkyrie was easy to fool, but he'd been worried about her sister, the Norn. Luckily the Norn had never given him any attention.

That one had secrets—more than her sister or the other females. He'd seen her more than once sneaking out late at night, or in the early-morning light. It hadn't occurred to him until now that she might know something that could help him in his quest to find and destroy the horn.

Just as she'd let her prejudices blind her, dismissing him as an old human of no merit or threat, he'd done the same. He had not even considered a female, especially a Norn, could be involved with the hunt.

Still thinking about this twist, Sigurd forgot his current disguise for a second and allowed his spine to straighten.

"Looks like the food did you some good." Geysa smiled at him.

Quickly remembering his act, he turned away and began shuffling into the darkness.

"The bar should be open now, if you want to come back," she called after him.

With only a grunt for a response, he stepped around the corner of the nearest building, and waited for her to give up on her good deed for the day. Whether she saw it or not, her sister was up to something. If that something involved calling up the hunt, Sigurd was going to stop her.

* * *

As the door to the bathhouse opened, Venge stepped behind the remains of an old rusted-out truck. Two wheels on blocks, two hanging precariously in midair, the vehicle was a risky hiding place at best.

The old human shuffled onto the porch, Geysa right behind him. Venge's gaze was instantly drawn to Geysa. She stepped close to the old man, her face tilting up, and even knowing there could be nothing between the two, something twisted in Venge's gut. He balled his fists and shook the irrational feelings away.

She wasn't his. One encounter didn't make her his.

The thought only made the twisting increase. Clenching his jaw until he thought it might crack from the pressure, he forced his mind back to why he was here—to find the horn. *Concentrate on the horn.*

Geysa gestured toward the bar, but the old man made no response, just shuffled away in the opposite direction. Geysa paused, a look of hurt passing over her face…or was Venge imagining that? Seeing hurt where there was none? To give him an excuse to hunt the old man down and crack his skull against a rock—to hear his spine crack, as Jora had claimed?

He suppressed a growl at the thought and forced his mind away from Geysa's aunt…and the truth of her words.

Caught up in his thoughts, he almost missed Geysa's approach. She was headed directly toward him. He thinned his lips at his sloppiness. Perhaps he could explain away his spying, but after Geysa's angry exit from the bar, he didn't think confrontation was the wisest choice right now.

Instead he decided on another little-known hellhound talent: blending. It wasn't effective against all beings…but Geysa? He had no idea what she was, what powers she possessed. No matter, it was his only choice. Drawing as lightly as he could upon the skill, he concentrated on not being noticed, on making any eyes directed his way skim over his body like so much background.

Geysa continued to move toward him, casting one last glance at the old man shuffling away, then hurried past Venge, her head down.

Venge curled his fingers into his palms and let the breath he'd been holding escape. Now what? Follow Geysa? Or return to the bathhouse—see if he could learn something from her sister?

As he was weighing his choices, the sound of feet striking packed dirt pulled his attention back to the street. Walking toward him in a hurried stride was the old human. The striped wool blanket was still wrapped around him, but the shuffling steps and hunched back were gone.

Venge froze, then quickly kneeled. This was no old man, not even a human, if Venge were to guess. The man approached from the direction he'd left, leaving Venge hidden from view behind the truck. The footsteps stopped a few feet away. Venge peered carefully around the end of a dangling bumper.

The man looked around then shoved the blanket off his head. Venge's eyes widened in surprise, but hatred quickly drowned out the softer emotion. *Sigurd.* Another hellhound in Lusse's pack. Second only to the alpha, Venge's father, in power and Lusse's trust. Sigurd had been the one to torment Venge in his father's absence, throwing Venge into the pit to be taunted and beaten by the rest of the pack.

Venge had last seen the older hellhound five years earlier on the day he had left Lusse's kennels. Venge had heard rumors that Lusse was gone, trapped in another world. When Sigurd's back was turned, he'd bolted, not knowing if anyone would follow, not caring. He could stand the kennels no more—death was preferable.

But no one had followed...until now.

Chapter 9

Sigurd pushed back the hood of his cloak and pulled the crisp mountain air into his lungs. His back ached from the constant stooping required by his disguise and his legs longed to stride purposely up the mountainside. He was tired of pretending weakness, of seeing pity in the eyes of the females and contempt in the eyes of the hellhounds.

Foolhardy as it might be, he needed a break. He tilted his head to the sky and stretched his neck. The Norn was the key. He knew that now. Perhaps in just hours this pretense would be over. The door to the bathhouse creaked. Sigurd pulled the cloak back around himself, stepped next to a tree and let the cloak's magic work to change his appearance into whatever Runa would expect to see leaning next to one of the ancient pines. He never knew what the others saw. Just that they didn't see him. The cloak was much safer than blending. He could move in the cloak and stay concealed, with blending he couldn't. Plus, it worked on all beings. Other hellhounds would see right through the less dependable talent of blending.

Runa stepped onto the porch, her eyes scanning the street. Apparently convinced she was alone, she reached back inside the house and pulled out a large canvas bag. After taking another glance around, she shoved her arm through the loop and took off down the street. Maybe ten yards along, she took a quick swing to the right, disappearing between two buildings.

Pressing his lips together to stop a curse, Sigurd silently jogged after her.

Venge waited, giving Sigurd and Runa both plenty of time to get ahead. Without the advantage of whatever magic Sigurd was using to hide his identity, Venge couldn't afford to get too close. Not until one of them pulled out the horn, that is.

Then, there'd be no need for secrecy. No reason not to release some portion of the hatred churning inside Venge. He would destroy Sigurd and steal the horn...all in just a few minutes' time.

It was going to be a good day.

Runa and Sigurd's paths wove up the mountainside, through trees and over slippery pine needles. Concentrating on tracking the two, Venge ignored everything except their scents and the slight imprint in the forest floor left by the weight of their feet. He didn't even allow himself to enjoy being on a hunt, following prey, knowing that soon he'd be on them. Hellhounds were born to hunt. Even hating what he was as much as Venge did, he couldn't deny that most basic part of himself. But for now, he could push it aside.

As he approached a small clearing, he heard voices—Runa and Sigurd. They were arguing. Shrieking, actually. At least Runa was. Keeping his footsteps soft, Venge picked up his pace.

Geysa was almost to the bar when she realized she had to go back to Runa's. She'd totally copped out on asking the hard question. She needed to pull the feather from its hiding place inside her shirt and confront her sister.

She didn't want to think Runa was behind the recalling of the hunt, but the feather certainly pointed in her direction.

Add to that her sister's reaction to the ErlKing and Geysa had to face facts. She didn't know what Runa was capable of, not really.

Turning on her heel, she pulled the feather from her shirt and began striding back to the bathhouse.

Venge stepped into the clearing. The remains of an old cabin were piled in one corner and a small stream bisected the space. On the far side near the cabin stood Sigurd. Hovering above him, covered in a flapping feathered cape was Runa. Clasped in one of her hands was a horn, silver and shining even in the little light that managed its way through the trees.

The cape moved upward like wings, and for a second Venge thought she would escape, but just as quickly as she rose, Sigurd yanked her back down by the ankle.

Runa shrieked, an angry unnatural sound that made the hair rise on the back of Venge's neck.

"Give me the horn and I'll let you leave," Sigurd called.

Runa made no response, just doubled her efforts. Her cape flapped in the wind, the noise so loud Venge was tempted to place his hands over his ears.

"The horn," Sigurd roared. He placed his other hand on Runa's calf, his hands climbing her leg.

Fisting her fingers around the edge of her cape, Runa jerked a feather free. Gripping it, she shrieked again—a gyrfalcon. Venge recognized the call. As the thought formed in his head, he heard the beating of wings, louder and louder until the sound all but drowned out the noise of Runa's struggles.

A line of falcons, birds that hunted alone, circled overhead. Runa screamed again. Her tone changed, more challenge than outrage, and as one the birds dropped from the sky, talons extended and directed at Sigurd.

His attention on Runa, Sigurd somehow missed their approach. As the first falcon hit, tearing at his flesh, Sigurd looked up, his eyes rounding in surprise. Still clinging to Runa, he bent, bowing his head. Another falcon struck, but as the bird's talon scraped over Sigurd's cloak, it screamed, not in pain but anger. The birds continued to soar toward Sigurd. Some hit the cloak, leaving Sigurd unscathed, but others found flesh and soon blood streamed down Sigurd's body, staining his shirt.

Venge clenched his fists at his sides, aching to join the fight, but seeing neither side as his own.

Runa screeched. Her eyes snapped with emotion. Her cape cracked in the wind. Then she gestured to her own leg—where Sigurd's hands still held her.

As one of the birds attacked, tearing at Sigurd but striking Runa, as well, she shrieked and Sigurd roared, but neither gave up their fight. Then as blood covered them both, Sigurd's grip slipped. Runa, a light of victory in her eyes, pulled back her free leg and smashed her heel into his forehead. Sigurd fell, Runa's leg slipping from his hold as he went.

With one final scream, Runa circled overhead, then with

a whirl of her cape, disappeared over the trees. The line of falcons followed.

Sigurd lay on the ground, his chest heaving, his eyes closed. Defeat. He reeked of it.

Venge stalked forward until he stood over the male who along with his father had made his youth hell. Sigurd's face was tired, his eyes filled with regret. He said nothing, just stared at Venge, not even giving Venge the gift of his surprise, much less his fear.

Venge cursed, wishing the other male was on his feet ready to fight. But he just lay there, giving Venge nothing.

Venge cursed again and started to walk away, but he stopped. Memories of Sigurd lining up hellhounds to beat him gnawed at his brain. Sigurd shoving him into a cage, taking charge of his imprisonment when the witch Lusse left. Sigurd was not his father, but he was the next best thing.

Venge turned back, spat on the ground inches from Sigurd's face, then pulled back his foot and kicked the other hound directly in the head.

Sigurd twisted. His hands still covered in blood, he grabbed Venge by the ankle. Pulling his legs back toward his chest, Sigurd flipped and jerked Venge into the dirt beside him.

Venge landed on his back, air swooshing out of his lungs, the back of his head colliding with rock. Sigurd, his hands still wrapped around Venge's leg, jerked Venge through the dirt toward him. Venge let him, waiting until he was close, when Sigurd would be least prepared….

With Venge beside him, Sigurd released Venge's leg to undo the clasp of his cloak then fling it to the side. Venge took advantage of the few seconds of inattention to surge upward and wrap his hand around Sigurd's neck.

"Long time no see," he muttered.

Sigurd smiled, his brown eyes changing, growing darker, burgundy as the bloodlust started. "Hello, pup. Looks like you've grown up."

"Count on it." The chain on Sigurd's neck bit into Venge's palm, reminding him of their connection. He snarled. "What brings you here? Hunting?"

Sigurd's eyes glimmered, his gaze dropping to Venge's neck, where Lusse's silver chain still lay. "I have no argument with you."

Venge laughed. "How nice, but I have plenty of argument with you." Unable to do more than squeeze Sigurd's neck in this position, he shoved the other hellhound away. He wanted a fight...a fair fight.

They both staggered to their feet. Sigurd rubbed his throat and wiped blood from his hands onto his pants. Venge's gaze dropped to the cloak at Sigurd's feet. "New toy?"

Sigurd kept his attention on Venge. "Why are you still here? The hunt isn't what the mongrels arriving here think it is. The horn promises freedom, but what it delivers is very different. Bondage...just like what you had in Lusse's kennels, but worse. Held by your basest desires, unable to travel of your own free will, bound to go where the horn orders you, to kill who the horn demands."

He took a step forward. "Nothing of *you* will be left. Not even the hellhound in you. Just instincts, desires. The hounds of the hunt are nothing but shadows of themselves, specters. Is that what you seek?"

Venge kept his face impassive. Sigurd lied; he knew it. The hounds of the hunt were revered in hellhound circles, beings of legend. But it didn't matter, because Venge had no intention of joining the hunt. He was going to lead it...once he had the horn.

"And you, you have no interest in the hunt?" he asked.

"Only in stopping it." Sigurd bent, scooped up a handful of dirt and threw it into Venge's face.

Momentarily blinded, Venge steeled himself for Sigurd's attack. He didn't have to wait. Sigurd hit him full force, his body slamming into Venge's. Again they were both on the ground. His eyes streaming, Venge grappled to find a hold. He could smell the blood on Sigurd's hands and knew at that moment those fresh wounds were Sigurd's biggest weakness. Venge waited for Sigurd to settle his hold, then moved his own hands to Sigurd's and dug his nails into the tears the falcons had started, clawing away the skin.

Sigurd grunted, but didn't loosen his grip. His fist balled around the chain at Venge's neck, twisted, tightening the chain until Venge gasped for breath. "Is this what you want? Bondage to a being even more callous than Lusse? The ErlKing may not share Lusse's love of torture, but in his kennel you'll be nothing more than a tool, not even something worthy of his taunts."

He twisted the chain again, leaned in and whispered in Venge's ear, "He won't even pay you the compliment of trying to break you. He won't have to.

"Go home. Or wherever you've been for the last five years. There's nothing here for you."

Then with a suddenness that made Venge fall back against the ground, Sigurd shimmered and was gone.

Venge leaped to his feet, spinning, sure Sigurd was still nearby, but the forest was empty—the only sound a faint rustling in the underbrush as some innocent creature recognized Venge's rage, his nearness to bloodlust, and ran.

Run. Sigurd *should* run. When Venge met him next he would… Venge stared at his hands, at the blood, Sigurd's blood, crusted under his fingernails. Sigurd had escaped. Runa, too…with the horn. But Venge had recognized her cape…it all made sense now. Only one type of being possessed such a cape. The tiny shields Geysa wore at her throat…Valkyries. Geysa and her family were Valkyries. Ancient enemies of the hellhounds who centuries before had stopped the Wild Hunt by stealing the horn.

Now apparently they'd lost it, and were trying desperately to retrieve it…so desperately they'd lie down with the creatures they despised.

His almost crazed mind focused on that thought, and he shimmered…his only focus Geysa.

Geysa shoved her knife blade into the space between the bathhouse's back door and the jamb. She'd knocked at the front and received no answer. She should have gone back to the bar then, waited until tomorrow to confront Runa, but she couldn't. She needed an answer now. So, she was breaking into her own sister's house, prepared to rifle through her belongings like a common thief.

After a few minutes spent jiggling the blade up and down, the primitive lock gave. Sucking in her breath, Geysa returned the knife to her boot and stepped inside.

The house was dark—all the windows covered by heavy blankets. Funny, Geysa hadn't noticed that before—that Runa had made such an effort to keep prying eyes out. Or were Geysa's suspicions causing her to invent motivations that didn't exist?

Not expecting to find herself alone in the dark, she hadn't thought to bring a flashlight today. Leaving the door open, she began a quick search of the kitchen drawers. On the third she hit gold—a stub of an old candle and a pack of matches. After melting enough wax to hold the candle upright on a dish, she shut the back door and headed into the main room.

The light from the candle barely cut through the surrounding gloom. Performing a slow spin, Geysa cataloged
the room's contents more from memory than sight. There
was really very little here…except Runa's fortune-telling
tools, but those would be of no use to Geysa. Besides, if
Runa were hiding the horn, she wouldn't keep it down here
where one of the hellhounds she read for might find it.

With that in mind, Geysa began to climb the stairs. The
steps were narrow and steep, another thing she didn't
remember from when the house was well lit and she wasn't
alone. She kept her hand on the railing, each creak of the
board beneath her feet causing her to stop and listen—sure
Runa had returned and would discover her.

And what would Runa do if she did? Did Geysa even
know her sister well enough to answer that question?

Shaking the doubts from her head, she gripped the
railing more tightly and continued her climb. Halfway
down the hallway leading to Runa's room, the candle came
loose from its wax moorings, fell over and sputtered out.
In darkness, Geysa placed a hand on the wall to keep from
toppling over.

She was sneaking around her sister's house, preparing
to go through her things to see if she could be responsible
for calling back the most feared force in the nine worlds.
The force responsible for their own mother's death. It was
impossible—crazy.

Geysa leaned against the wall and pulled in a deep
breath. It was crazy, but that was good, right? She would
just continue what she started—take a look in Runa's room.
She wouldn't find anything, then she could mark Runa off
her list and concentrate on really finding the horn.

Balancing the plate with the candle on one knee, she

struck another match. The candle hissed into life. Her fingers wrapped around the plate, Geysa continued her trip down the hall.

Venge shimmered back to his room. The bar had been empty…. Geysa's room had been empty, increasing his suspicions that she knew more than she'd let on. But if she knew her sister had the horn, why ask for Venge's help?

He was reaching for a match to light the oil lamp beside his bed when he heard a noise—the sound of a match striking and a few mumbled words.

Runa. Had she come back? Would finding the horn be this simple? Leaving the lamp unlit, he edged the door of his room open and peered into the hall. A few feet away the door to Runa's room was open, too—only a foot or so, but enough to see light coming from within.

Venge shimmered.

Geysa turned in a circle, studying her sister's room— bed, table, trunk. Nothing more. Made searching simple.

She knelt in front of the trunk and placed the candle on the floor next to her. Licking her lips, she grasped the heavy iron clasps and flipped the lid open. The top banged against the bed with a thud. She jumped.

Once her heart had resumed its normal beat, she retrieved the candle and held it over the open trunk so she could see what lay inside.

Very little. Nothing except a few changes of clothes. Geysa frowned then leaned in farther and ran her free hand over the top of the twin stacks of clothing. Something soft tickled her fingers. Exhaling through her nose, she closed her fingers and pulled the object out…. She didn't have to look to know what she held: a gyrfalcon feather.

She pulled the one she'd found earlier from her shirt and laid them both on the floor. She couldn't look at them, not yet. Instead she returned to the trunk. "No horn. No horn," she whispered.

This time she dug deeper, running her hand along the side of the trunk, under both stacks of clothing and between layers. She was ready to let out the anxious breath she held, when she felt something…not the horn, but something just as damning.

A bag—small and made of velvet, with a silk drawstring cord. The bag that had housed the Wild Hunt horn for the past three hundred years. She jerked the sack out from under a pair of jeans and stared at it with the same loathing she would have the ErlKing himself.

Runa…her sister…who she had known all her life… who she loved…had stolen the horn and was now using it to unleash the Wild Hunt. Something inside of Geysa cracked, leaving her exposed and lost.

Hoping to surprise Runa, Venge shimmered into a corner of her room. She was kneeling in front of a trunk, her head bowed, a candle flickering beside her on the floor. Barely giving his body a chance to materialize, he shimmered again, this time solidifying directly behind her.

He wrapped his arms around her body to grasp her wrists. He knew from his experience with Geysa the Valkyries weren't slow to react, and their reaction could be painful.

Runa was no different. As soon as his hands touched her, she swung her body to the side, knocking him off balance and into the burning candle. Wax sputtered; smoke filled the air. The woman in his arms struggled against him, her hand moving toward her boot. He pulled her between his legs, her back to him. She bumped against him again. This time, as the candle made contact with his leg, his jeans caught on fire. Knowing flames couldn't harm him, he ignored the growing heat, but the woman he held gasped, a soft sound that caused his head to tilt in recognition. His body tensed.

Not Runa…Geysa. What was she doing here? And what was he going to do with her?

Chapter 10

Geysa rounded her eyes as fire crept up her captor's leg. She hadn't meant to set him on fire, but now that she had, she knew she had to take advantage of the situation. Ignoring the red glow and smell of burning cotton, she twisted inside his arms, trying to throw him off balance and free herself.

They both hit the ground, Geysa on top. She couldn't see his face, could only feel his body beneath hers, strong, broad, and intimidating. She reached for her knife, but as if able to read her mind, his hand grasped her wrist.

"I told you it was time for a new trick." Venge's voice rumbled in her ear.

Venge. Relief, then apprehension, rolled over her—one following so quickly after the other she could do little more than blink trying to still her spinning mind. When she'd last seen him, she'd been angry. How did she feel now? How did he feel?

He sat up, taking Geysa's weight with him, and clapped his hand over the fire that was busy consuming the wax-coated denim. She started to help, reaching her hand toward the flickering glow, but he stopped her with a shake of his head. "Fire's no threat."

She pulled her hand back, her fingers curling into her palms. That's right. He was a hellhound. Nice of him to remind her. She needed that.

She watched as he systematically suffocated the fire with his bare palm. When he was through, her gaze darted to the open trunk and the velvet bag that was draped over its edge. Runa. The horn. She'd almost forgotten.

"What are you doing here?" she asked.

"I live here." He wrapped an arm around her waist, pulling her tighter to his body. "What about you?" The words and action could have been playful, but they weren't. His voice was steady with no hint of teasing, no emotion at all.

Geysa swallowed. "Visiting…my sister."

"Really?"

"She isn't here." With the fire extinguished and the candle out, it was dark again, dark enough he couldn't see the flush she could feel creeping up her neck. At least she hoped he couldn't. "I'd better leave." She started to stand.

His grip didn't lessen. "I've never met a Valkyrie before. What's it like to lure a man's soul from his body?"

Geysa stiffened.

"You're rare, you know. I didn't think Valkyries existed outside the walls of Valhalla. Didn't really know if you existed at all. But…" His hand cradled the back of her head. He brought his face close, brushed his cheek against her hair. "What powers do you have besides luring men? Or is that enough? Is that why no matter how I try, I can't get you out of my mind, my soul…what little there is of it?"

She felt his breath on her face, his hand trailing down her cheek, then her neck and shoulder.

She opened her mouth to tell him…what? What did she want to tell him? He was a hellhound. She was a Valkyrie. A pairing that would never work. Valkyries had hated hellhounds for as long as either had existed—for destroying souls when Valkyries cared for them. And hellhounds had killed her mother. She clung to the thoughts, trying to burn them into her brain, tried to stop the flow of emotions and sensations that threatened to push her under, to make her forget everything but Venge.

Then he kissed her, a soft movement of his lips on hers, testing, tasting, making her want more. She blinked back tears of frustration, muttered a small prayer of forgiveness for forgetting herself yet again and gave herself up to the warmth of his body beside her.

He hadn't meant this to happen. Not again. Yes, he'd wanted to find Geysa, to let her know she could drop her act…that he knew she was a Valkyrie…that she couldn't care about him—not that he'd ever really believed she could, but he'd hoped. Somewhere deep inside himself he'd hoped. And when he'd realized the truth—that she was the one being who could play his emotions against him and that he was a tool to her just as Sigurd had said he would be for the ErlKing—he'd hated her. Not because of what she'd done, but because of what he'd wanted…believed possible if only for a second.

And damn the tiny speck of his soul that struggled to exist, that still longed to hope she could care, even now, knowing what she was.

Shoving all thoughts of hope, need and manipulation out of his head, he moved his lips over hers and stroked the backs of his fingers down her cheek. Soft, feminine, but still warrior strong. No wonder generations of heroes had followed her ancestors, leaving behind everything they'd ever loved or struggled to be.

Right now at this exact moment in time, Venge would have taken on an army of ale-crazed dwarves just for a few more moments in her arms.

"Venge," she murmured.

"Shh." He didn't want to hear words, didn't want to think right now. He rose to his knees and pulled her with him until they both kneeled in front of the trunk—her back pressed against it, his hands on either side of her keeping her from leaving.

"But I…"

"Shh," he repeated. She smelled good, as always. And she felt good—as always. He ran his palms down her body, along her sides, barely skimming the curve of her breasts. She pushed closer to him, her breasts flattening against his chest. She tilted her head and pressed tiny kisses to his neck. Her tongue flicked out, danced over his skin. A shiver passed over him and he moved his hands to her front, cupping her breasts.

She followed his lead, her hands skimming over his body, pulling his T-shirt free from his jeans. Her fingers slipped under his waistband, stroked the sensitive skin there. Another shiver. Her nails scraped against him. Pleasure, not pain, made his erection strain against his fly. Her fingers slipped lower until she caressed the tip of him. His groin tightened. His entire body tightened with need. He moved his hands to her butt and pulled her against him until her pelvis ground against his.

The pressure…so intense…

She tugged on the front of his jeans, pulling them away

from his body until her fingers could work the button. His zipper slid down, his penis pushed free, and something inside of him relaxed and tightened at the same time. Relief and anticipation rolled into one overwhelming need.

Venge's hands moved from Geysa's buttocks to her stomach, his thumbs catching on her shirt and pushing it along as his hands roamed her body. She arched her back, pushing her breasts forward. Cool air hit her heated skin.

She sucked her lower lip into her mouth and moved her hips against his, bumping into the trunk behind her as she did. The sharp edge of the iron clasp dug into her back, reminding her where she was, what she had been doing.

The bag.

Venge's lips traveled down her neck, his hands finding her breasts, pushing up the human bra she chose to wear. His head lowered, his mouth finding the aching tips that he had uncovered.

A gasp escaped her lips, but her thoughts detached her from the moment. The bag. Would he know what it was for? He'd claimed he would give her the horn…but was it true? Was anything true?

Her heart racing, she pulled her hands free of his pants and slipped them behind her, first undoing the hook that held her bra, then pulling both the undergarment and her shirt over her hand. She dropped them onto the floor then casually let her hand fall to the edge of the trunk where the bag still lay. She knocked it over the edge, back inside the trunk.

Another puff of air left her lips, this time a sigh. Venge massaged her breasts, his hands warm and strong, making the rest of her body scream for attention. Attention she didn't deserve. He knew her first lie of omission, but now she had added another. She bit her lip.

Venge murmured against her skin, his mouth roaming from her breast down to the indentation of her belly button, his hand unsnapping her pants. She wiggled her hips, willing the material to fall. He grasped her by the waist, his tongue darting into her belly button then sliding lower.

His thumbs hooked the thin strips of material that held on her panties and all her thoughts of lying and the feelings of guilt were gone. All she could think of was how much she wanted him, right now…and forever.

As her clothing slipped away she worked on freeing him from his, as well. First his shirt, her hands pausing only briefly to appreciate the indentation of his abs, the solidity of his chest. Then his pants, her frustration making her growl when he refused to move away from her long enough to complete the task. Instead he scooped her into his arms and shimmered.

The magic in the movement added to her excitement— every inch of her body, inside and out, tingling. Still kneeling, they materialized on his bed. He laid her down, smoothing her hair around her head, brushing his fingers over her brow. Then he stood and finished removing his clothing. There was more light in his room, enough so she could see him, appreciate him.

He stood for a second, looking down at her, his face serious, his gaze intense. Then, without a word, he knelt over her, his knee going between hers.

Her heart fluttered and her fingers curled into the blanket beneath her. She had never wanted anything as badly as she wanted this man…this hellhound.

The thought scraped at old wounds, but she shoved it aside, instead concentrating on Venge…only Venge. He lowered his head first, capturing her lips, then lowered his body until his weight pressed her into the mattress. She could feel his erection nudging against her. She opened her thighs, inviting—no, begging—him to enter.

Her hips arching upward, she ran her fingernails down his back, found the indentations above his buttocks, then walked her fingers across and down until they rested in the tiny space between his buttocks, over his tailbone.

A breath shuddered out of him and she moved one hand to his erection. As he stared into her eyes, she positioned him against her folds and he plunged inside.

He moved slowly at first, then faster, his gaze holding hers as his rhythm increased. Her breath came quicker, too, erupting from her throat in heavy pants. She tilted her hips, increasing the pressure, taking more of him inside her. Sweat clung to her body like a veil and the musty scent of the two of them joining filled the room.

Faster and faster he moved, the pressure inside her building with each of his thrusts—until she could feel herself floating overhead, spinning, still aware of each of his movements, while pleasure sent her soaring. Her body began to shake, to tighten around him. He shuddered, too, his gaze burning into her, saying something she couldn't understand, then together they plunged over the side and settled back down.

A soft sigh fell from her lips as Venge lowered his body onto hers.

Venge lay next to Geysa, the sweat on her body mingling with his own. Neither said a word. Venge's heart hammered in his chest. He reached out to stroke Geysa's hair even as his brain told him not to—to distance himself instead.

But he couldn't. He knew he couldn't. Whether it was Valkyrie magic or a weakness inside him, he couldn't let go of how he felt, how much he wanted her to share that feeling. Love? He clenched his jaw. He wouldn't go there, couldn't.

So, here he was—stuck. Couldn't give himself over to a feeling he wouldn't name, and couldn't let that feeling go, either. He was caught with no visible escape.

Geysa turned and pressed a kiss to his shoulder. "I'm sorry I didn't tell you that we're Valkyries," she murmured. "My aunt, she thought it best. When the hunt was running, well…and then when the Valkyries took the horn…" She looked up at him, her eyes huge and filled with regret.

"Are the stories true? Can the Valkyries control hellhounds?" The words came out clipped. Even with her nestled against him, Venge couldn't stand the thought of being under someone else's control, especially a control he couldn't see. At least Lusse's bonds had been visible, obvious—honest.

"Control?" She frowned. "Not control, more influence. Luring men has always been one of our skills. We couldn't pull warriors from their bodies and bring them to Valhalla without it. But with hellhounds it's more than that." She exhaled through her mouth. "More of an obsession than an enticement. We have to keep ourselves shielded constantly. When we first came, we didn't realize how bad it would be. There were fights—"

"With hellhounds there are always fights," Venge interrupted, his fingers balling around her hair.

"This was different. You saw it."

"The first day. When I arrived." Venge stared at the wall beside them. "I felt different."

"And then, the first time, when you came to my room." She moved as if to sit up, but his hand in her hair held her down. She fell back, her expression cautious. "I was sleeping. I didn't think… As soon as I realized what was happening, I put up my shields, but it was too late. You'd already succumbed and I…" She looked down and back up. "I didn't want to stop you."

Venge smiled. The first real smile he remembered ever experiencing. "You didn't want to stop me."

She looked away, her tongue darting out to moisten her lips. "It was selfish. Since then I've been more careful."

He leaned down and pressed his lips against hers, silencing the misplaced guilt. Little did she know how much he wished he could blame his reaction to her on her Valkyrie powers, but he couldn't lie to himself that way. Not anymore.

Geysa slumbered beside Venge, her breath soft and even. She murmured in her sleep and nuzzled closer. Her twin shield charms shone against her throat. Venge touched them lightly.

They both wore chains around their necks, but how different their meaning. He touched his own chain, his fingers wrapping around it, gripping it. The metal was heavy and cold, even though it had lain against his skin.

The chains were just another sign of how different they were, how whatever was between them couldn't be.

Geysa's chain symbolized love and loss, Venge's hate and bondage.

Geysa chose to wear her chain with the tiny gold shields. Venge... He pulled back, realization hitting him. He chose to wear his, too, but he hadn't...not originally. It wasn't his choice to put the links around his neck. But now he needed it to remind him of what had happened, of what he needed to do.

Geysa stirred, her hand fluttering against his chest. He twisted his chain around his neck, clung to the reminder.

Venge had just settled down, his arm behind his head, when he heard it...the horn. His heart froze, the hair on his arms standing up. He looked at Geysa, but she hadn't moved.

Runa was using the horn. If Venge wanted it for his own,

he needed to leave now. But…Geysa. He hadn't yet told her that her sister was calling up the hunt, and he had agreed to take Geysa with him when he did hear the horn.

But that was before he knew about Runa. His gaze dropped back to the tiny shields nestled now in the hollow of her neck. Geysa loved her family. There was no way she would be part of what he was about to do.

He had to get that horn…one way or another. Concentrating on that thought, he shimmered.

Sigurd was already on the mountainside when Venge arrived, as were at least a dozen other hellhounds. Runa soared overhead, her feet skimming through the air just out of Sigurd's reach. The horn at her lips, she glared at the hellhound, then inhaled through her mouth and blew. The silver peal stopped Venge midstride.

The scent of blood, wind rushing through his hair, cool earth beneath his feet—the sensations hit so quickly he staggered backward, was barely able to stop himself from falling.

Around him the other hellhounds didn't show as much restraint, as one by one they Changed. Until only Sigurd and Venge maintained their human forms.

Runa's cape flapping above them, the horn still sounding, the hellhounds began to snarl and growl. The peal was stronger than it had been before…more intense.

"She's learning how to use it," Sigurd yelled over the sound of raging hellhounds. "Before none Changed." He shook his head, then looked up at Runa, his eyes snapping with anger.

One of the youngest hellhounds leaped, trying to reach the horn or take flight…which one, Venge wasn't sure. Instead, the pup fell onto a group of other hellhounds. As one, they turned, teeth flashing and hackles raised, then jumped on the intruder. The sound of their roars as they ripped him apart filled the glade.

"You see? You see what it does to us?" Sigurd yelled again. He held up one hand, pointing to Runa.

Venge ignored him. He could handle the horn, but… He glanced at Runa, flying back and forth over the clearing. The sound and sight of the hellhounds ripping into each other below seemed to intensify her efforts. Her eyes gleaming, she raised the horn again.

Five more hellhounds shimmered into the clearing and instantly Changed.

Sigurd stared up and cursed.

Runa soared up and over the trees, then back down.

Venge followed her with his gaze. A pattern. She was following a pattern. He waited and she proved him right, swooping low again.

Which meant… Venge shimmered, rematerializing midair just above the tree line, right where Runa should be…. He began falling before the tingle of the shimmer had passed. Arms outstretched, he opened his eyes and concentrated on the feathered cape fluttering beneath him. Air rushed past him as he fell. He kept his eyes open despite the speed of his descent—the surety that he was plunging to his death.

In an explosion of feathers, he hit. His weight collided with Runa full force. Together they tumbled toward the earth, Runa shrieking and scratching as they fell.

"Geysa, wake up."

Geysa blinked, the urgency in the voice bringing her instantly awake. She sat up.

Her aunt stood in front of her, holding a lantern. "The hellhounds are gone." Her gaze flicked from Geysa's bare breasts to the empty pillow beside her. "All of them."

Geysa stared at her aunt, her mind struggling to process what she was saying, what was happening. She twisted at the waist, placing her hand on Venge's pillow. It was cold. He was gone, and had been for how long?

She looked back at her aunt. Jora waited, her eyes cold. "You have clothes somewhere? Or you want to go like that?"

Ignoring the judgment in her aunt's eyes, Geysa leaned forward. "Go where?" Where was Venge?

"The hellhounds. They've all disappeared. You think it might have something to do with the horn?" The dryness of her aunt's tone told Geysa more than her words. She thought Geysa had slipped.

Geysa glanced back at the pillow where Venge had laid beside her. Maybe she had.

Chapter 11

The ground rushed toward them. Runa lashed out, her nails scraping across Venge's face. He cursed, struggling to maintain his hold on her. He meant to shimmer to bring them both down to the earth softly, or even miles away where he could take the horn from her without others' interference, but her struggles stopped him. If he miscalculated, shimmered just as she pulled away, she'd fall and Venge would lose her...and the horn.

As trees zoomed past, Venge heard Sigurd roar. Venge surged forward, grabbing Runa in a bear hug. His arms wrapped around her body; his hands locked around each other over her chest. He looked up. The earth— Venge flipped, hitting the ground with a heart-stopping jolt. Runa lay atop him, completely still except her heart, which beat like a bird's in her chest.

An ache spread through Venge's back, his head felt as

if it might explode, but he couldn't rest, not now. Already, Sigurd stood beside them. His hands covered in some kind of mesh gloves, he reached for the horn.

Venge flipped again, rolling Runa beneath him, pushing her face into the dirt to keep her from shrieking, from calling the falcons she'd set upon Sigurd before. With her contained as much as he could, he lifted his head and snarled at Sigurd. "It's mine," he said.

"You don't want it," Sigurd replied, tension making the muscles of his chest and arms bulge.

"Trust me, I do, and I'm willing to kill to get it."

Runa began to struggle beneath him. His gaze still on Sigurd, Venge relaxed his hold enough to unlatch the feathered cloak around her neck. She turned her head, her teeth sinking into his bicep.

Venge cursed, his attention switching to the female. Sigurd didn't hesitate. He threw himself onto Venge's back, knocking him off Runa. Venge cursed again as Runa's teeth finished the job, ripping the skin she held between her teeth free. A hot pain pierced his arm like a brand burning into his flesh, but Venge kept his hold on her cloak, pulling it with him and out of her reach.

Sigurd glanced down at Venge, his gaze shooting from the empty cloak back to Runa, who, still holding the horn, scrambled up the steep slope of the mountain. Without the cloak to aid her, her feet slipped on the blanket of pine needles covering the forest floor and she fell. Her free hand shot out to break her fall, but her forehead still collided with a rock. She glanced back at them, her eyes wild. Blood streamed from a cut at her hairline. The horn cradled against her chest, she wiped the back of her other hand across her forehead, swiping away sweat and blood, and resumed her attempts to escape.

Sigurd turned on Venge. His body seemed to vibrate with rage, the smell of it clouding around him. He shoved his hand into a small bag that hung from his belt and flung something at Venge. "Here, at least use these."

Two objects, like pebbles, struck Venge in the chest. With a frown, he kneeled and retrieved them from the dirt. Small and soft with a piece of twine sticking from their ends.

"Earplugs, for the horn." Sigurd motioned to Runa, who had given up on climbing the mountainside and instead sat, the horn rising to her lips.

Venge hesitated.

"Are you blind?" Sigurd yelled, his arm sweeping toward the other hellhounds who were now so fully engaged in battle it was difficult to tell one squirming body or set of flashing teeth from another.

Gritting his teeth, Venge slid the plugs into his ears.

Silence. No gnashing of the hellhounds' teeth, no wind whispering through the trees. Nothing. Another sense lost. Venge reached up, ready to pull the plugs out…to assure himself the loss was temporary, but Sigurd held up a fist and pointed to Runa, stopping him. The mouthpiece of the horn was pressed against her lips, the bell pointed at the sky. With her stiff posture and the squareness of her shoulders, there was no mistaking she had restarted the call—and this time she was putting her all into it.

Venge took a step forward, ready to shimmer. As he did, a new fervor broke out among the hellhounds. The group closest smashed into him, knocking him to his knees. Dirt flew into his eyes, his mouth, and his open wound. Knocking the nearest hound away, he spat and pushed himself to a stand.

He was barely upright when the air around him began to shift and cool. His gaze shot to the sky. Above him, some in feathered cloaks like Runa's, some astride massive horses, the Valkyries circled. And in the lead, her hand wrapped around a gleaming sword, her legs around a snorting destrier, rode Geysa.

Geysa flew over the clearing, her heart pounding, her eyes darting side to side. She had told Jora what she'd found, that she suspected Runa of having stolen the horn. Jora hadn't replied, just thinned her lips and ordered Geysa to join the others.

Their horses and battle gear had been waiting in the street below. It had been centuries since the Valkyries had ridden this way. Modern times had changed how they were perceived, forced them to be less grand in their retrieval methods. They still took the spirits of the worthy, but secretly without the pomp of their feathered cloaks and stamping destriers.

But today they were riding against the Wild Hunt, and Jora had wanted everyone to know it.

As Geysa reined her horse around a tree so she could see all of the clearing, Jora dropped from overhead, her cloak flapping behind her.

"You were right. It's Runa." Jora held out one hand, pointing to the side of the mountain where Geysa's sister sat, the horn pressed to her lips. Geysa's heart sank as surely as if it had been filled with lead. "And—" Jora spat "—your lover."

Geysa's head snapped to the side. Venge stood swaying, pressed all around by snarling, snapping hellhounds—beasts. He caught her gaze. She felt her hand begin to rise—to what? Call for him? Assure him that she—

"Geysa, now." Jora swooped down, her hands like talons in front of her. But toward who? Geysa couldn't see. Runa,

Venge or another hound she could see standing near them? Who was her aunt's target?

Geysa's blood pounded through her veins; her entire body quivered with each pulse. The rushing wind, the flapping of the capes around her and the heavy breath of the stallion she rode drowned out all other noise. Unsure what she planned, she followed her aunt's lead and reined her horse toward the battle below.

Geysa was coming. Venge could see her falling toward him. He stood frozen for a second, indecision nipping at his resolve.

A hellhound slammed against him and Venge stared down into the beast's glowing eyes. Eyes aware of nothing but the lust for blood. Hatred rippled through Venge. Hatred for his father, his own kind…himself. With emotion still pouring through him, he shimmered, wrapped his undamaged arm around Runa's neck and squeezed.

She fought back. The horn dangling from one hand, she clawed at his arm with the other. He ignored the pain, and focused on the horn. So close. He twisted at the waist, reaching for the horn. As he did, the air shifted around him—Sigurd shimmering.

Sigurd struck at Venge, the mesh metal gloves he wore dragging across the open wound on Venge's arm and hitting the horn.

All three froze, their stares following the horn as it flipped end over end through the air.

Out of nowhere, the air seemed to split, changing from hot to cold in the time of one breath. Venge's senses screamed at him…something unnatural…lethal…was coming. His head jerked upward, his eyes searching for Geysa. She was still there, astride her stallion…safe. A trickle of relief made its way past the pain and adrenaline filling Venge.

As he watched, she threw her hands over her ears and, her eyes round, she also searched the sky.

A figure, so dark he seemed to suck all light from around him, plunged toward them. The gray stallion he rode pawed at the air and flung its head upward, steam flowing from its nostrils. The Valkyries' horses pulled back, their riders fighting to keep the steeds calm. Venge could understand the horses' apprehension. The Valkyries' mounts, impressive though they were, appeared like ponies in comparison to this storming beast.

Runa twisted in his arms, a gleam of victory in her eyes. She batted at Venge's arm, which still held her. Without thinking why, he released her.

She stood, teetering as if her knees couldn't hold her weight. Her gaze on the figure zooming toward her, she reached into the sack strapped across her chest and pulled out a crossbow.

Unable to stand the lack of hearing any longer, Venge tugged the plugs from his ears. The sound of rushing wind as the horseman plowed through the sky knocked against him.

In front of him, Runa pulled an arrow from her bag and notched it into the crossbow. Her eyes still glimmering, she raised the bow's butt to her shoulder and pressed the tiller to her cheek. Her body rigid with concentration, she waited.

From the side, the Valkyries moved in, Jora in the lead. She plunged, heading toward the horn. Venge shimmered, landing beside the horn seconds before Geysa's aunt. He reached out, his fingers within an inch of touching the relic, and was hit from behind. Sigurd, snarling curses, knocked both Venge and Jora away from the horn. They landed in a pile, Jora cursing as strongly as Sigurd. Her hand flying to the scabbard at her waist, she leveled her gaze at Sigurd and charged.

Venge leaped to a stand. The horn lay in the dirt halfway between himself and Runa. Geysa's sister still sat with the crossbow pointed toward the sky, her lips drawn in a thin line.

Venge darted forward, bending as he ran, ready to scoop up the horn and shimmer, but as he did a horse landed next to Runa—the rider leaping from her steed to the ground. Geysa. Even dashing across the ground, Venge couldn't miss her. He could feel her. Either she'd forgotten to raise her shields or he was immune to them. Her fear hit him square in the chest, stopping his forward movement like a wall. He jolted to a stop, his gaze dashing from the horn to Geysa—unsure where to go first.

As he watched, Geysa hurried forward and lay a hand on her sister's shoulder. Runa shoved Geysa away, her hand catching in Geysa's shirt, pulling her sleeve off her arm. The white piece of cloth flapping from her hand, Runa glared at her sister, her eyes wild...lost. Venge recognized the signs. Lost in the lust to kill. He'd been there—too often.

Geysa pulled back her hand as if burned, and looked away, directly at Venge. Her eyes, huge and filled with panic, stared at him. She glanced down at the horn only feet away from him and her emotions morphed from fear to sorrow. Sorrow caused by him. By his greed—no, *need*—for the horn.

She had no right to judge him, didn't know what he had been through.... He fought to cling to the thought, to be angry rather than moved, but he couldn't hold on to the emotion. He felt himself slipping.

The sound of the crossbow, vibrating with power as its arrow shot skyward, pulled Venge's attention back to Runa. Shoving her hand back in the bag, she cursed.

Geysa spun, her neck craned and her eyes on the sky. The horseman dove downward, one arm outstretched. His target was obvious…the sisters.

The ErlKing. Geysa stared up at the dark figure racing toward them. It had to be. No one else except a god had such power. Wind swirled around her, so cold she couldn't move. The sound of hooves pounding and the wind whistling overrode all else. He was coming…for Runa.

She tried to move, to warn her sister, but her legs wouldn't budge. She could only stand by and watch as the dark form changed to the shape of a man, clothed in dark armor, the head of a boar placed on his head like a helmet. The animal's tusks curved upward, the ends tipped with silver. Razor sharp, Geysa knew from the tales. Not that he needed the added defense. Once a being was in the ErlKing's sight, had his awareness, it was over. No one had ever returned from his hunt.

As he approached, so close Geysa could smell the sweat from his horse and see the vacant blackness of his eyes, an arm wrapped around her and tugged her away. She fell, her attacker falling with her. She tried to break away, to get back to Runa, but it was useless. The pair rolled like logs down the hill.

They came to a halt, knocking into a group of pines. She jumped to her feet, ignoring the ache in her muscles, the bruises she could already feel forming. "The ErlKing," she muttered, her heart dropping. There was no way Runa could get out of this intact.

The man who had taken her from her sister's side stepped next to her. "I couldn't let him take you," Venge murmured.

"But you could her?" Geysa bit her lip, watching as the ErlKing leaned sideways in his saddle, his arm sweeping out. Runa, realizing her peril too late, dropped the cross-bow and took off across the clearing in a run, the sleeve from Geysa's shirt still trailing forgotten from her fist. Her feet seemed to barely touch the surface of the dirt, but she wasn't fast enough. The ErlKing reined his horse around and kneed him into a gallop.

Each pounding hoofbeat seemed to smash into Geysa; she closed her eyes. She couldn't watch. Couldn't see her mother's fate repeated by her sister.

"Gods be damned," Venge swore beside her.

"What?" Geysa's eyelids flew open, her hand curling around Venge's arm for support.

The ErlKing, with Runa draped across his lap, bent from the saddle again. This time, he scooped up the deserted horn before pointing his mount back to the sky.

Geysa watched, a hollowness filling her chest. She'd lost her. First her mother, now Runa…. What did she have left?

Geysa stared vacantly ahead. Venge glanced from her face to her nails cutting into his skin. Pain rolled off her. He tensed his arm, concentrating on the physical hurt she was causing him rather than getting lost in the sensual pull of her emotions.

"She's gone," she murmured. As if suddenly realizing where she was, she dropped her grip on Venge's arm and turned to face him. "Why did you stop me? I could have—"

"Been taken, too?" Venge pulled a strip of cloth off his shirt and twisted it around his arm, over the missing skin where Runa had bitten him. Geysa barely glanced at the wound.

"He didn't want me. He wanted Runa."

"How can you be sure? Maybe he just took her because you weren't there."

An impatient huff escaped Geysa's lips. "The ErlKing

wouldn't give up that easily. I moved twenty feet. My mother crossed three worlds…and he still got her. Besides, if he wanted me, don't you think I'd have rather he took me…than take my sister instead? Do you think that little of me—that I'd trade her life for my own?"

Venge stared; no reply seemed adequate. Geysa loved her sister—truly loved her. Seeing the anguish in her eyes, smelling it…he wished he could be sorry for interfering, but he wasn't.

Geysa might regret her sister's loss, wish she had been taken in her place—but Venge would never regret what he had done. Geysa could despise him because of it, and still, he wouldn't be tempted to go back and change his actions.

Her face turned toward the spot where Runa had last stood, she swallowed. "Why were you here? Why didn't you wake me? I thought we had an agreement."

He stood beside her, less than an inch separating their physical bodies…but so much more separating their realities. Unable to keep the truth from her any longer, he sighed. "I never meant to honor it."

She turned then, her eyes wide and filled with disbelief…then pain…again. "I believed you."

"I know." He crossed his arms over his chest and turned so he didn't have to look at her face. It was bad enough smelling the betrayal wafting around her.

"I need the horn," he continued.

"But the horn calls up the Wild Hunt." He could hear the frown in her voice.

"And I need it."

"For what?"

He dug his fingers into his arms. She wouldn't understand…couldn't understand. She loved her family, was willing to die to save them. How could she even begin to understand his need to destroy his own? He turned back toward her, shale crunching under his heel as he moved. "It doesn't matter. I need the horn. I came here to get it."

She stared at him, confusion clouding her eyes. "Would you use it? Would you call up the hunt?"

He inhaled through his nose, his nostrils flaring with the effort. "Yes. I would definitely use it."

Her lips parted as she took in a tiny breath. Then her expression changed again—from confusion to realization.

She was seeing him clearly now. Whatever illusion she had built around him, that he had helped her to build—it was gone. She was seeing the real Venge...the hellhound...the monster.

Her lips snapped shut and she spun. Her heels dug into the earth as she strode away.

Venge just watched her, knowing she wouldn't be back. At least not as the soft Geysa he had held in his arms. No. If Geysa returned, it would be as a Valkyrie...and he'd have to meet her as she knew him now. No more lies. No Venge...nothing but hellhound.

Sigurd pulled the hood of his cape back before entering the bar. No reason for pretense now. His cause was lost if he didn't act soon. But Sigurd wasn't one to give up easily.

The bar was dark and empty—of patrons, that was. The Valkyrie leader who had been posing as a bartender was here, scowling as he stepped inside. Since the Valkyries had revealed themselves, the hellhounds had avoided the place, instead converting an empty barn into a makeshift hangout. Most of them were there now, drunk and brawling...waiting to hear which of them would be chosen by the ErlKing for his pack.

Idiots. Sigurd wrapped his fist around the chain at his

neck until the metal nearly glowed with the heat pouring from within him.

"We're closed." Jora, the fraudulent bartender, slammed an empty beer mug, bottom side up, onto the bar top.

"Should have locked the door." Sigurd strode forward, his cape flowing behind him.

Jora snorted. "Like that would have made a difference. What do you want? Why aren't you with the others—celebrating your victory?"

"Victory. That's one way to term it." Sigurd picked up the empty beer mug and flipped it over.

Jora cocked one brow.

Sigurd leaned forward, both palms pressed onto the varnished wood. "Believe it or not, we both want the same thing—to stop the hunt and destroy the horn. I'm willing to work with you...or not." He slid the mug toward her.

Jora stared at him a moment, her index finger tapping lightly on the bar. "Do I know you?" she asked.

With a smile, Sigurd flipped up his hood. "Perhaps," he replied.

Jora spit out a curse and yanked her sword from its scabbard. The tip pressed against Sigurd's jugular, she asked, "A hellhound impersonating a human, now I've seen it all. Who are you? And why shouldn't I kill you?"

His gaze holding hers, Sigurd brushed the sword away from his neck, but made no move to disarm her. "Too many questions. Let's take the second first." He shimmered, rematerializing behind her, the dagger he'd hidden in his sleeve before entering the bar pressed to her throat. "Because you can't."

She laughed, an exhalation of air from her pursed lips. He slid the sword from her hand and placed it out of her reach on the bar top, then pulled his dagger away and slipped it back into the scabbard strapped to his forearm. She probably had an arsenal of other weapons hidden around her, but he'd made his point. Hopefully, well enough her curiosity would force her to listen.

He stepped back and held out his hand. "Sigurd Bjorstad."

She ignored it. "Hellhound."

"Of course. How would I be of help otherwise?"

She glanced at his outstretched hand, then slowly slipped her work-calloused fingers into his. "Don't make the mistake of thinking this means I trust you, *hellhound*."

"I think you missed the point. I'm a hellhound. I don't know the meaning of trust." He squeezed her fingers until he could see the first flash of pain in her eyes.

She squeezed her fingers in and out of a fist, her lips twisting to the side. "So, you want to help. What makes you think we need help?"

It was his turn to laugh. "So, the Valkyries all got together and decided they wanted to come down from their golden hall just to wait on us hellhounds. I'm flattered."

"We needed to be where the horn was."

"And?" he prompted.

"We needed a way to know when it was being used."

"So you…?"

She kept her lips firmly sealed.

He took a step closer, knowing he'd made his point. "You still need us, and none of the other hellhounds are going to help you. They think the hunt is the height of honor. They'll be working against you, not with you."

"But you're different?" Jora did not look convinced.

"I want to stop the hunt as much, if not more than you. And I'm willing to partner with the enemy to do it."

Jora crossed her arms over her chest, her expression assessing. "My niece put her trust in a hellhound, but we saw him fighting for the horn…as were you."

Sigurd pulled back. "Venge. Yes, he's another problem I need to address. But—" he touched the chain at his neck "—there may be someone better equipped than I to take on that issue."

Chapter 12

Geysa tiptoed toward the barn where, according to her aunt, the hellhounds had taken up residence. She had lost Venge, both as a partner in finding the horn and— She jerked her chin up, not allowing the thought to fully form.

He was out of the picture; that was what mattered. He had lied to her, wanted the horn for himself. Perhaps she could forgive the lie, gods knew she had lived with deception her entire life, and was plenty guilty of it herself, but letting the ErlKing take Runa? Venge had said it was to save Geysa, but then admitted that he still wanted the horn—he had cursed as the ErlKing flew off with it. How could Geysa believe anything he said now?

Jora was right. Hellhounds were…hellhounds. Geysa might not ever again hate them as blindly as she once had, but she couldn't choose one over her family. That would be too complete of a betrayal to even consider.

Now the ErlKing had the horn and Runa, magnifying the need to recover the horn to the point of desperation. The Valkyries wanted both back…. Geysa curled her hands into fist…. No, the Valkyries would *get* both back.

But the loss of Venge as informant had put them back where they'd started…no way of knowing when the horn reappeared. And worse, the hellhounds, their only connection to the horn, now avoided the bar *and* the Valkyries like death. Geysa had no choice but to spy on them. She'd fumbled her first job by falling for Venge. This new one was her chance at redemption.

Parting the long grass that separated her from the barn, she crept toward the building.

Venge leaned against a piece of rusty mining equipment and studied the interior of the old barn. Light leaking from gaps in the log wall revealed twenty or so hellhounds in various stages of drunkenness sprawled around the room.

Apparently, they had been celebrating.

Venge suppressed a growl. Only necessity brought him to this place…to his own kind. He needed to convince them to resist the lure of the horn, at least long enough for Venge to take it from the ErlKing. If the ErlKing used the horn and the hellhounds answered, his chances of recovering the horn would be greatly diminished—most likely obliterated.

This morning, he hadn't gone in search of Geysa, hadn't tried to convince her that she should still trust him. No. That would have been just another lie and he was done with lying. She shouldn't trust him. She shouldn't be with him. Just as he shouldn't be with her…even thinking of her.

He'd screwed up; he'd let the horn almost literally slip from his grasp. At most, he had one more shot at commanding the Wild Hunt. The ErlKing would be back to call up his pack, and Venge had to be ready for him.

So, this morning, instead of searching out Geysa, Venge had made a trip to a human city and a number of hardware stores. The sack at his waist now bulged with earplugs. He only had to convince the drunken louts at his feet to use them.

He pushed away from the piece of equipment and stalked to the nearest fallen male, the one with a clipped beard and an earring. The hellhound lay chest down, his head turned to the side; a soft snore rumbled from his throat. Venge shoved his boot against the hellhound's side and rolled him over, faceup. The male barely stirred.

Mumbling a curse, Venge grabbed a bucket half filled with rain water and tossed it in his face. The hellhound leaped to his feet, his fist swinging in protest. Venge caught his arm by the wrist, halting his blow. "Nap time is over," he said.

The hellhound blinked, recognition slowly making its way past the fog of alcohol. Venge grabbed a second bucket and shoved it into his hands. "Time to wake the others." Not waiting for him to respond, Venge tacked his way through the stuporous hellhounds and strode outside to a metal horse trough. After dredging the bucket through the murky water, he returned inside to awaken more of his pack. They'd chosen him as alpha. Now they had to follow his lead.

Geysa pulled back as Venge strode into the sunshine, a metal bucket in his hand. Her heart leaped into her throat, and she swallowed hard. She hadn't expected to see him here. Silly. He was a hellhound. Why wouldn't he be here working with his kind? She focused on the thought…*his kind.*

It didn't help. The resolve she'd built around herself began to crumble. Her tongue darted out to moisten her lips, her eyes tracking each of Venge's movements. He stopped next to a metal trough filled with water. After filling the pail, he stood, his biceps bulging as he turned to re-enter the barn.

She let out a sigh of relief as he disappeared.

A few seconds later another hellhound followed, repeating Venge's errand. Geysa tried to concentrate on what the hellhound was doing, what might be happening inside, but her mind drifted back to Venge—what *he* was doing. How he'd looked—healthy, strong. Relief pattered through her and she frowned.

Weak. She was weak. Perhaps she should leave, go back to Jora and explain—

What? That she had let herself get too close? That she couldn't even spy on Venge without wanting to rush to him, to tell him…

No. She could do this. She had to do this. Squaring her shoulders, she lowered to a crouch and began creeping toward the barn.

Venge tossed the new pail of water across a group of hellhounds who were passed out, their bodies overlapping like a basketful of kittens. He huffed out a disgusted breath. "Get up," he yelled. They stirred, less alert than the hound with the earring. He glanced to his right where the other hellhound had just dumped his own pail of water on an unsuspecting group.

"What's your name?" Venge asked.

Surprise darted across the other male's face, but he replied, "Marius."

Venge grunted and tossed the empty bucket to a dark-haired hellhound. "Fill it," he ordered. Dropping his gaze, the male hurried from the bar.

As each hellhound woke, the noise inside the barn escalated—and so did the smell of lethargy and pain. Venge had to get the hounds past this. Continuing to smell their own wretched state would only prolong the process of reviving them.

To Venge's left was a window covered with a swinging wooden door. A rusty lock held it closed. Venge grabbed it in his hand and let his anger—at his situation, at losing the horn, at losing Geysa—escape his self-imposed controls. Heat raced from his body, into his hand. With a quick twist, the softened metal snapped free.

He shoved the window open and stood there, the fresh air rolling over him…calming him. He had never hated who he was, what he was, as much as he did right now.

Behind him, hellhounds, energized by his anger, surged to life. Yells sounded. The smell of adrenaline and sweat replaced the earlier stench of lethargy, and the air vibrated with energy.

Venge kept his back turned, pulling in a breath to calm himself before addressing the other hellhounds.

A bottle smashed against the log beside him, spraying him with beer.

He spun. "Enough." He kept his voice low, controlled. But as a hellhound whirled by, Venge grabbed him and the one who followed by the shirt and jerked them forward. "Sit."

As if their legs had lost all strength, their knees folded and they hunkered on the ground. Slowly, the rest mimicked their actions. Once they were all seated, or at least standing still, Venge leaped onto a wooden box and held up his hands.

"Do you see this?" He pulled the silver chain he wore away from his neck. "Anyone know what this symbolizes?"

There were mumbles, but no one answered.

"Bondage. To another being. I was property, owned. With no rights of my own. Ordered as to when I could or couldn't fulfill the most basic needs of existence. Anyone here want that life?" He let his regard wander around the group, fall heavily on the few who still wore the cocky air of a newcomer. After the last challenger had dropped his gaze, Venge continued. "Each of you wants to be part of the hunt. Am I right?"

A wary cheer arose.

"But does anyone want it bad enough to turn over their existence to a being who doesn't know what it's like to be a hellhound…to need to run free…to hunt…to kill…?" He let the sentence die off. He was using Sigurd's words. He recognized them as they fell from his lips. And why not? Sigurd believed them, maybe these hounds would, too.

The hellhounds' eyes narrowed to suspicious slits; a grumble rolled around the room.

"We don't have to. As your alpha…" He paused, having to swallow his discomfort with the term before continuing. "I have a plan. The ErlKing isn't undefeatable. The Valkyries beat him before, stole the horn and hid it for centuries. None of us want that to happen again." He waited, letting them agree and their eagerness to build. "But why give our power to the ErlKing? Hellhounds *are* the hunt. Why shouldn't we not only run in it, but lead it, as well?"

Understanding and excitement lit their eyes, and began to fill the barn. Venge smiled, knowing he had won. No one, not Sigurd, not the ErlKing, could stop him now.

He pulled the earplugs from his bag, and continued. "When the horn is sounded, we will go. But not as the ErlKing will expect."

Not as anyone would expect.

* * *

Geysa dragged an old tire closer to the barn and shoved it under the open window. Bent at the waist, her head just below the window opening, she listened to what was happening inside. A familiar voice rumbled toward her, sent chills of longing over her skin. Venge. He was talking, and surprisingly the hellhounds appeared to be listening. In the few weeks the Valkyries had been here, Geysa had never seen the hellhounds listen to anyone. One spoke a word, and another took offense. They had been in a semiconstant state of drunken brawling, adding to her perception of them as little more than beasts.

But now, miraculously, a group of all of the hellhounds in the town were sitting, listening, and in their own way…showing respect.

It was disturbing, frightening actually. A shiver traveled over her body, brought the hair on her arm to a stand. The desire to peer through the window, to look at Venge, to see if he was the same man she had made love to, almost overwhelmed her. To have such control of a group of hellhounds…their respect…what had he done to earn that? Surely something she didn't want to imagine.

She curved her fingers around the weathered log wall she leaned against—felt the smooth, dry wood. Reality. She had to face it. Venge was a hellhound, their leader. How much more proof did she need that he was dangerous, someone to avoid?

None. Swallowing the hurt, she concentrated on thinking only of Venge as what he was—a threat—and listened to what he was saying.

Ten minutes later she'd heard enough. She'd heard his plan to beat the ErlKing and the Valkyries, to take the horn as his own and lead the Wild Hunt.

It was enough. Her eyes still on the window, her ears still trained on the masculine voice rumbling inside the barn, she stepped off the box backward.

A rough hand slapped over her mouth, and a hand wrapped around her leg, grabbing her by the thigh. With a quick jerk, her back was pressed against an ungiving body. A man, he smelled of sweat, beer and dirt, as if he'd been wallowing in the three for days. A hellhound, and...her gaze darted to the window...it wasn't Venge.

Venge tossed the earplugs into the group, a handful at a time. The hellhounds had bought his speech, swallowed it whole. They would wait for the horn to sound, slip in their earplugs then shimmer to its origin. Once there, as a group they would attack the ErlKing, and Venge would take the horn. All he owed the others in return was a chance at making the hunt. And that wasn't a decision he would have to make. The hellhounds would settle it themselves, fighting until the needed nine rose to the top.

He glanced around the room, taking in the gleam in each of their eyes, the assuredness that they would prevail. He knew better, as did a few of the older hounds. Ranking would happen quickly. A bloody process, but part of hellhound life. All would learn their place. Some would even survive to enjoy it.

His bag empty, Venge strolled to a corner where he could keep an eye on the group. They accepted him as alpha right now, but he knew better than to take the position for granted. Their brains were muddled with alcohol, but soon that would wear off. They would start to think...why him, why not me?

Then the challenges would start anew.

Venge just hoped he didn't have to kill too many of the

best. He'd need them later, when he led the hunt against his father. After finding a place in the shadows, he waited—for the horn to sound or the challenges to begin.

He was ready.

The hand pressed tightly against Geysa's lips. She could feel each finger where it pushed against her cheek. Her assailant's skin was rough, his hand so big it blocked her nose, making it hard to breathe. He still held her by the thigh, making it impossible to reach her dagger which was tucked inside that boot.

All manners of curses bounced through her brain… curses at herself, her stupidity. She'd been focused on Venge—totally. A child's mistake.

Her body twisted back and forth as the hellhound walked backward away from the barn…where? Panic began to rise up, but she tamped it down. Calm was her greatest defense right now.

"The alpha's bedmate. Spying. He know what you're up to?" The voice was accented, nasally. "Could score me some points I'd bet, turning you over."

She curled the knee of her free leg into her chest, then propelled her foot down, aiming blindly for his kneecap.

Her assailant barely grunted.

"'Course, like he said in his big speech, you Valkyries want to stop the hunt altogether. Seems to me the best plan would be to get rid of all you first—kill some time while we wait for the ErlKing to get done with the one he took."

Anger at the callous mention of Runa hummed through Geysa. She wedged her jaws apart, not much, but enough. One of his fingers slipped between her lips and she bit down with every bit of hatred she felt at that moment.

With a curse, he flung her to the ground. Her shoulder

hit first; pain pulsed down her arm, into her chest. She tried to stand, using her hand to push herself up, but fell, the arm dropping uselessly at her side.

His eyes blazing red, the hellhound pulled back his foot to kick her in the stomach.

She rolled, his boot grazing over her side as she moved.

Fingers dug into her hair and, using her one vanity against her, he dragged her to her feet. "One less Valkyrie it is." He held his hand to her face, his finger dripping blood from where she had bitten him. Then, slowly, he wrapped his hand around her throat and began to squeeze. She tried to plan an escape, to stay calm. He held her sideways, her good side away from him. She kicked, landing a blow to his leg, but again he showed little sign of the impact. With her good arm, she clawed at his forearm. Useless. She was panicking. She had to stop. She pulled in a breath, but little air could make its way past the fist around her throat.

She began to curl into herself, her knees lifting to her chest. If she'd been able to do this earlier… The knife. She could reach the knife. Darkness edged at the side of her vision as she fumbled her good hand inside her boot. She was rewarded with the reassuring feel of the bone handle against her palm. She edged it out and, with all the strength left in her, she twisted, plunging the knife into his side.

With a roar, he dropped her again.

Venge heard the roar. He recognized the voice—Bjorn, a grizzled hound who had seen his share of battles. Bjorn would be either a powerful adversary or a dangerous enemy. Circumstances hadn't told Venge which yet.

Bjorn was normally calm and quiet…never giving a hint as to what was going on in his mind. For him to roar…

Venge tensed, his gaze darting around the barn. The hell-hounds inside the barn made no sign they'd heard the noise, or more likely just didn't pay it any notice.

But… Venge waited.

Nothing. Whatever had disturbed Bjorn had either passed or been killed.

Venge took a step back into the shadows. Whatever Bjorn was doing, it didn't involve Venge. For his plan to work, Venge needed to stay alert, on task. His arms crossed over his chest, he leaned against the wall…and heard another sound, this time a feminine peep.

Dread clutched at his chest. *Geysa.*

He shimmered.

As Venge materialized outside the barn, a form flew past him. A hellhound, the singed scent they all shared wafting after him. But the shape passed too quickly for Venge to identify which hellhound he was and thus how dangerous.

The unknown hellhound smashed into Bjorn who stood over a prostrate Geysa, her dagger in her hand dripping with blood. The force of the moving hellhound's strike pro-pelled Bjorn into the side of the barn. The pair hit; twigs and dirt fell from a winch that jutted out of the wall above their heads. Another strike and a length of oiled rope followed the other debris.

Venge ignored the two grappling against the logs, his attention focused on Geysa. She staggered to a stand, one arm hanging limp at her side. In her other hand she still held the knife, the veins in her forearm protruding from the strength of her grip.

She stumbled backward. Her gaze locked on the two males fighting only a foot away, she didn't even notice Venge.

He shimmered again, this time behind her.

Sensing his presence or perhaps the shimmer itself, she spun, the knife held forward, to her side, ready to slash at whoever snuck behind her.

Venge blocked her attack, his fingers wrapping around her wrist. "You're hurt," he muttered. She stared at him, her eyes wild. Pain, anger and fear all rolled off her. Venge shut his eyes briefly against the onslaught.

"I'm fine," she replied, attempting to jerk her wrist free.

He opened his eyes, saw her standing there, the light striking her hair, strands of copper reflecting back at him. Her body was taut as if with anger, but her eyes held uncertainty.

He loosened his hold on her wrist. A white band, where his fingers had wrapped around her, glowed back at him. She dropped her arm to her side. Her hand shook, her entire body beginning to shake. The knife wavered, the blade tapping against her leg, leaving a smear of red as it did.

Her eyes were big, too big. Sweat covered her body, causing her shirt to cling to her breasts and stomach.

"Geysa," Venge said, placing a hand, soft this time, on her shoulder.

The knife fell from her fingers into the dirt, but she didn't look down and didn't reply.

"Geysa," he repeated, a tremor in his voice.

"You messed up." Sigurd pulled Bjorn behind him, the oiled rope in a noose around Bjorn's neck.

Venge blinked at him, his mind registering that the form he'd seen when he arrived had been his old rival. Sigurd had been there first…and had probably saved Geysa when Venge didn't.

"Take her to her aunt," Sigurd said. Bjorn jerked against the rope, but Sigurd just slid the noose tighter. "Go," he added.

Venge was alpha and he needed the pack's loyalty. He should be the one to take care of Bjorn, to make sure every hellhound in the town knew the price for hurting Geysa, but he didn't care. Didn't care about anything but saving Geysa from the pain, bringing her back from wherever her mind was right now.

With a short nod to Sigurd, he slipped an arm around Geysa's waist and shimmered them to the bar.

Jora pierced Venge with a glare, then motioned for him to lead Geysa to a chair. "What happened?" she asked, her voice brusque.

Venge shook his head. "What's wrong with her?" His fingers swept over Geysa's brow. She glanced up at him, but with a frown, and he could see confusion in her eyes.

Jora muttered something then jerked a dented metal case from under the bar. "Looks like shock. She's been through a lot of emotional stress lately. Probably didn't take much to send her over the edge." Her voice slid into him like a knife.

Her lips thin, she tossed the case over the bar. Venge held out both arms and caught it with a grunt. Not bothering to acknowledge his actions, Jora swept her body up and over the bar. Once on the same side as he and Geysa, she jerked the box from his hands.

"Geysa?" she murmured, her gaze turning gentle. She flipped up the lid and pulled a vial of gray powder from inside. "Get me some water," she ordered.

Venge shimmered behind the bar and back, a glass of water in his hand. Jora dumped the powder into the glass and stirred the mixture with her finger. When she was done, she held the glass to Geysa's lips. Then, muttering words of encouragement, she poured it bit by bit down Geysa's throat. Within seconds, the sweat had disappeared from Geysa's body and her pallor had lessened.

Venge stepped closer, taking the empty glass from Jora's fingers and setting it out of the way.

"How is she?" he asked, his hand reaching toward Geysa's hair, then falling back to his side.

"Move." Jora jostled the metal box closer and pulled out a strip of material.

Venge frowned, but said nothing. Jora hadn't asked him to leave, and she had every reason to. He wouldn't squabble over her treatment of him…not as long as Geysa was getting care and he didn't have to fight to stay with her.

Jora placed a hand on Geysa's arm, the one hanging limp at her side, then muttered under her breath. Pulling air into her body, she looked up at Venge. "You want to help?"

Venge could see each word pained her.

He nodded.

"Her shoulder's out of place. I'm going to move it back. Once I've done that and she's had some rest, she'll be okay. Valkyries heal fast."

Afraid she'd change her mind if he spoke, Venge nodded again.

Jora squared her shoulders and pointed to Geysa's waist. "Hold her. I'll do the rest."

Venge wrapped his arm around Geysa, pressed his face against her hair. Jora scowled, but Geysa moved closer until her body was curled against his.

When she was settled, Jora grabbed Geysa's useless arm above the elbow and pulled. Something popped and Geysa jolted against him, but she didn't cry out and he caught no scent of pain. She seemed numb to the pain and unaware of what was happening around her.

"There." Jora wrapped the strip around Geysa's neck and tucked her arm into the loop. The makeshift sling complete, Jora stood. "You can leave now."

Venge's hand splayed across Geysa's stomach. He felt his lip lifting in a snarl. He didn't want to leave, and there was no being in the nine worlds that could make him.

"Go back to your kind." Jora's gray eyes turned steely.

Geysa moved in his arms, her hair tickling his cheek. He closed his eyes, pretended for a second they were alone and she was well.

"Unless you want to hurt her more…" Jora's voice deepened. "Leave."

Venge opened his eyes and stared at Geysa's aunt, then, his gaze lowered, he shimmered.

Chapter 13

Venge sat alone in the darkness. With Runa still missing, the bathhouse was empty. He'd been here for two days. When he'd first left Geysa and her aunt, he'd returned to the barn, planning to find Bjorn and tear his limbs from his body. Unfortunately, Sigurd had stolen the opportunity. Neither Sigurd nor Bjorn had been seen—at all. The other hellhounds hadn't even realized the fight outside the barn had happened.

Venge scoured the area for either, but had turned up nothing. Wherever Sigurd had gone and presumably taken Bjorn, it wasn't in this town—perhaps not even in this world.

Resolved to the loss of his revenge at least for the time being, Venge had returned to the bathhouse—only leaving periodically to search for Sigurd. Two days later and still no sign of his old enemy.

Venge's visits to the barn, or infrequency of them, had elicited no comments from the other hellhounds. They were so caught up in challenges among themselves, he doubted they noticed the passage of time, much less the disappearance of their alpha. Not that he cared. He'd had enough of his kind to last him ten hellhounds' lifetimes.

He wouldn't have mourned the loss of the entire species…not even at the cost of his own life.

So, he waited…alone and in the dark…for the horn to sound.

Something stirred outside, a knocking sound. He walked to the window and peered into the night. The Valkyries continued to come and go, their numbers increasing each day. Getting ready for whatever attack they had planned for stopping the ErlKing, Venge assumed. Luckily none had entered his hideout. Geysa had lost her sister partially because of him. He didn't want to be responsible for the death of anyone else important to her.

Geysa. He pressed his hand against the window's glass. Was she okay? Her aunt had seemed confident she would recover, but was she wrong? The thought gnawed at him.

He curved his fingers toward his palm, his nails scratching against the smooth surface. What if Jora was wrong? He pulled back his arm, ready to smash his hand through the thin glass.

"What good would that do?"

Venge spun.

Sigurd stood, hands in his pockets, his cape shrugged back from his shoulders.

Venge eyed the cape. "Have you been hiding from me?"

Sigurd glanced around the dark room. "Me, hiding? I think you might be confused."

Venge curled his fingers into his palms, all the anger he'd been nursing for the past two days bubbling to the surface. "Where'd you take Bjorn?"

"Away, and I had another errand to run." Sigurd wandered to the round table where Runa kept her cards and runes. He flipped over a card. "She's a Norn, you know. I didn't know Norns had it in them."

Venge assumed he was talking about Runa, but he didn't want to talk about her or Norns. He didn't want to talk period. He wanted to rip someone apart with his hands… Bjorn preferably, but in a pinch, Sigurd would do. Venge took a step forward.

"You left her," Sigurd said, his gaze on the table as he continued to flip cards.

Venge flexed and unflexed his hands.

"I guess I was wrong." Sigurd looked up, his finger resting lightly on the last card he'd placed.

Venge tried to ignore him. Sigurd's attempt to divert him was blatant, but his words still rankled.

"First, you left her unprotected and vulnerable, an easy target for Bjorn. Then—"

"Geysa is not vulnerable." Venge refused to listen to such a statement. He'd seen her fight. To call her vulnerable was an insult—another reason to attack Sigurd. Venge's anger wasn't directed at Sigurd, a part of him realized that, but a bigger part, the part in control at this moment, didn't care, was just happy to have a target.

Venge wrapped his fingers under the lip of the table and tossed it onto its top. Cards fluttered into the air and stone runes clattered to the ground.

"Feel better?"

Venge could hear the boredom in Sigurd's voice. It should have added to his anger, given him the last nudge he needed to grab his old enemy by the throat and squeeze the arrogance out of him. Instead Venge spun and rammed his fist into the nearby wall.

Plaster cracked and fell in hunks onto his feet.

"Have you seen her?" Sigurd picked a rune off the ground and tossed it in the air.

Venge pressed his fingers against the wall. His head hanging between his arms, he took in a deep breath. He didn't want to see Geysa—couldn't.

"She's hurt." Sigurd caught the rune and held it up, pinched between two fingers. "Did you know that?"

Venge shoved himself away from the wall, tried to summon the anger he'd felt earlier. "Of course I know that. I was there, remember?"

Sigurd tossed the rune onto the floor with the others. "There are other types of hurt, alpha. You should know that." Then he shimmered.

Venge stared at the space where Sigurd had been. What had he meant? Why had he come here?

Venge strode across the room, shimmering to avoid the table, then reforming once past it. He slapped both palms against the far wall. The anger was gone, but some new emotion had replaced it...a restlessness, a need to *do* something.

He'd been right. Sigurd had been trying to distract him—and he'd succeeded. Once Geysa was mentioned, Venge had totally forgotten about hunting down Bjorn.

He should leave now, find Sigurd before the wandering hellhound left again. He was most likely at the barn, lecturing the fallen.

Venge should, but he wouldn't. There was only one place Venge wanted to be...with only one person...Geysa.

But he couldn't. He had to stay away...he had to.

Geysa picked up a glass and threw it into the bar's wall. The answering crash made her feel better—for a second.

Her aunt had left her here alone, gone to a meeting that Geysa was not invited to attend.

With Runa's disappearance, and the attack on Geysa, Jora's attitude had changed. Valkyries had been arriving steadily for the past two days. No longer content to sit and wait, Geysa's aunt had called in as many Valkyries as she could from Valhalla. And there was something else.... Geysa frowned at the line of glasses still sitting on the bar. A few days earlier, Geysa had noticed a hellhound leaving the bar. Only seeing him from the back, she'd been unable to identify him, but after his visit, her aunt's demeanor had changed. As though she had direction again, a plan.

That was when the Valkyries had started arriving. And Geysa had been told nothing. Nothing. At first she had assumed it was due to her injury, but her shoulder was basically healed...well enough she could... She picked up a second highball and sent it flying. Slivers of glass exploded against the wall.

Which meant there was another reason, and Geysa thought she knew what it was. Despite the fact that she suspected her aunt had teamed up with a hellhound in some way, Geysa feared her exclusion had nothing to do with her injury and everything to do with—she picked up a third glass—Venge.

The Valkyries didn't trust him. And because of that, they no longer trusted Geysa.

The glass left her hand. As it winged across the room, the space in front of the wall began to shift...shimmer. A split second before the glass should have collided with the wall, Venge materialized. The glass zipped past his head and crashed into the wall behind him, sprinkling him with thousands of tiny fragments. He took a step, into the light, his arms sparkling as if he were dusted in diamonds.

Geysa's heart leaped to her throat.

Venge flicked his gaze from the remnants of the broken glass beneath his feet to Geysa. "Your arm's better." There was no expression on his face, no hint of a smile or glimmer of relief…nothing.

Geysa turned her back on him and began lining the remaining glasses on a tray.

"I heard you were hurt." He stepped closer. She could feel his presence as clearly as if he had touched her, but when she glanced over her shoulder, he was still standing at least six feet away.

"I'm fine," she replied, twisting her head back to stare at the tray.

"Good. Then…"

She waited, not moving.

"Bjorn, the hound who attacked you, he's gone," he continued.

She shrugged and reached for the last glass. A stab of pain shot through her shoulder. Her repayment for destroying the barware.

Venge was next to her instantly. "You are hurt."

As he stood beside her, as she inhaled his scent, she realized he was right. She was hurt, but not in the way he meant. She tilted her face to his, caught his gaze with her own and lowered her shields.

He *had* hurt her. It was only fair he knew how much.

Venge skimmed his hand over Geysa's injured shoulder. She should have healed by now—her aunt had said she would heal quickly. But she was still in pain; he'd seen her wince.

His lips parted ready to say…what? He didn't know. She lifted her face upward, a space between her lips, too.

Her breath passed through them with a gentle huff. Her eyes were huge, soft and gray. They glimmered up at him.

Then he felt it, like a kick to the stomach. Pain. Her pain, but not physical—worse, much, much worse.

"I miss…" she started.

He stepped back, unable to take the intensity of what she felt. "Your sister. I know. I'm…sorry." It was a lot for him to say. He didn't understand their relationship, couldn't fathom the loss she felt, but she did…feel it, that was…and for that, for her pain, he was sorry.

"Runa? Yes, I miss Runa, but…" She licked her lips. "I miss…" She dropped her gaze.

Venge froze; even his heart seemed to slow.

"I know I shouldn't. I think my…feelings are costing me, not just here." She held her closed fist to her chest. "But here, too." She opened her hand and motioned around the room. "I don't belong anymore. They don't trust me. Even though I've lost more to the hunt than anyone, they think I might risk even more, to be with you."

She stood quietly, her hands falling to her sides.

Venge forced a dry laugh from his lips. "That's crazy. You already told me how you feel."

"Did I?" She glanced away. "I don't think so. When I first figured it out, I kept it to myself. Then after Runa…" She flicked her gaze back to him, then away again. "I thought I could forget."

An emotion Venge hadn't experienced before meeting Geysa, one he was afraid even now to name, began to build inside him. Despite attempts to deny what *he* was feeling, his heart began to beat loudly.

"How about you? How do *you* feel?" she asked.

Venge didn't move; for a second he thought he couldn't, like a deer frozen in the first few seconds when it realized it was caught…trapped, as the creature decided how to escape…if it could escape.

He looked at Geysa again, truly looked at her, and he knew the answer—there was no escape. He was well and truly caught.

He closed the space between them, cupped her chin in his hand and tilted her face to his.

"What am I going to do?" Geysa murmured. She didn't seem to expect an answer. Venge brushed his thumb over her lips, his mind grappling with the same question.

He couldn't love Geysa. He couldn't love anyone. The thought went against everything he had ever believed. He just…

Geysa pressed her hands against his chest, her lower lip trembling slightly. Venge stared at her mouth, wished he knew what to say. What the easy solution for the two of them was, but the only answer that came to mind was walking away, forgetting each other. Their worlds would never mesh.

He started to do the right thing, to tell her he didn't care about her, he was sorry if he'd hurt her, but hellhounds didn't love, couldn't. But even as the words were bouncing through his head, his hands moved to her hips and he pulled her closer, until her hips were snug against his.

She looked up at him. "This won't work, will it?" she said, her hands slipping around his neck.

"No. It won't." And he lowered his mouth to hers.

She was an idiot. Geysa knew that, but she didn't have the strength to stop her hands from slipping behind Venge's neck, from pulling his head toward hers. She lacked the resolve to keep her lips from opening beneath his, her tongue from darting inside his mouth.

He pulled her closer, a sigh passing between them, as if both were taking this moment for what it was… precious. Something never to be repeated. The horn would sound soon. The ErlKing would come and both the Valkyries and the hellhounds would answer. Both she and Venge would fight, but not together. Never together… again.

Venge lifted her onto the bar. Her thighs parted and he stepped between them. His hands skimmed up her sides, his thumbs catching on her shirt, tugging it away from her skin. She dropped her head to his shoulder, her lips grazing along his neck. Her hands traveled over his body, exploring every plane and indentation of his chest and back. And she inhaled, bringing the scent of him deep inside her. But she kept her eyes closed, using her other senses to taste, smell and feel. Even her ears… She could hear the steady in and out of his breath, the growl he made when her fingers roamed too low…or not low enough. She memorized every sensation, knowing she had to, would have nothing but memories once she returned to Valhalla.

"I…" Venge began.

Geysa stopped him, pressing her fingers against his lips. "Not now. Anything we say now…it won't necessarily be true later. Let's not lie to ourselves, just enjoy what we have…" For now. She left the last unsaid.

Her fingers still against his lips, they looked at each other. His hazel eyes, more green than brown right then…she wanted to remember that, too. She wanted to remember everything.

He grasped her hand in his, kissed her fingers, then the back of her hand, her forearm and up to where the short sleeve of her shirt covered her shoulder.

"You won't forget?" he asked.

She shook her head. She wove her fingers into his hair, pressed her lips to his ear. "Will you?"

He nibbled on her shoulder. "Never."

Venge ached with need. Not just sexual...but Geysa was right. Why put voice to something that wouldn't be true in the future...maybe in just moments?

The thought of how quickly everything could change intensified his need. He placed his hands back at Geysa's hips, pushed her shirt over her head.

She seemed to share his desperation. She helped him jerk her shirt free, throwing it across the room, onto the floor. Not pausing between, she moved her hands to the tail of his shirt, pushing it up his chest. This time he assisted, tugging it off his body and letting it sail. Her bra was next, then their pants and her underwear, until both of them were completely nude.

He ran his hands up her front, cupping her breasts. Their tips were peach-colored, perfect...her skin smooth. He moved his hands and gaze downward, to her waist, then between her legs where red curls covered her sex. His hands traced the muscle on the tops of her thighs, his thumbs brushing her curls.

She put her hands on his shoulders and edged her butt forward, until she almost slipped off the edge of the bar. His erection brushed against her as she moved still closer.

Her nails ran down his sides, scratching into his skin, causing him to shiver.

Venge lapped his tongue gently, reverently, around her nipple. His body was ready, eager to be inside her, but his mind knew if he rushed this moment it would be over too soon.

She seemed to feel the same, her hand drifting down to

capture his erection, then pulling back to trace the base of his shaft. A touch so light, he might have imagined it, but still he shivered.

He murmured her name, heard her sigh in response. Her nipple erect against his lips, he suckled, drawing the pebble into his mouth and letting his fingers drift back to her curls and the heat they concealed.

Slowly he parted her folds. She was wet and hot. He slid his finger against her, felt her tremor as he circled the kernel hidden there.

She panted against his throat, tiny breaths that begged for more. His finger twirled against her, the smell of her arousal calling to him, causing his shaft to harden even more, almost painfully.

He groaned, but waited, slipping his finger inside her instead, felt her tighten around him. With his thumb he continued his attentions to her nub. She arched her back, drawing his hand closer, deeper. She tightened again, his erection jerking in response. Then her neck lolled back, her fingernails digging into his shoulders and three tiny *ahs* escaped her lips as she relaxed against him.

"No one's ever… I…" She spoke against his chest.

His own need was still visible and growing more urgent each second that her breasts were pressed against him, that the scent of her climax clouded around him. He slipped his hands behind her, under her butt, and nudged his erection against her.

"Ah." She wiggled, her folds slipping over the sensitive head of his shaft. Teasing him.

He wanted to plunge inside her, but he waited, each excruciating second he did so increasing his need…and his anticipation.

She wrapped her legs around his waist, her thighs

strong, pulling him toward her. The tip of his sex slipped inside her. He groaned, but waited still, making sure she was ready, wanting this as much as he did.

She swirled her tongue over his chest, up his neck. "Now," she murmured.

Unable to wait a second longer, he plunged his length into her wet heat. Sucking in a breath at the perfect feel of the two of them together, her body squeezing him…her legs, her arms and her sex. He squeezed her, too…didn't want to let go, but he had waited so long, his body was too eager. The need to drive into her faster and faster became overwhelming and he succumbed. Grasping her by the hips, he held on to her, lifted her off of the bar, off of him, then back down. Over and over until he could feel his heart hammering inside his chest, hear her breath exploding from her lips.

Her tone grew higher, her movements frenzied. Venge pulled back one last time, felt his climax coming upon him. As he did, when he knew he could wait no longer, she threw back her head, let out a last urgent cry, and joined him—her body tightening around his shaft as release swept over them both.

As the waves rippled around them, Venge pulled Geysa close, ran his hand over her hair and squeezed his eyes closed. Her body was hot and sticky. The smell of sex hung around them. He pulled back her hair and pressed a kiss in front of her ear, beneath her cheekbone. She tasted of salt, but not just from sweat. Her cheek was damp. He pulled back, concern making his eyes widen.

"What…?" he started, but she shook her head, her lower lip between her teeth, and pulled him back close again. He knew the answer, had just forgotten for a second. He clenched his jaw, angry at everything and nothing at the same time.

After a few more minutes she pulled back, stared at the floor where their clothes were piled. "Jora could be back anytime. If she finds you here…"

"She'll kill me?" Venge laughed. Maybe that was the solution. Throw himself on her sword. End the almost psychotic swings between his desire to be with Geysa and his lifelong need to kill his father. End the pain he saw in Geysa's eyes. With him dead, she'd move on. She'd move on anyway…he didn't fool himself that she wouldn't. But with him dead, the trip would be easier—no risk of turning back, faltering as they had today.

But dead he would get nothing he wanted…no Geysa… no revenge. He thought of the Wild Hunt, of Sigurd's warnings. Maybe there was another way, a way to get his revenge and something Geysa wanted—her sister.

There had to be a way to get her that at least.

Chapter 14

Something clicked behind Venge's eyes. Geysa could feel him pull away from her, not physically so much as mentally, emotionally.

So that was it. Her last few moments pretending they had a chance were over. She tilted her head, letting her hair fall over her face, hiding the tears that still welled in her eyes.

Valkyries didn't cry. Not even when another died. They were stoic; they went on. Geysa was tired of being stoic. Maybe her mother's Norn half had leaked into Geysa, after all. She was tired of pretending loss had to be taken with strength. She wanted to embrace it, fall to her knees and crumble under its weight—just once.

But she didn't. Instead she slid from the bar and Venge's arms, then bent to pick up her clothing. "We'd better get dressed." She pulled on her pants and shirt. Behind her, she could hear Venge doing the same.

Once they were done, she turned back to him, expecting him to leave. Wanting him to. Not wanting to face what would happen if the Valkyries returned while he was still in the bar. Would they try to kill him? Would he kill in return? Would Geysa stand by and let the slaughter happen? Or make a choice she'd be unable to live with?

Of course, whether it happened now or later…the confrontation would happen. And Geysa would have to choose. *But, blessed gods, don't let it be now.* She needed time…to think.

"What do you want?" he asked.

She jerked her head up, surprised by his question. "Want?" She laughed. The impossible, was that too much to ask?

"What do you want the most? The horn or your sister?"

She frowned. His question was simple, too simple for all the wants Geysa had roaming through her head and her heart. But the answer was simple, too. "My sister." Of course, she wanted to stop the hunt. But not at the cost of one of the few people left to her.

He stepped forward, an urgency in his posture. "If I can do that, if I can get you your sister, will you be happy?"

Happy? Could she be happy? Had she ever been? She'd never questioned the state before, just taken her life for what it was. But now, after being with Venge, after seeing what life might hold, could she be happy?

He apparently took her silence as assent.

"I'll do it. No matter what it costs. I'll get your sister back for you." Then, without waiting for her to reply, for her to ask what cost he meant, for her to make yet another heart-wrenching choice, he shimmered.

Venge returned to his room at the bathhouse. Sigurd was lying on the bed, ankles crossed and cape tossed back so it covered the mattress.

"Is she better?"

Venge prowled across the room and pulled his bag from beneath the bed. After a quick check to make sure Sigurd hadn't rifled through his belongings, he addressed the other hellhound.

"What do you want?"

Sigurd stared at him, his expression tired. "You wouldn't believe me if I told you."

Venge shrugged. He was right. "So go. I have things to do."

"You're leaving?" Sigurd swung his legs over the side of the mattress.

Ignoring Sigurd, Venge tied the bag back on his belt.

"You've given up on the hunt? How about the girl? Is she going with you?"

The knot secure, Venge locked his stare onto Sigurd. "What's it matter to you?"

Sigurd shrugged. "It doesn't, not if you're leaving."

Venge kept his face blank.

Sigurd stared at him for a second, then swore. "You still plan on joining the hunt." He stood, his fists balled at his sides. "Maybe you aren't worth saving."

A rough laugh fell from Venge's lips. "Now you're saving me? How sweet."

"The hounds of the hunt—" Sigurd began.

"I don't intend to join the hunt," Venge said.

"You don't? But then—"

"I plan to control it." Venge walked to the bed and threw the pillow Sigurd had been reclining against onto the floor, then leaned back against the metal headboard, arms over his chest. "I agree with you. Hellhounds shouldn't give up their souls to another being. I don't plan on running in the hunt. I plan on manning the horn.

"There are enough of us here. We can take the Erl-King. The Valkyries defeated him once. Why can't we?"

Sigurd stared at Venge, his head shaking. "What did Lusse do to you? Shock you with one of her little toys once too often? You think an object as laden with magic and as ancient as the horn can be used by anyone? You think the gods who endowed it with its power didn't consider just such a move? Do you even know who the ErlKing is?"

Venge rolled his hands into fists. "I know I can't trust you. I may have had reason to hate you before, but I never doubted your strength. But somehow, you've forgotten what it is to be a hellhound. The anger that rules us."

Sigurd stepped forward, his hand going to the chain at his neck. "You think I've forgotten?" Red simmered in his eyes. "I've just chosen a new path. Hell knows the old one didn't get us anywhere."

Venge thinned his lips. He didn't want to listen to Sigurd, didn't want to hear his plan wouldn't work, but he was no fool. He wouldn't have survived life in Lusse's kennels or his travels if he was. "So, tell me your truth and why my plan won't work. Geysa's sister was able to blow the horn."

"She isn't a hellhound."

"So, only hellhounds can't use the horn? Convenient." Venge tilted one eyebrow.

Sigurd leaned against the wall, his cape flowing back over his chest. It made him look bigger somehow, ominous.

Venge frowned. "Quit your games."

Sigurd twisted his lips in a crooked smile, but shoved the cape behind his back. "I don't know who can man the horn, I only know hellhounds can't. The horn was designed to control our kind. If you so much as touch the horn, you'll be prey."

"Prey?"

"The hunt will turn on you. Your own pack will tear you to bits and take your soul back to the ErlKing."

Venge exhaled, studying Sigurd for some sign he was lying. "And if I join the hunt?"

"A hellhound doesn't just join the hunt…it isn't a club. He becomes the hunt—everything he hears, smells, tastes, has to do with the hunt. All a hound of the hunt cares about is the hunt. You'd tear your own mother to pieces and not bat an eye." Sigurd tapped his chin. "Of course, you'd probably do that anyway."

Venge growled, showing his teeth. "Wrong parent."

"Ah, yes. You were our own little Oedipus."

Venge's hand wandered to the chain at his neck. "Not quite. I had no mother to love. My father took care of that."

"Or so you were told."

Venge dropped the chain. "What do you mean?"

Sigurd shook his head. "Who told you your father killed your mother?"

A frown lowered Venge's brow. "Lusse, but my father didn't deny it."

Sigurd turned away and strolled to the window, his gait casual and unhurried. "I was there. Didn't see the actual event, but I saw Risk right afterward. Lusse had him so crazed he didn't even answer to his own name. He has no more idea what happened than you do."

"But—" Venge twisted to the side, his legs swinging over the edge of the mattress until his feet landed on the floor.

"But Lusse told you. Yeah." Sigurd pinned Venge with his gaze. "Then it must be true."

Venge's fingers curled into the sheet beneath him. "Still, he left me there."

"You think he had a choice?" His eyes staring out the window, Sigurd laughed. "She really did do a number on you, didn't she?"

Geysa sat by the front window, staring into an empty beer mug. Her third. Too bad alcohol had no effect on Valkyries. Jora and the others had returned hours ago, only a few minutes after Venge left. Geysa's aunt was suspicious. Geysa could feel Jora's regard on her back while she sat at a front table nursing her ale. Her aunt should be happy Geysa was leaving her and the others alone. She could hear them whispering behind her, still plotting, and not letting Geysa in on their plans.

Finally the whispers became too much, the gazes on her back too heavy. Geysa slammed the mug onto the table and strode into the bright sunshine. With no destination in mind, she found herself striding down the path that led to the stream, to the spot where she had first kissed Venge, first realized her life was as purposeless…as fake as the false fronts on the buildings that lined the town's main street.

Next to the creek she stopped, picked up a stone warmed by the sun and tossed it back and forth between her hands. The Valkyries didn't trust her. That fact should have bothered her more than it did.

She wrapped her hand around the rock, let the remaining heat radiate from its smooth surface into her palm. Heat. Venge. She squeezed the stone harder, squeezed her eyes closed, too.

How could the Valkyries' lack of trust bother her? She didn't trust herself.

"Nice day."

Geysa's eyes flew open. The hellhound she'd seen

fighting with Venge over Runa and the horn stood in front of her. Her grip on the stone tightened even more.

"Glad to see you're feeling better."

Geysa frowned. Something about this hellhound was familiar, but she knew she hadn't served him at the bar. At least not… "Audun?" she murmured.

He acknowledged her guess with a slight incline of his head. "Sigurd, actually. Sorry for the deception, but I had my reasons."

"Like eavesdropping?"

"Valkyries do tend to talk more around…" He whipped his cape around his body. Instantly the feeble human she'd known as Audun stood hunched in front of her. She took a deep breath and held it. The next instant Sigurd, the hellhound, was back in Audun's place. She let out the breath with a harried huff, then turned on the ball of her foot to leave.

His next words stopped her. "So you're well now? You were a little worse for wear last time I saw you."

She turned back, the stone in her hand moving to her lips. "You were there…" Geysa remembered very little of the attack that had dislocated her shoulder, a side effect of shock, her aunt said, but still a memory tickled at her brain, began to solidify.

He stared back, his dark gaze neither confirming nor denying.

"You saved me from—"

"Bjorn. He won't bother you again."

She dropped her hand to her side. "Why save me?"

Sigurd cocked an eyebrow. "Why not?"

Geysa angled her head and studied him out of the side of her eye. "Hellhounds aren't known for their good deeds."

He scooped up a stone similar in size and shape to the one in her hand, and held it up to the light. His eyes still focused on the rock, he replied, "And you're an expert on hellhounds?"

"I—" She stopped. She didn't know this male. He may have saved her, but that didn't mean she could trust him. "I've met a number since we've been here."

He tossed the stone once, then twice. On the third toss he appeared to catch the rock again, but held up his fist, fingers out. "Doesn't make you an expert. Or even that you know anyone as much as you think you do. Appearances…" he nodded toward his upraised fist "…can be deceiving." He opened his fingers, revealing nothing but air.

Geysa's gaze dropped to his feet and the dirt beneath them. There was no sign of the rock.

"Do you care about Venge?"

She jerked her gaze back to Sigurd.

"Do you know what he has planned?"

Her fingers clung to the stone she still held. The warmth, the specialness, was gone. Nothing but a cold, smooth rock lay in her grip.

"Do you know why?" Sigurd continued.

Geysa turned her head to the side, cast her gaze toward the stream. Water gurgled over rocks, kept moving no matter what else happened around it. She tossed the stone she held into the flowing water. One quick plink of sound and the stone was gone, not even a ripple in the water's surface marking where it had hit.

She took a breath. "Does it matter?"

"Which? Whether you care, what he has planned, or why?"

"Any of it. What I feel, what I know…neither is going to change anything."

Sigurd glanced from Geysa to the creek and the boulder that jutted from the precipice above. In the space of two breaths, he shimmered, rematerializing next to the massive rock. He placed his hands on the backside of the boulder and shoved. The stone rolled forward a few inches; a vein in Sigurd's neck bulged from his efforts. Geysa took a step back, her hand drifting to the space over her heart.

Sigurd shoved again; this time the boulder rocked in place and smaller pieces of stone and dirt tumbled down the hillside. Her eyes wide, Geysa watched the determined hellhound. He backed up, dusted his hands against each other then carefully reapproached the stone. His hands placed shoulder-width apart, he shoved. The earth groaned and the rock broke free, rushing toward the ground, then landing in the stream with a shuddering splash.

Water sprayed across Geysa's face. Her heart pounding, she pulled in a breath. The giant stone settled into the creek bed, instantly diverting the water into two smaller streams that poured around each of the boulder's sides.

Sigurd shimmered again, into the dry space directly behind the rock. He held out both hands, showing his skinned and bleeding palms. "Some changes take more effort than others. I think you underestimate yourself."

Geysa stared at the two rivulets of water, at the damp earth where the bigger stream used to flow.

"What does he have planned?" she asked.

Sigurd shimmered, solidifying next to her. "He thinks he can take the horn and run the hunt himself."

Something inside Geysa squeezed shut. She'd already known this. Venge had told her as much himself, but she'd guarded his secret, not let the Valkyries know his plan. If they learned Venge planned to steal the horn, run the hunt, he would quickly take a place next to the ErlKing as a Valkyrie's target. Who else had Sigurd told?

"Why?" she murmured.

"To kill his father."

Geysa's gaze snapped to Sigurd.

"Venge believes his father murdered his mother."

Geysa nodded. "He told me." But she hadn't realized that was Venge's motive—hate. So different from her own motive—love for her mother, stopping anyone else from suffering the loss she had.

Surprise flitted behind Sigurd's eyes, but he continued. "And he blames his father for…things that happened to him in his past."

"He wants revenge," Geysa concluded, her gaze moving back to the stream.

"Not unusual for a hellhound," Sigurd added. "But in this case…"

"What?" Geysa asked. The stream was gurgling louder now that the water had to batter its way around the boulder.

"The horn. It was designed to control hellhounds. If a hellhound touches any part of it with his bare skin, the hunt will turn on him, with abandon. His body will be destroyed and his soul will belong to the ErlKing."

"But you were fighting with Venge. For the horn?" She frowned. Although it hadn't occurred to her at the time, it was the only explanation that made sense.

"I took precautions…." He held up his hands. An image of linked metal covering his fingers flashed through Geysa's mind. "And I never planned to blow the horn. I don't know what would happen if a hellhound did, but I can't imagine it would be anything good—for the hell-hound or the nine worlds."

"So, we need to stop him." She flattened her hands against her legs and tightened her jaw.

"Not we. I've tried. At this point I think any further *friendly* input from me may have the opposite effect to what I want.

"So, assuming you care, *you* need to stop him. I've made contact with someone who might be of help, but he's having a few difficulties getting away. And trust me—" Sigurd flicked a piece of skin from his torn palms "—it would be a lot less…explosive, if you were able to stop Venge. But either way, he has to be stopped."

Geysa bit the inside of her cheek.

Sigurd turned his regard to her, his eyes somber. "I want Venge to survive and the hunt stopped, but more than that I don't want to see what happens if a hellhound gets hold of the horn. I'll do whatever it takes to keep that from occurring."

Geysa took a step forward. "Who else knows—" Before she could finish, Sigurd shimmered and was gone.

Geysa stood for a second, the sounds of the creek filling her ears. The Valkyries could not learn Venge's plan. The town was swarming with her people, all of them eager to begin the battle against the ErlKing. If they knew of Venge's plan they would—

"Geysa, what's going on?" Geysa's aunt peered at her over crossed arms.

Geysa jumped. How long had her aunt been standing there? What had she heard?

Attempting at casual, Geysa replied, "Walking. The water's so peaceful. It reminds me of…" What? Valhalla wasn't peaceful. "I like it," she added.

"Really?" Jora's gaze shot to the boulder. "What happened?"

Geysa stooped to retrieve a round stone and slipped it in her pocket. "Things change."

Her body tense, Jora studied Geysa. "Is there something you want to tell me?"

Geysa kept her eyes in a steady stare. "No. Nothing. Why do you ask?"

Jora looked back at the boulder. "You know I love you, right?"

Surprise pulled a tiny breath through Geysa's lips. It was the first time her aunt had said those words.

Jora turned back, an intensity in her eyes Geysa hadn't seen there before. "There are things about me you don't know, and as leader of the Valkyries, I have to do things you might not understand. But no matter what happens—with Runa, the horn, any of it—I want you to know…I love you and your sister." Her hand resting on the handle of her sword, Jora turned on her heel and left.

Geysa stared after her aunt, tendrils of fear spiraling around her. It was the first time her aunt had ever said she loved Geysa or Runa. The admittance should have been re-assuring, but somehow it just made Geysa all the more con-cerned—for everyone.

Her dagger in one hand, Geysa pushed open the bath-house door and crept inside. Venge wasn't at the barn with the other hellhounds. At least the Valkyrie Geysa had sidled up to at dinner claimed he wasn't. The young female, along with a dozen others, had been assigned the duty of watch-ing the barn for movement.

According to the girl, no one fitting Venge's description had been near the barn in days. Which meant either he had left or he'd chosen somewhere else to wait for the horn's call.

Geysa was betting on the second.

She'd waited until dark, when the Valkyries left for yet another meeting from which she was excluded, and this time, she'd brought a flashlight. Inside, with the door closed behind her, she switched it on.

The table was overturned, rune stones and cards were

scattered all over the floor. Someone had been here. She let the light dance around the room quickly, then headed for the stairs.

Venge sat on the floor of his room, his chin on his knees and his gaze on the door. Someone was in the house. A Valkyrie most likely. With their increasing numbers in the town, it was only a matter of time before they gave up whatever prejudice they had against Runa's house, and moved in.

He hadn't expected them in the dead of night, though. And he wasn't exactly in a mood to leave. He knew they were monitoring the barn. Watching the hellhounds like animals in a zoo.

Another reason not to join his pack.

He was tired of waiting for the ErlKing to sound the horn. His time with Geysa, followed by Sigurd's visit, had put him even more on edge. Both confused him. He didn't want to be confused. He wanted to act.

The door to the room edged open; the sound of a foot sliding across the wood floor followed. There was a gleam—a length of metal in the dim light.

With a growl, he sprang forward, lunging toward whoever invaded his space.

Chapter 15

Geysa heard the roar echo through the building. Her heart surging to the top of her throat, she sprinted up the stairs. She raced into Venge's room, her dagger clutched in her hand.

Venge flew backward, propelled by Jora's foot on his chest. He smashed into the wall, next to the window, but sprang to his feet, his lip curled in a snarl. Jora stepped forward, her sword held in front of her, gripped by both hands.

She pointed the weapon at his chest. "Time to move on," she said.

Venge lunged to the side; Jora followed.

Jora widened her stance. "I don't want to kill you, but I know what you're doing. And I can't let it happen."

"Kill me then." Venge took a step toward her.

Geysa stood frozen, her fingers cramping where they wrapped around her dagger. Her aunt had heard Geysa talking to Sigurd—and now Jora or Venge was going to die because of it.

Jora's sword lifted, less than a quick thrust from Venge's heart. Both still unaware of Geysa's presence, they stood unmoving.

Fear clenched like a fist around Geysa—fear for Venge, her aunt, for all of them. Why didn't he shimmer? He could escape. It would be so easy.

Venge jerked as if startled, his head twisting toward Geysa. Surprise rounded his eyes. Then, as he held her gaze, resolve clicked into place, hardening his face, his body, his entire demeanor.

Shimmer. Leave, she willed, praying he understood.

The air turned to waves she could feel as much as see, and he was gone. Geysa breathed in a second of relief before feeling the second shimmer—Venge reappearing next to her aunt. His eyes simmered with red, the red of a hellhound intent on killing.

He reached out, his hand skimming Jora's hair, heading for her throat… Geysa clenched her jaw, trapping the scream forming in her chest. Screaming would just startle them, cause more carnage.

She had to stop them, to shock one or both of them out of their actions. Her teeth ground together so tightly a band of pain began to weave around her head. Sucking in a breath, she pulled back her arm and let her heart guide her dagger.

Venge saw Geysa from the corner of his eye—her hair slipping free to fall around her face, her breasts jutting forward as she pulled in a breath. He'd shocked her, scared her—just as he'd meant to do.

Her arm moved, silver flashed, and her dagger flew across the few feet separating them.

He waited, let the blade pierce his flesh as it had before, but this time it was more than a wound. It was a choice. He stared at the handle protruding from the back of his hand, let his gaze catch Geysa's. Let her see the truth of what had happened—had to happen.

She'd chosen the Valkyries over him—they both knew it. The bright red hellhound blood dripping onto the wood beneath his feet made denying it—by either of them—impossible. Ripping the dagger from his hand, he let the weapon fall with a clatter onto the stained floor, then shimmered.

Geysa stared at the dagger, her dagger, streaked with Venge's blood. Her aunt spun, her sword raised, ready to hack through anyone who stood in her path.

Geysa held up a shaking hand. "He's gone."

Jora frowned, her gaze following Geysa's to the knife… the blood…the story. Her aunt bent, picked up the dagger and wiped the blade clean on her pants. She took a step forward, the knife held toward Geysa, handle first. Geysa stared at the dagger, then her aunt expecting her to say something…anything about what had just happened.

But Jora just nodded toward the blade in her hand, urging Geysa to take it. Her voice firm, she said, "You may need this again."

Geysa took the dagger, her fingers so limp she was surprised it didn't clatter to the floor. Instead, still sticky with Venge's blood, the weapon clung, like a burr she would never be able to shake free.

Jora strode past her, her heels clicking against the floor in determined strides.

Geysa turned to follow, but couldn't, not without casting one last glance back to the stained floor.

"Geysa! Something is happening. Come now." Her

aunt's voice rang up the stairs. Knowing her decision had been made, Geysa slid her dagger back into her boot. Jora was right. She might need it again.

Venge wrapped his hand in an oily cloth he had found lying on the barn floor. The other members of his "pack" were still in much the same state as the last time he'd visited—drunk, dirty and fighting at every opportunity.

He kicked a prostrate hellhound out of his way and strode to the back. Behind him the male he'd struck roared and lurched to his feet. Venge spun, his lips pulled back in a snarl. The hellhound froze, his gaze dropping to Venge's hand. Venge took a step forward, letting the other males know his injury was not an opportunity to challenge him, not a weakness.

No. Venge's true injury, his true weakness, wasn't anything anyone could see.

The other hellhound acknowledged Venge's threat and superior rank. Shuffling his feet, he turned on the next hellhound he encountered.

Growling under his breath, Venge continued stalking toward the back. He had barely turned to face the front of the barn when a voice called out....chilling him to the depths of his soul.

"I heard you wanted to see me."

Venge spun, his lips pulling back in a snarl, the muscles in his back tensing. His father stood in the middle of the barn, his arms hanging casually at his sides.

"Why are you here?" Venge asked.

"Why not?" Risk glanced around the barn, his expression cool, disinterested.

"I haven't seen you since Lusse—" Venge snapped his teeth together. There was no reason to talk.

"I didn't think you would be particularly eager for a family reunion." Risk stared back at Venge with the same bored regard Venge remembered from his last encounter with his father—right after he had ground Venge's face into the mud, then ordered him locked in a cage barely big enough in which to turn.

The hellhound who had thought to challenge Venge earlier stumbled into Risk. Venge's father wrapped his hand into the front of the wayward hound's shirt and tossed him into a group that sat watching their exchange. To Venge's surprise, no scuffle broke out, the other hellhounds too intent on what was passing between Venge and his father.

They thought Risk could defeat him—that Risk would become the new alpha. Venge narrowed his eyes, his anger for his father bubbling anew.

"So, why did you want to see me?" Risk held out both hands, one eyebrow raised in a question.

Rage poured from Venge's core into the rest of his body—down his arms and legs until he felt he might explode with it. A growl erupted from deep inside him and, head bowed, he rushed his father.

His head collided with Risk's stomach, knocking the older hellhound into a forgotten tractor. The machine shuddered, a fender falling onto the ground with a clang.

"Forandre rules?" Risk's voice rumbled into Venge's ear.

"Forandre rules," Venge agreed, already pulling back to face his father, to give Venge the distance he needed to kick Risk in the gut—to end their feud once and for all.

Risk stepped to the side, his gaze dancing over Venge, gauging his son's next move.

The other hellhounds had gotten to their feet, forming a circle around father and son. The room filled with the scent of aggression, rage…anticipation.

Venge swung his fist, the one not wounded by Geysa's blade. His father ducked. Venge's fist struck the tractor, sending reverberations down Venge's arm, into his body. He gritted his teeth, the pain only increasing his determination.

Risk lunged to the left, his foot hitting the fallen fender. "Use it," Venge urged. He wanted his father to take every advantage, wanted the joy of knowing he had killed him without tricks. He had thought he simply wanted his father dead, that using the hunt would be rewarding enough. Now he realized the real satisfaction would be in tearing Risk's body apart with his own hands.

Risk tilted his head toward the twisted piece of metal. "You." He bent, picked up the fender and tossed it toward Venge.

Venge moved to the side, letting the fender sail into the line of hellhounds behind him.

Risk cocked a brow. "I heard you wanted me dead—that you were willing to take stupid risks to get me that way."

Venge kicked, his foot slicing through the air toward his father's head. Risk moved, dropping to a one-legged squat. His other foot shot out, hitting Venge in the side of the leg. Venge fell, but rolled to the side and back to his feet.

"You don't fight like a hellhound anymore. Who have you been learning from?"

Venge ignored the question, instead looking for an opening, a weakness. Everyone had one—his father included. He just had to find it.

"Elves?" Risk plucked an old metal tool off the ground and twirled the two-foot-long piece in one hand. "They use weapons. Why won't you?" He let the length spin free, toward Venge's head. Venge reached out, stopping its momentum with his hand.

"Because…" Venge dropped the tool onto the ground. "I don't want to."

"But you would use the hunt?" Risk asked.

Venge feinted to the left, then struck from the right; this time his foot collided with Risk's head. His father's neck snapped backward, a dribble of blood forming at the corner of his mouth.

"Maybe," he said with a smile, "I won't have to."

"Maybe you won't." Risk stepped forward as Venge kicked again. A second blow to Risk's head—harder. So hard, Venge felt something in his own knee pop. Knew he'd damaged something. But with the adrenaline pumping through his veins, he couldn't feel the pain—only the hum of excitement from being part of the battle. The one he had dreamed of.

The two approached, both with their fists up—protecting. Risk swung. Venge dropped to the side and led with his elbow, using the point to slash into his father's face. His father kicked at the same time, his foot making contact with Venge's shoulder but without the full strength Venge knew his father could deliver.

Venge staggered back, watching as Risk fell to the ground, then waiting for Risk to stand, to come back at him, harder…stronger, as he always had before, but his father didn't. He just lay on the ground, propped on one elbow, the hand beneath him curled into a fist, the side of his face already swelling, his eyes closed…as if he were concentrating on something, saying something to himself.

Then he opened his eyes, one barely more than a squint past the swelling, and Venge saw it—the first glimmer of the Change. His father was going to Change. He'd lose. Venge would win and the other hounds in the barn would tear Risk to bits. But it was a lie. Venge knew his father better than this—had seen him endure the unendurable. There was no way he would give over this fast—not unless he was throwing the fight.

"No," Venge yelled, throwing himself toward Risk. He wanted to beat him. He wouldn't let Risk take this victory from him.

As the tips of his fingers brushed against Risk's shirt, as Risk stared back at him, his eyes almost solid red, Venge felt something else…like twin kicks in his chest. He flew backward, his breath rushing from his lungs, his arms going limp—useless.

Power. He'd been hit by power. His brain recognized the feel even while it struggled to compute what was happening. A witch. Only a witch could strike like this.

He flew backward, into the wall, heard the logs crack as his back smashed against them. Rage surged through him. A trick. His father had tricked him…made Venge believe he was here to fight, then had his witch wife attack when she saw he was losing.

He looked down; two white streams of power pressed against his chest, holding him to the wall. He roared, his control of the beast inside him breaking.

Then the pressure on his chest was gone and he fell to the ground, his head bouncing back against the logs as his body rebounded off the floor.

He leaped to his feet, his fists balled, rage simmering inside him. The witch…where was she? He spun and saw her. His father was at her side, his arms wrapped around her, holding her with her back pressed against his chest, her arms pinned to her sides. She vibrated against him, seemed to be yelling, but Risk ignored her—his brows lowered and his attention on Venge. Venge started forward, fury propelling him, but before he could reach them or think enough to shimmer, his father moved first, shimmering and taking the witch with him.

Venge was still trembling with anger, blood still buzzing through his veins, his mind unable to focus on anything except the opportunity that had been taken from him when the horn's call began…warm and fluid, like blood flowing fresh from a kill's throat.

He stood for a moment, the call coursing over him, calming him, drawing him with the sweet promise of the hunt. His lips tilted into a smile—all wasn't lost. His father was close, and the hunt even closer.

The other males in the barn heard the call, too, turned to watch Venge. He clutched his good hand over the one Geysa had wounded earlier. Let the pain shoot up his arm, reminding himself he had control. He pulled a pair of earplugs out of the sack at his belt and shoved them into his ears. The other males followed suit. Then, after a nod from Venge, they all shimmered.

Venge solidified at the top of a mountain, above the tree line. Piles of snow still decorated the otherwise barren terrain. The ErlKing had selected a spot more deserted than any Runa had chosen before.

Venge waited, his encounter with his father increasing his commitment, his focus. The earplugs blocked all sound—the tingle of magic alerting him the other hounds had materialized behind him. When the shimmering had stopped, and the magic from the act dissipated, Venge signaled for the other males to wait as he looked around.

There was a path leading, Venge suspected, to the rocky summit. He started up, rocks rolling beneath his feet. It was predawn, the first rosy glow of daybreak just now visible. Red like the blood Venge had lost to Geysa's blade, that he had taken from his father—that others would most likely lose before ownership of the horn was settled.

There was movement beside him. A tree. Venge frowned. No. There were no trees here. He focused harder and was able to see past the disguise. Sigurd already here.

"Go away," Venge called.

"I can't," Sigurd mouthed, lowering his arms, all pretense of being anything but hellhound gone.

"You can't stop me." Venge unwrapped his wounded hand and left the bloody rag lying on the ground behind him. Nothing could stop him now.

Sigurd held up one arm, pointing beyond the mountain's side.

Pouring out of the town below were the Valkyries. Hundreds of them. But only one caught Venge's eye. Geysa, back on her stallion, her sister's crossbow strapped to her saddle, her hair snapping free behind her.

There was no hesitance in her posture, no sign of indecision.

Venge exhaled and curled his injured hand toward him. It had worked. Attacking her aunt in front of her. Reminding her exactly what a hellhound was—would do—had cut any bond she thought they had, had freed her to forget him and go back to her kind. To be accepted. Venge's face hardened with grim resolve. He had done the right thing, and now he was free, too—to complete the rest of his task.

His father was near—near enough that tracking him once Venge controlled the hunt should be no issue.

Everything was falling into place. Geysa would forget him, and Venge would get his revenge. Everything would be as it should be.

All he needed now was the ErlKing.

* * *

Geysa rode at the head of the Valkyries. She could feel each movement of the horse beneath her, hear his breath as his hooves ate away the sky beneath them. A mountain loomed in front of them, higher than the others, spotted with snow.

Her aunt raised a hand, signaling for them to wait, to circle like the birds of prey they emulated.

Geysa, hollow inside, fell into line behind her aunt. Waiting had never been her forte, but today she could have waited for eternity. Today, no matter what happened, who won—Geysa would lose.

To Venge's right, a few feet from Sigurd, the air shimmered, pulling his gaze from Geysa. A band tightened around Venge's center. He knew instantly who was arriving….

Risk materialized, his feet moving in long strides toward Venge as he did. Venge growled. Did his father really think he would fall for more of his tricks?

Above them the air darkened, black clouds moving in with no warning. The Valkyries continued to circle, but only a few on the whitest of horses or wearing the brightest cloaks were visible. Geysa, on her dappled destrier, all but disappeared. A sliver of panic shot through Venge but he fought it off—she was fine, still flying overhead, not visible, but safe.

He turned his attention back to his father. Risk yelled something, but the earplugs blocked the sound. Venge shook his head, motioned to his father to save his breath—it was too late. The ErlKing was coming; Venge could feel it in his blood, in the way his pulse jumped against his throat.

The horn sounded again—closer. The earplugs blocked the sound, but Venge could feel the call trilling through his body and saw his father stiffen then clap his hands to his ears and curse. Sigurd tossed his father something…and Risk shoved the items into his ears. The other hellhounds, the ones Venge had left farther down the mountain, appeared, tramping forward trancelike, the horn…even muffled…calling to them.

The air turned cold. The ground shook as if struck by lightning. Venge widened his stance to keep from falling, saw the other hellhounds stumble into each other, a few dropping to their knees.

They should have been yelling, running back down the mountain confused, but they all stood or sat where they had fallen, their eyes cast toward the sky…waiting.

The sky broke open, a wind brushing aside the Valkyries like a hand waving away a gnat. A wedge of silvery gray split the darkness, and the ErlKing appeared astride his gray horse, Runa lying limp across his lap and the horn held to his lips.

Geysa wrapped her hand in her mount's mane—the wind shoving against the Valkyries with such force they couldn't maintain their form. First one then another fell back, a few tumbling, almost falling from their capes. Others battled against the rippling currents of air to grab those who seemed most lost, most at risk of being taken by the wind and whirled to the earth below.

The current pulled at Geysa's hair, yanking it with such force tears of pain welled in her eyes. She hunkered against her horse's neck and urged him down, toward the ground and away from the screeching wind.

She could hear the others following, their horses screaming as they followed her path.

Jora dove from above, until she flew next to Geysa, the feathers of her cape brushing against Geysa's cheek. "Runa," she yelled. "He brought her."

Geysa turned in her saddle, struggling to see without losing her seat. Sensing her movement, her horse swerved, forcing Geysa to adjust again, to flatten her body against his neck.

"There." Her aunt pointed, but Geysa could see nothing but the upward movement of Jora's cape. The wind cut into Geysa's eyes, the cold air taking her breath and causing tears to stream down her cheeks.

"Damn it," her aunt yelled. Jora flew closer, so close her cape flapped over Geysa's back as if she wore it, too.

Geysa's horse jerked, frightened. Geysa screwed her eyes shut, blocking the wind, and prayed he somehow found his way to the ground.

The horse jerked again, but this time a shorter movement as if directed and Geysa felt his flight change, become more controlled. They dropped beneath the wind, and Geysa opened her eyes. The ground zoomed toward them. Panic welled within Geysa, but she quickly tamped it down, realized her aunt had her hand wrapped around the horse's bridle and was guiding him to the earth.

With a jolt, his front hooves then his back landed on the hard, rocky dirt—the impact tearing Geysa's arms from his neck and dropping her onto the ground with a bone-jarring thud.

She stared at the sky…at the growing triangle of white against black…at the blurry outline of the ErlKing wearing his boar-head helmet, riding his stallion down to the earth. Her breath was already gone, stolen by her fall, but seeing him, her heart froze, too. She could only lay there wide-eyed, watching, dread covering her like a blanket.

Slowly her eyes adjusted and her brain focused—tearing her out of her fog.

The ErlKing performed a figure eight above them, one

hand held up, grasping the horn, the other pressed against the squirming form draped across his saddle in front of him.

Runa.

Geysa sprang to her feet.

Chapter 16

Venge pulled in air…thick and cold…and growing colder with every stride the ErlKing's mount took. The ErlKing was stronger now—with the horn, Venge realized. It was as if the instrument completed him somehow, added to his might. Clamminess crawled over Venge's skin.

How strong would the ErlKing be with the horn and the hounds—actually running the hunt? The thought held Venge frozen for a moment.

From the corner of his eye he saw movement—his father and, now beside him, the witch. Venge's doubts disappeared.

They were too late. They couldn't stop him.

He clenched his fist and glanced back at the hellhounds who had made their way to the top. They had done as they were told, broken into two groups so they could approach the ErlKing from both sides. The plan was for Venge to speak first, to make the ErlKing believe the hellhounds were ready to follow him—then when he least expected, they would attack.

The ErlKing flew lower, his figure eight growing smaller. The darkness behind his helmet seemed to scan the crowd waiting for him on the ground. He leaned forward and whispered something in Runa's ear. Venge could see her jerk, as if trying to fight him, but her movements were cut short, as if she were bound by some invisible rope.

Then Venge felt it—the ErlKing's gaze. The clamminess that had crawled over him earlier was nothing compared to the feeling that accompanied the ErlKing's regard— like an icy slime sliding over Venge's body, heavy and damp, weighing him down, making it difficult to breathe.

"You," a voice boomed in Venge's head. Deep and reverberating, the sound seemed to go on long after Venge knew the word had stopped. His hands flew to his ears, checking the plugs, but they were still there. The ErlKing had done what Venge thought only forandre could—speak inside another's mind. And even forandre couldn't use the talent in human form.

The ErlKing was nothing Venge had ever encountered before. Without realizing he'd done so, Venge took a tiny step back.

The ErlKing laughed, a dark, bottomless sound. Venge squared his jaw and took a bigger step forward.

The ErlKing laughed again, then reined his horse in and brought him to the ground—his iron-tipped hoof landing inches from Venge's foot.

The air around the ErlKing vibrated and buzzed—as if he carried with him the power of ten thousand bolts of lightning. Venge's heart jumped in his chest, like a rabbit darting back and forth, searching for a hole to escape down.

The ErlKing leaned forward, resting the side of his forearm on the horn of his saddle. "Are you the alpha?"

Venge tilted his head slightly, and slowly, with a concentrated effort, unclenched his fists.

"You think to outsmart me?" The ErlKing nodded and Venge knew he was referring to the earplugs.

"I have no desire to be trapped," he replied.

"Trapped?" The ErlKing pulled back, as if surprised. "Riding with the hunt is the greatest of honors."

"Perhaps." Venge shifted his feet so his body moved closer. He covered the action by crossing his arms over his chest.

The ErlKing's helmet hid his face, with only black holes where his eyes and mouth should have been, but Venge sensed a lightening of his mood. He held up the gauntlet-covered hand that held the horn and twirled the instrument between his fingers. "You want this?" Then he leaned down again, the horn held in front of him. "No reason for games. Just take it."

Venge could feel his smile… *Trust me.* The words hummed low in Venge's head.

Venge stared at the silver horn, so close. His hand rose, his fingers uncurling from his palms. He wanted to touch the ancient instrument, to own it. The horn called to him. A hellhound should own it—who else could understand what the artifact needed…the chase, the blood, the hunt.

He should own it. He stretched forward, the tips of his fingers seconds from brushing the gleaming metal of the horn.

Geysa paused in her race up the mountain, her heart pounding, her breath coming quick and hard. The ErlKing had come to a halt, too, his horse landing in front of Venge. Runa still tossed across the ErlKing's saddle, he leaned forward—seemed to be talking with Venge. Something silver sparkled in the sun. The horn. The ErlKing twirled it overhead, then leaned forward again…the horn in one hand. He was offering it to…Venge.

Sigurd's warning roared through her mind. One touch. Just one touch, he'd said.

Venge reached out, his fingers moving toward the horn.

Something inside Geysa screamed. She broke into a run, picked up her pace, ran until her thighs screamed and she thought her lungs might burst.

Then, just as she realized there was no way she could make it, something blue and hot shot from beside her, slammed into Venge and sent him flying backward—away from the ErlKing and his horn.

Venge's feet flew from under him, a bolt of power knocking into his chest. His body cupped and he zoomed backward. Then, as quickly as the magic had hit, it was gone, and Venge dropped like a stone onto the ground. He scrambled to a sit, his fingers getting caught in the strings connected to his earplugs as he did. They fell to the ground, but caught up in what had just happened, in his desire to get back to the horn, he took no notice.

Within seconds, Sigurd was beside him. "What are you doing?" he growled.

Venge stood and, shaking the other hellhound's hand off his arm, started to stride back to the spot he had left. The ErlKing still waited there, his horn latched to his saddle and his dark gaze following Venge as he walked ever closer.

"What do you want?" the ErlKing asked inside Venge's head. "The horn?" He dropped his gauntlet-covered hand to the instrument and stroked the metal.

Venge paused, his gaze latched onto the horn.

"I'll bring it to you." The ErlKing applied one heel to his mount's side and within seconds he was back in front of Venge, as if he had been there all along. "They can't stop you." The ErlKing raised his hand and made a swirling motion overhead. The wind picked up, began to twirl around them, as if he and the ErlKing were standing inside a tornado—trapped or safe, Venge wasn't sure which.

He could see the hellhounds, Sigurd, his father, the witch, all of them, but he couldn't hear them, and he knew they couldn't get to him. He could feel whatever power the ErlKing held swirling, cutting him off from them and any actions they might choose to take.

"Here." The ErlKing held out the horn again. The silver shone as brightly as before; the call would sound as sweet. Venge reached out, ready to claim it. Then, from the corner of his eye, he saw movement…. Geysa, her mouth open in a plea. He squinted, trying to discern her words, trying to decipher what was causing her such distress. Her mouth opened again, and her gaze locked on his, connecting them, an almost physical sensation…like a metal wire vibrated between them, linking them together. She wanted him to stop…not to take the horn, but she'd known his intention before, hadn't pleaded with him then. Why now?

He paused, his brow lowering in confusion. Something was wrong. Geysa was telling him that. He glanced at Sigurd. The other hellhound stood stiffly, his cape stirred by the ErlKing's wind flapping around him, and his face somber, concerned. Sigurd's words…his warning…returned to Venge.

Venge looked back at the ErlKing and the horn he held. This was easy—too easy. Why would the ErlKing give him the horn? Why give it up?

Venge licked his lips, his mouth dry with the desire to

touch the instrument, to just stroke one finger over the cold metal, to hold it to his lips…just once.

"Venge, no." Geysa's voice broke through the wind, slicing into Venge, cutting him free from the spell.

He jerked back his hand—the motion surprising him. He hadn't realized he'd been reaching for the horn again.… He shifted his focus to the ErlKing, anger beginning to bubble inside him. The ErlKing watched him, the darkness behind his face guard enigmatic, but Venge sensed something…a shift in how the ErlKing held himself, almost a sigh. Disappointment?

A growl formed low in Venge's throat.

Another trap. The ErlKing, like Venge's father, sought to trick him. And Venge had almost fallen for it. But… Venge frowned. If the ErlKing had been trying to trap him with the offer of the horn, then Sigurd had spoken the truth.

Could his old enemy truly have been trying to help him? Venge shook the thought from his head. Right now he couldn't sort that out…had to concentrate all his energies on where he was and the being he faced.

The ErlKing slid from his saddle, landed on the ground next to Venge. Venge had never felt small, but even though the ErlKing in his armor stood only an inch or two taller, Venge felt inconsequential…like he was an ant staring up the trunk of the tallest and oldest of trees.

The ErlKing peered down at him. "What do you want?" Again in Venge's head. "You must want something, or you wouldn't be here…and I need an alpha. So, tell me what you want and in return I will give you the most honored position a hellhound can obtain—alpha of the Wild Hunt." The ErlKing's voice rose as he spoke; the last few words came out with a boom.

Venge glanced around, past the swirling wind that separated them from the others. Confusion, anger, even fear, he could see on their faces, but no one moved—no one made any sign of hearing the ErlKing's words.

A sound pulled Venge's attention to the horse behind the ErlKing and the female draped across its saddle. Runa twisted back and forth, her hands stretching away from the horse's side. The ErlKing arched one brow, and Runa's hands snapped back against the horse's side.

"What is she to you?" the ErlKing asked.

Startled, Venge shifted his gaze back to the armored form in front of him. "Nothing." She was nothing to him...but what was she to Geysa? And what of the promise he had made to himself earlier?

"Really?" Without turning his body, the ErlKing placed a hand on Runa's back. She jerked, her legs kicking out. The horse stirred, stamping his feet, but the ErlKing made a low, mumbling noise in his throat and the beast stilled. "So, you won't care if I send her to join her mother? I brought her as a reward for my new pack. Their first kill— always the sweetest." He paused, his helmet dipping as if in thought. "Perhaps I don't need you. A morsel this tempting...tossed in their midst...one hound would surely battle the hardest, come out on top."

The ErlKing's hand lowered again, to a thin tie Venge now realized looped around Runa's waist, holding her to the saddle. Venge's gaze shot back to the swirling wall of air— to Geysa. She stood close now...too close...her hands extended in front of her as if pressed against a glass window, her eyes huge and her lips parted. What was she saying? For some reason Venge couldn't hear her anymore, just see her, see the pain she'd endured etched in the tense line of her body.

He tore his attention away, back to the ErlKing. "I want her, but free and with a promise."

The ErlKing tilted his head. "A promise?"

"You'll remove her from the hunt. You'll never target her again. Safe. She has to be completely safe from you."

"Safe?" The ErlKing turned so he could reach Runa while still keeping Venge in his sight. He tilted her head until Venge could see her gray eyes…so like Geysa's. "She's so like her mother…such a waste."

Then, with no warning, he pulled his hand back, let Runa's head fall against the horse's side. "It's a bargain. Give yourself to the call and I'll free the Norn."

With a short nod of his head, Venge agreed. Then he held out his hand and let it be captured by the mail gauntlet the ErlKing wore.

His hand still wrapped around Venge's, the ErlKing released the horn from his belt and lifted the instrument to his lips. The call started low, soft, and full of promise. Venge didn't fight it this time…just let himself go. The call grew louder, more demanding. Venge could feel his blood thickening, his body changing—shifting from man to canine. His senses increased…he could smell everything, the leather of the ErlKing's saddle, the sweat from his horse, the dirt they stood upon. All of it filled him with excitement. Then the sounds came…the pattering flight of Runa's heart, the steady breaths of the ErlKing's horse…and finally, far away, almost outside of his new hearing…a scream…from…Geysa. He knew the sound, recognized the name, but the new Venge, the hound of the hunt, was already forgetting who she was or why he'd cared enough to save her sister.

The ErlKing had been right…such a shame, a waste…but no matter. Venge had the rest of eternity to run, to hunt.

"And soon," he heard the ErlKing whisper, "the hunt will ride again."

With Venge as its alpha.

* * *

Geysa stood with her hands held toward the wall of swirling air. She wanted to touch it, to break through, but she couldn't—the fast-spinning air held her at bay, making actual contact impossible.

She looked over her shoulder at Venge's father, Risk. She'd only met him moments ago and, based on what Venge had told her, she had no trust for the intimidating male, but she was desperate. "Can you shimmer?" she yelled. "Get past it that way?"

The burly blond hellhound shook his head, his face grim. "I tried. It's not just air…I don't know what it is."

Magic. Geysa bit her lip, tears of frustration seeping from the corners of her eyes. The ErlKing had them both—Runa and Venge. How could Geysa lose so much to one being? What else could he take from her?

He couldn't. She wouldn't let him.

With a scream of rage, she backed up and raced toward the gyrating cone of air.

Chapter 17

Running at a speed she didn't know she was capable of, Geysa hit the wall. She felt herself slip, felt the air whip through her hair, tear at her clothes, and for a second she thought she'd made it through. Then, just as quickly, she realized her mistake, felt the spinning air shove her sideways and up until she spun like a top—twirling so fast the world below her was a blur and she could feel herself slipping…losing consciousness.

She closed her eyes, felt herself slowing, stopping for one brief second, before air rushed past her again, this time swooshing past her body as she plummeted back to the earth. The wind roared; she could hear nothing but it whooshing past her ears.

Pinpricks of air assaulted her, stabbing into her skin wherever it was exposed. Her shirt flew up, leaving more of her body vulnerable. She wanted to open her eyes, but couldn't, some deep part of her knowing it was better not to know what was coming, not to see her own death written on the faces below her.

Then her body jerked upward, something sharp cutting into her sides, tearing into her skin. Her descent stopped; instead, her body moved sideways in long, jerking movements, as though whoever held her was fighting to move forward.

Her heart pounding, Geysa opened her eyes. The mountain where the Valkyries and hellhounds had gathered was still dangerously far below, but she was descending now—in slow, controlled movements. There was the sound of flapping—strong and steady, the tempo too even to be a Valkyrie's cape. But what?

She tried to turn, to see who held her, but pain shot from her sides where she was gripped. Instead, she moved her hands there, felt her own skin, the warmth of blood, and…

Something hard and smooth penetrated her skin, into her muscle.

Her mind jumped. Not a rope or arms…but some kind of claw had captured her, saved her from falling. A claw…attached to…

She twisted her neck, this time ignoring the pain, and stared into Jora's gray eyes…framed in the giant feather-covered face of a gyrfalcon.

The wind quit swirling around them. Venge shook his head; his body relaxed into his hound form. The dirt was dry under his feet, but it was a petty annoyance—scratching against his pads. The air was thin, but it didn't matter—he no longer needed such things to exist. Not air, not food, not anything weaker corporeal hellhounds needed.

He wasn't there yet, wasn't fully spectral like hounds

of the hunt became, but he was on his way…could feel his physical body fading, his spectral form growing. Soon he would feel nothing but the rush of the hunt, *need* nothing but the hunt. He would forget everything he'd left behind in this dry, unsatisfying existence.

Except…something tickled at his brain…something he didn't want to forget, not yet, not ever….

"Venge." The ErlKing's voice broke through his thoughts. "It's time." He held up the horn. "Call your pack."

Venge stood, his legs stiff, his tail held straight, and stared at the hellhounds gathering closer. "I was wrong," he said in their heads. "The ErlKing can not be beaten."

"But…" One of older ones stepped forward. "The Valkyries—"

As if his words urged them to action, the Valkyries began to move, to gather closer together. Venge waited, expecting their attack—wanting it, but they turned away, their gazes shooting to the sky. He started to turn, too, to see what could pull their attention away from something as important as the reforming of the Wild Hunt, but again the ErlKing spoke.

"Now, Venge. While the Valkyries are occupied saving one inconsequential speck of existence."

Knowing he was right, that nothing could be as important as what he was in the process of doing, Venge turned back to his pack.

"Join me." Then, Venge closed his eyes and let dreams of the hunt, the promise, flow through his thoughts, into the mind of every hellhound in front of him.

One by one they pulled the earplugs from their ears—all but two, Risk and Sigurd. Venge could feel their resistance, but their opposition—their very existence—was nothing more than a tiny irritation now, a gnat buzzing in the background.

As the other hounds Changed, Risk and Sigurd stayed in human form. Afraid of the horn, Venge realized, his lips curling into a smile. They didn't realize the call wasn't meant for them, that they weren't part of its invitation, its promise. Venge was in charge—the ErlKing had given him that power and he had no desire to share this newfound exhilaration with his father or old enemy.

He felt their anger, though, their frustration that he was experiencing what they couldn't. They both raced toward him, stupidly thinking they could touch him.

He started to turn to rip their souls from their bodies, but the ErlKing acted first, holding up one hand and with it unleashing a wind. The two flew back, out of Venge's sight.

He watched, disinterested again, then turned back to the others. "We'll fly now. The final choices will be made later." He pinned each with a look. They knew what his words meant—the moment they'd been awaiting was almost here.

He shook his body, then widened his stance and let a howl pour from within him—the howl all beings, whether they knew of the hunt or not, feared instinctively. One at a time, each of his pack echoed the sound.

The sound rolled down the mountain, causing everything living to scurry for a hiding place. As the last howl faded, he let the ErlKing's magic flow through him—then lifted his front paws off the ground and took to the air.

Behind him the other hellhounds followed—making a gray spectral trail across the sky.

Geysa felt the ground looming beneath her. Her aunt swooped through the dawn, accelerating again as she approached the earth. Then, with a shriek, she pulled her talons free and Geysa slipped from her grasp.

Geysa's breath caught in her throat, sure at the speed they were traveling she wouldn't survive the landing. She felt the ground graze then grate against her skin...a hiss escaping her lips as she skidded across the dirt. Pressing her hands to her face, she forced her mind to stay calm and her body to turn until she could log roll across the rough ground. Painfully, but steadily, her speed lessened and she drifted to a stop.

Instantly the other Valkyries crowded around her. "Was that Jora?" "Did you know she was a shifter?" "Can Runa shift?" "Can you?" Geysa could feel their gazes on her, curious but also afraid.

She sat up and pushed herself backward with her heels—away from the Valkyries and their pounding questions. No, no, no, no, she wanted to yell. She knew nothing, suspected nothing. Had no idea her aunt had been hiding a secret this huge.

"What were you thinking?" Back in human form, Jora strode across the ground. Geysa could only blink, her mind grappling not only with the knowledge that the legends were true, that there were Valkyries who could actually change into the massive birds whose cloaks they wore, that her aunt was one of them, but also that Geysa had been ignorant of the fact. How could she have not known?

The Valkyries parted, allowing Jora to pass. Most stared at Jora with the same round-eyed disbelief Geysa felt herself. A few shot veiled glances at companions.

Jora encompassed them with a sweeping glare, then, addressing Geysa, she said, "Did you think you could take the ErlKing alone?"

Still not fully grounded as to what had happened, was happening, Geysa's lips parted, but no words came out. Her aunt, however, didn't wait for her reply. She spun, turning on the other Valkyries instead.

"And you. Did none of you think to do anything besides stare at me?"

Mumbles and a few curses answered her. An older Valkyrie stepped forward. "How could we not stare? We all know what this means—why you've been hiding it from us."

"Nothing. It means nothing." Jora took a step forward, her stare moving with precision from one Valkyrie to the next. "That's why I've been hiding it. I knew you'd all jump to conclusions—think this meant I was losing my focus, my strength. Why right now more than any other time I didn't want to reveal…" She gestured toward the sky. "But if any of you have doubts, let's settle it right now." She stepped backward, opening her arms, inviting someone—anyone— to challenge her. One by one, the Valkyries' gazes dropped.

There was a flicker of relief in Jora's eyes, but the emotion disappeared so quickly, Geysa questioned its existence as soon as she noticed it. Her face stoic, Jora continued. "Good. Then we have a hunt to stop."

The mention of the hunt brought Geysa stumbling to her feet. "Venge? Runa?"

"Gone…and here." Venge's father shoved his way past the Valkyries. Behind him the witch who had hit Venge with a stream of power, stopping him from taking the horn when the ErlKing first offered, hurried to keep up. Sigurd followed, one burly hand wrapped around Runa's upper arm. Geysa's sister pulled away from the hellhound as they walked, her eyes snapping.

"And you were no help." Jora turned on the three outsiders.

"The worst didn't happen," Sigurd replied, giving Runa's arm a squeeze as he did.

Jora ignored her niece, instead shifting her regard to Risk and the witch. "Who are they?"

"Venge's father," Geysa murmured, staring at the broad-shouldered blond male. What had he done to make Venge hate him so much?

"And his—" Sigurd began, but the witch cut him off.

"Kelly. My sister's married to him." She jutted her head toward Risk.

Jora studied the petite but confident witch for a second, then spoke to Sigurd. "They need to leave. The hunt's been called up. Our deal is off."

Geysa tilted her head. Jora had made a bargain with a hellhound. She was beginning to wonder if she knew her aunt at all.

"He didn't take the horn," Sigurd said.

Glimpsing at Runa, Jora pursed her lips, then looked back at the three. "As if that makes a difference to us. He followed, and provided the ErlKing with a full kennel. The hunt could be running at any moment."

"He didn't take the horn?" Geysa looked at Sigurd.

He shook his head.

"But he joined the hunt. We have to find a way to release him." Venge's father took a step forward.

"We are not worried about saving a hellhound." Jora shoved her cape back over her shoulders. The other Valkyries murmured in agreement. Geysa curled her fingers into her palms until her nails cut into her skin.

"It can't be done." Sigurd's lips formed a grim line.

"There's nothing that can't be done." Risk pointed to the chain around Sigurd's throat, then to his own unadorned neck.

"We'd need Kara." The witch crossed her arms over her chest. "Is it worth it? She's nine months pregnant."

A muscle in Risk's cheek began to jump. "Kara can't come here. You know that. Aren't you witch enough on your own?"

Kelly leaned forward. For a second Geysa thought she might attack Venge's father. "My sister sent me here to save you—not some ungrateful pup intent on his own destruction."

Risk stepped closer, his voice softening. "Do you think if my wife were here, she wouldn't *try* to save my son?"

Kelly crossed her arms over her chest and turned a rocky gaze to Geysa. "I can try."

Jora shook her head. "There is no trying. A hound of the hunt comes here and we kill it. It's that simple." She glanced at Geysa. "It's what has to be done. I doubt my sanity to have trusted any hellhounds to begin with…" She glanced at Sigurd. "But once one's joined the hunt, he has to be destroyed—it's the only option." Then she turned to Runa. "Your actions have cost us…" She glanced around the group. "All of us, a lot. You'll get a chance to explain yourself, but for now you're a prisoner." She nodded to two Valkyries. They stepped forward and reached for Geysa's sister.

Sigurd hesitated, his gaze moving from Runa to the Valkyries.

"They won't kill me," Runa said, her voice low, almost bored.

Sigurd stared at her for another second, then released his hold, letting the Valkyries wrap a silver cord around her wrists.

"Today," Runa finished.

Cold fingers grabbed Geysa's heart. Runa was joking—she had to be. Jora would never kill Runa, no matter what she had done. She had told Geysa she loved Runa. Geysa glanced at her aunt for confirmation.

Jora stared back; her face gave away nothing. "We have to stop the hunt. If we don't…" She watched as Runa was led away. Her jaw firm, she looked back at Geysa, the first hint of regret showing in her eyes. "There is no if, we have to stop it. There's no other way. If the hunt actually rides, the worlds will want answers—and someone to pay for its return. If we eliminate Venge and the other hellhounds, we can at least buy some time, and the ErlKing will be weaker without them. It's the only solution." Then she strode away…following Runa and her guards.

"She'll be fine." Sigurd lay a hand on Geysa's shoulder.

Her heart in her throat, Geysa didn't reply.

"What now?" Kelly asked, her gaze shifting between the two men.

Sigurd sighed. "Jora may be right. It may be too late."

"It isn't." Geysa lifted her chin, the strength of her own voice surprising her. "It can't be. If we can bring Venge back…would the other hellhounds come, too?"

"You mean, desert the hunt?" Sigurd frowned. "It depends on how strong his hold is on them. He hasn't been alpha that long."

Geysa wrapped her fingers around her arms and winced. She'd forgotten her trip sliding across the dirt…but her body hadn't.

Kelly angled her head toward her. "You're hurt. I'm not the most nurturing twin, but I'm married to a Guardian. I'm used to patching people…beings—" she corrected "—up. Let's go somewhere—" she glanced around "—other than this. Maybe with water and clean rags."

Geysa started to object.

"And we can figure out a way to save the unsavable while we're at it." Kelly shot Risk a long-suffering look. "Heaven knows we've done it before."

But Risk didn't seem to hear, his attention on the spot where the ErlKing had stood next to Venge. Without warning, he shimmered, reappearing in the smooth circle of dirt. Sigurd cocked an eyebrow and followed.

With a huff, Kelly turned to Geysa. "Annoying, isn't it?" Then started back up the mountain, where the two hell-hounds now stood holding Venge's clothes and some kind of sack.

By the time Geysa had joined them, they had the sack open. Inside was an assortment of weapons and tools.

"Your boy has been busy," Sigurd said.

"Yes, he has." Risk picked up a particularly deadly-looking dagger between his thumb and index finger.

Kelly reached to test the tip, but Risk pulled the blade back. "Don't," he said.

His face serious, Sigurd explained. "Poison."

Kelly and Geysa stared at the knife, then the other things spread out on the ground.

"You still think we should save him?" Kelly asked.

Risk looked up, not a trace of doubt in his eyes. "Yes, I do."

Jora did not agree. Geysa had left Risk, Sigurd and Kelly at the bathhouse that, with Runa under guard at the bar, had been empty. Then, trying to stay as unobtrusive as possible, she'd slipped into the bar herself. Not that stealth was a huge matter. The Valkyries were too busy arguing amongst themselves over the best way to eliminate the ErlKing and his team of hellhounds to give Geysa much notice.

"What about the knife? We still have it."

"Yes, but…" Jora glanced at Geysa, who kept her gaze lowered. "It won't work for us. It has to be held by the prey of the hunt. With Runa not talking, we have no way of knowing who that might be. And, even if we did, we can't be sure the target could wield the knife. Most of the hunt's prey never fight back. It's too risky. Besides, we need to do something *before* the hunt rides."

The group barely paused to take in Jora's words before beginning to yell again. "Let's search for the ErlKing's hiding place and destroy the hounds while they sleep."

"Do they sleep?"

Unknowing mutters were the only replies.

"Why not lure the hellhounds away from the ErlKing and eliminate them first? Before the hunt has been called— before they've turned completely spectral?"

"Let's just wait for the hunt. Take the ErlKing on and destroy him once and for all."

The arguing went on and on, none having a solid idea of how to defeat the hunt, but all seeming to think Geysa would acquiesce and help destroy not only the ErlKing, but also Venge and his pack.

She poured herself a glass of water from a battered metal pitcher and took a sip. A millennia of history said that she would do whatever the group deemed necessary. As far as she knew, no Valkyrie had ever blatantly gone against the group.

Except Runa. The first of their own to turn on them, and now Geysa was considering following suit. Maybe their mother's Norn blood did something to them; made them rebellious...stupid.

The water was cold sliding down her throat, but it didn't lessen the burning discomfort she felt even considering going against her aunt's wishes.

Jora ran her gaze over the group of Valkyries. "The knife isn't dependable. We'd have to know who the target of the hunt was, and convince them to use it. Much better if we can lure the hellhounds to us."

"But how?" Mist, a young Valkyrie who had arrived after the hellhounds took to the barn, glanced around the room.

Jora placed her hand on her sword's hilt. "They're simple beasts—even more so now. We learned when we got here that they have no resistance to our lure. In fact, their resistance is so low, it was a problem. We had to keep our shields in place every second we were near one. A few times…" she looked at Geysa "…we forgot. They'd almost kill each other trying to get to us."

"That's the solution then. We find a way to amplify our lure—broadcast it so it reaches wherever the ErlKing is hiding," Bryn, another Valkyrie, added.

"And once they're here, we won't have to lift a sword. They'll turn on each other, saving us the trouble." Jora patted the hilt protruding from the scabbard at her side.

Geysa set down her glass. "What of Sigurd and Risk—the two who didn't join the hunt?"

Jora turned, her eyes patient. "Every battle has casualties. Besides, they're hellhounds—not innocents."

Another Valkyrie spoke, drawing Jora's attention back to the group.

Geysa wrapped her hand around the empty glass and squeezed. Everything was simple for her aunt, so cut and dried. But no matter how much Geysa thought about things, they weren't for her—and never would be again.

As the Valkyries continued their argument, she slipped her glass behind the bar and crept out the back door.

Venge paced back and forth down the central run of the kennel. Cages flanked him on both sides. Inside each was a snarling hellhound, trapped and hungry for the hunt. When they arrived, the fights had started, hellhounds lunging at each other with little control and no organization. It was like nothing Venge had seen before—not even in the pit where his old owner, Lusse, "exercised" her pack.

He stopped for a second to shake his head. A buzzing sound had invaded his brain a few hours ago. He'd been trying to drown the noise with his own thoughts, but it was getting stronger, making it harder to concentrate. He screwed his eyes shut and willed his mind back to what had been happening. The buzzing faded, slightly.

Slowly, he opened his eyes, and his mind, free to return to his thoughts. He resumed his journey down the run.

There were rules to forandre battles—order. This had been nothing but an orgy for blood. Venge was not averse to killing, but this had been senseless and so chaotic there was no way of knowing the strongest would win—completely defeating the purpose of the face-offs.

Venge had brought it all to a halt, choosing the lucky few to run in the hunt himself. Lusse would have punished him for such an act, but the ErlKing seemed undisturbed...disinterested. The chosen had been assigned a cage; the rest... Venge didn't know what the ErlKing had done with them. Some small piece of him chafed at that, but he shoved the feeling aside. He was the alpha of the hunt. That was where his concern had to lie.

One of the hellhounds behind him took a running start and rammed his head against his cage door. Venge spun, his lip curling. The other hellhound snarled back. Venge pressed his snout against the wire, let his eyes glow with his demand for obedience. The caged animal's snarl changed to a grumble, then he lowered his head and slunk to the far end of his allotted space.

Venge paced back to his starting point, snarling into each cage as he did. The floor under his pads was cold, the air inside the kennel bitter. He'd started his pacing to stay warm, to keep his muscles from cramping, but as time went on, the pains had faded. Some piece of him realized they were still there, as were issues that had nagged him when he first arrived—the fate of the other hellhounds, of Runa, and…Geysa.

He jerked his head higher, his eyes narrowing. *Geysa.* Memories of her and everything to do with his life before the hunt jumped in and out of his brain, like a disk caught on a scratch skipping ahead, then stopping. But even when he could remember, his thoughts were clouded, confused. He had been watching Geysa, was concerned with what she was doing, he knew that. But he couldn't remember seeing her after he'd joined the hunt. Was she there? Had she left? Did he care?

The buzzing started again…stronger. He shook his head, but it didn't stop. He lowered his face to the ground, rubbed his paw over his eyes. Not buzzing so much as a chant. Hunt. Kill. Hunt. It was growing louder, blocking everything else. Hunt. Hunt.

He growled, wanting it to stop, sensing he was losing himself in its never-ending hum.

If anything, it grew louder, each word more distinct. He shifted his paws to his ears, moaned. The noise didn't lessen.

Soon it would be all he'd hear…all he'd know.

Geysa walked down the path toward the creek. It was twilight—cool, but not cold—and quiet. No arguing Valkyries—well, they were somewhere, but for now Geysa couldn't hear them.

Once she reached the water, she stopped. The boulder Sigurd had moved to make his point was still there, the water still flowing around it. Geysa stepped into the small stream and pressed her hands against the stone. Water flowed over her feet—cold even over her boots. She wanted to pull the leather off her feet and feel her bare toes sink into the mud, feel the pebbles that littered the stream bed cut into her soles.

But she couldn't. She was here waiting…bait.

Praying Venge would forgive her, she laid her forehead against the rough boulder and did her job—she lowered her shields.

Chapter 18

Someone was calling him. Who? What?

Venge staggered to a stand, blinking—confused. Almost dazed. He glanced around the kennel. The other hounds were still in their cages, most huddled in the back, their eyes glowing, their bodies shaking with some kind of internal struggle.

Venge walked the length of the run; not a hellhound challenged him.

No problems here, everything was as it should be—as the ErlKing would want it. Or not… Venge tilted his head. The pack seemed weak, not strong. Didn't they need to be strong to fly, to hunt?

Hunt. The buzz. It was starting again. Venge shook his head, trying to dislodge the noise. Hunt. Hunt. He swayed to the side, knocking against the door of a cage. The hellhound inside stirred, his eyes glimmering at Venge.

Venge snarled, felt the heat build inside him…the hunger. Hunt. He needed to hunt. That would stop the buzzing, bring back his strength. That was what the ErlKing wanted…what Venge wanted.

Then he heard it again, or felt it. A call. A call for him. Someone wanted him to come. Someone he could hunt.

His mind latched onto the solution. Follow the call. Fulfill the hunger. The thought became obsession.

He spun, searching for an exit. He had to get out, but the small building had no doors, no windows.

How had he gotten in? He frowned. The ErlKing had pointed the way, a door had opened, but closed—and it was gone now. Or was it?

Hunt. Hunt.

He growled, frustration eating away what little control he had left. The hellhound in the nearest cage lifted his head, stirred as if to stand. Venge spun, his lip rising, his body again knocking into the cage…except it didn't. Instead it passed through…as if the cage were constructed of nothing but air.

Or…Venge stared down at his paws…as massive and covered in fur as normal. He lifted one and shoved it against the gate nearest him. It passed through…and the color. His fur was changing, not the ginger-red he was used to. Now it had a new gleam, and—he held his paw up again—translucent. He could see the web of the cage in front of him through his paw.

Spectral. He was becoming spectral…like a hound of the hunt. His eyes darted back and forth, checking the state of the other hellhounds. They all seemed solid for now.

So, Venge was the first. He smiled.

No walls could contain him. No prey could evade him. He was a hound of the hunt. The hound. The alpha.

And somewhere out there, someone was calling him.

With a roar, he leaped forward, his front feet then his back leaving the ground. Adrenaline pumped through him. The ceiling of the kennel was only inches away. He passed through as if it were no more substantial than mist.

Air tore through his fur. He soared above the kennel, through the clouds and into the growing night. He could fly…and now he could hunt.

Everything went quiet. No birds…no animals…no wind. The forest around the creek stood perfectly still.

Geysa froze, her heart beating and her own breath the only sound except for the water still sluicing around the boulder. The desire to survive urged her to reach for her knife—or to run. She wasn't sure which instinct was stronger.

But she did neither; she just willed her heart and breath to slow…and she waited. Something was here.

She prayed it was Venge.

Within seconds, the temperature dropped. Not drastically, but enough that goose bumps rose on her arms—the hair on the back of her neck coming to a stand.

Slowly, so as not to startle whatever waited for her, she dropped her arms to her sides and turned.

The hellhound she'd first encountered at the stable what seemed like a lifetime ago stood staring at her. Venge, in canine form, but different. He looked… She swallowed. He didn't look like himself. His body shimmered, and…she pulled back, realizing she could see through him, not completely, but enough to distinguish where the path beneath his feet wove to the left, cut through the grass—as if his body was formed of nothing more substantial than a thick fog. His eyes were the biggest difference, though, the most chilling. They darted side to side, as though his mind couldn't pick just one thing on which to focus.

"Venge?" She spoke softly, afraid if she put more strength in the word, she'd scare him…scare herself. This couldn't be the man she'd made love to, the one other hell-hounds followed, it couldn't—but it was.

She held out her hand. Venge…the beast, it was less painful to think of him like that…staggered forward, his head low and swinging side to side, like he expected an attack at any moment.

"Venge, is that you?"

She saw a flicker behind his eyes, or thought she did, hoped…

"Are you…?" She watched the way he swerved as he walked, the way he kept his tail and head low. She wasn't used to dogs. Valkyries only dealt in horses and falcons, but something about the way he was acting—

"Geysa, get back." Sigurd appeared beside her. His arm shot around her waist before she could stop him, tell him she wanted to stay.

Venge looked up. He pulled in a breath, his nostrils flaring and his eyes glimmering red. Then he lunged, his feet leaving the ground. He flew at them, mouth open and gums pulled back to reveal impossibly long canines.

Sigurd cursed, and Geysa's body began to tingle. Then, just as Venge's feet would have touched her, he was gone. Or…Geysa glanced around…she had moved. She'd shimmered, or been shimmered by Sigurd. They now stood twenty feet away, beside a small grove of aspens.

Venge landed where she and Sigurd had stood just seconds earlier. His head swung side to side. He tilted his neck to the sky and let a chilling wail escape his throat.

Geysa shivered, her arms wrapping around her body.

She had never heard such a sound, but it brought forth images from old nightmares. She closed her eyes and it came back as if real.

She was being chased. She ran, clawed her way through foliage and underbrush. Something was tracking her—slower than she was moving but with such calculation she knew it would find her, no matter her speed. Fear closed off her throat. She couldn't breathe; her hands shot to her neck as she gasped for air.

"Geysa." Sigurd shook her arm. "Snap out of it—you're safe."

She opened her eyes, round with the horror of what she had felt. Venge prowled in a tight circle, his nose skimming over the ground as if searching for a scent—her scent, she knew it.

From the corner of her eye she saw movement. Kelly, a stone in each hand, stood maybe ten feet from Venge.

Geysa opened her mouth, a warning coming to her lips, but she bit it back. Kelly knew what she was doing—it was all part of the plan. And Venge—she glanced back at the beast still sniffing for a scent—if Venge was still in there…would be unharmed.

Sigurd gave her a quick look, intense and questioning. She nodded.

Then, so quickly she would have missed it if her gaze wasn't glued to the scene in front of her, Sigurd shimmered, appearing beside Kelly. At the same moment Risk shimmered, materializing in front of Venge.

Venge looked up, started to surge toward his father, but at the same instant Sigurd touched Kelly and they shimmered, too—so they were only a few feet behind Venge. Kelly bent, dropped a stone into place, then nodded at Sigurd. They shimmered a second time, back to where they had started.

Venge flew toward Risk, the tension in his body leaving no doubt in Geysa's mind that he intended to kill his father.

Geysa's breath caught in her throat, her hands balling into fists so tight her knuckles cracked. *Let it work.*

With a roar, Venge hit the barrier Kelly had snapped around him when she dropped the final rock, sealing a magical circle. He bounced back, smashing into the ground. He lay there for less than a second before springing back up. His hackles raised, he ran at the invisible wall of power, hitting it and bouncing backward—over and over. Finally he seemed to give up, instead pacing 'round and 'round, his fur flattening when it touched the circle's boundary.

Sigurd, Risk and Kelly approached the circle. Geysa ran to meet them, elation and fear mixing, making her words come out short and choppy. "Now what?" she asked, her gaze on Venge. He stopped his movement for a second, his glowing eyes lighting on her. His brow lowered, he tilted his head. She sucked in a breath. Did he recognize her?

She took a step forward, but Risk stopped her with a hand on her arm. As he did, Venge pulled back and rushed the wall again. Geysa jerked, but again when Venge hit the barrier, he fell back to the dirt.

This time, though—Geysa blinked—*anxiety at work.* The circle had held, would hold. Kelly had said she'd used it on forandre before, but just for the second that Venge had hit the wall, Geysa had thought his fur didn't flatten—as if some of it managed to break through. *Impossible.* It would be all or nothing—surely.

Still, she turned to Kelly to ask.

Kelly, however, was in another heated discussion with Risk. "We need Kara. I trapped him, but without Kara I can't do much more. I don't even know if *with* Kara I can do any more."

"Are you suggesting we leave him like this?" Risk gestured to Venge.

Geysa broke in. "How long will the circle hold?"

Kelly gave her an impatient glance. "As long as no one moves those stones. They can't be moved from the inside, but they can from the outside."

Still unsure, Geysa turned her attention back to Venge. He sat in the center now, his gaze distant, like he was deep in thought or…he twisted his head…hearing something. Something Geysa couldn't.

"Do you hear that?" Geysa interrupted again, this time addressing Sigurd and Risk.

"I don't hear anything," Sigurd replied. "Why?" He turned, following her line of sight to Venge. As the words left his mouth, Venge lifted his head again, then slowly began to walk backward.

"What's he—" Kelly started.

"Running start." Risk reached out, placing a hand on both Kelly and Geysa.

"It'll hold," Kelly said. Her voice was low, little more than a rough whisper.

"Maybe." Sigurd stared at Venge, a furrow between his brows.

"But you said—" Geysa started. As the words left her mouth, Venge charged across the grassy space. His front feet left the ground, then he used his back to spring farther into the air. Geysa placed a hand on Sigurd's arm.

Something was different. Venge was almost completely translucent now…thicker than mist, but thinner than the heavy fog she'd compared him to when he had first appeared. As he flew toward the barrier, Geysa knew what she'd seen earlier hadn't been wrong—he was going to pass through.

He would escape…then what?

* * *

Venge felt the change…the total loss of the restrictions that came with being locked in a corporeal form. He'd rejoiced in what he thought was freedom before, but it had been nothing like this. And when he'd returned to this place, seen the female—Geysa, even her name was fading again—he'd lost some of his newfound strength, slipped ever so slightly back to what he had been before. Then he'd felt the shift—his pack making the change, too. It was like a plug being pulled from a sink, releasing a flow of energy and strength he'd never dreamed existed. And now, the ErlKing was calling him back—him, no other hellhound, just him, the alpha of the Wild Hunt.

That call and the final formation of his pack had given him the focus needed to escape the witch's trap. He soared over the group's heads, out of their reach. They stared up at him, shock and awe on their faces. They'd thought he would attack them—and they deserved it, trying to cage him, to keep him from his destiny, but the ErlKing's call saved them.

The Wild Hunt was ready to ride…and the ErlKing needed his alpha to lead the way.

Geysa shoved open the door to the bar and slunk inside. It was over. Their plan, or the closest thing they'd had to a plan, had failed.

"There she is." Bryn stood, her gaze shooting to Geysa.

"We're ready to start." Jora stepped forward.

Geysa walked past her aunt without lifting her gaze from the ground. "It won't work," she murmured.

"What?" Jora crossed the space between them and grabbed Geysa by the shoulder.

Geysa lifted her chin, stared her aunt in the eyes. "It

won't work. He's different now. Things that affect other hellhounds, don't affect him. Lowering your shields will just draw more hellhounds here...and not the ones you want." She started to turn, to leave, but her aunt gripped her harder.

Her fingers digging into Geysa's shoulder, Jora asked, "What have you done?"

Geysa spun, her hand finding Jora's where it held Geysa's shoulder. She wrapped her fingers around her aunt's wrist and jerked it away. "Nothing. I've done nothing." Nothing that would change anything. Nothing of any use.

"You know something." Jora's voice was softer now, less demanding.

Geysa sighed. She did...more than she wanted to. She looked at her aunt, then at the rest of the Valkyries. Expelling another breath, she told them everything—how she had tried to help Risk, Sigurd and Kelly, how they had failed, and how she now believed there was no Venge left to save.

When she was done, silence greeted her. She felt empty inside. She knew she should care...she'd lost Venge and now she'd admitted to the Valkyries that she had planned to betray them—had betrayed them. But she felt nothing, no sorrow, no anger, nothing. Just a void where her heart should be.

With a slight shake of her head, she reached for the clasp of her necklace.

"What are you doing?" Her aunt reached for Geysa's wrist this time.

"I betrayed you. No one has ever betrayed the Valkyrie—gone against the group."

"Except you, your sister...and your mother." Jora's gaze

held Geysa's, but there was no anger in her eyes. "It must be the Norn blood."

Geysa lowered her arms. "Mother?"

Jora nodded. "We knew the hunt was after her. The ErlKing had made no secret of his intention of taking what he considered our greatest strength—a Valkyrie who could see the future. It gave us an advantage over the hunt. We knew when battles would form, where the best and bravest would gather.

"He couldn't stand that." She pulled out a chair and sat. The few other Valkyries who had been standing followed suit.

"But how did Mother…?"

"When we got wind of the rumors, we told her to stay in Valhalla. We thought we could protect her there, but you and your sister were visiting the Norn at the time—your other family."

Geysa blinked; she had no memory of ever meeting other Norn.

"Your mother, against direct orders, left Valhalla. Later, we found her note. She knew she wasn't coming back. She'd had a vision. The hunt was after you and Runa—she thought it was her destiny to save you. She was right. The ErlKing had wanted your mother, but he was willing to target her daughters to get her. The fact you were children meant nothing to him."

The nightmare Geysa had remembered when Venge faced her flooded back to her. "Where did it happen?" she asked. She'd never heard this part of the story, never been given much detail on anything.

"In the woods of this world. The Norn had brought you here. I never knew why."

"Training." It was coming back to Geysa. "They were

showing us how they deliver destinies. I had no talent for it." She smiled. "Maybe I have no talent for anything."

"You had no talent for Norn work because you're a Valkyrie. A far better existence." Jora squeezed Geysa's arm, using it to pull her close, almost into a hug, then shoved her back to her original position.

"So Mother died…"

"Saving you and Runa. But she took many of the hellhounds with her. That's how, when we arrived, we were able to get the horn. Without your mother, the hunt would never have been stopped."

"And without Runa—"

"It never would have started again." Jora nodded, her face grim. "But what you did and what your sister did are in no way the same thing."

Something caught next to Geysa's heart. "Does that mean Runa—"

"It doesn't mean anything except what I said. Runa is locked up, and she's going to stay that way until we get the mess she made cleaned up." Jora's brows lowered. "No matter how much she rants."

Runa, ranting? Geysa opened her mouth again, but her aunt held up a hand, stopping her. "The question right now is, are you ready to follow us? To do what we say? Because that's the only way we can stop the hunt."

"And save Runa?" Geysa asked.

Jora's gaze drifted to the other Valkyries. "It would certainly help her case."

Geysa tightened her jaw. Venge was gone. There was nothing of him left in the spectral hound she'd seen. The realization made her want to crumple to her knees—but she couldn't. Her sister was still very much alive and Geysa could still help redeem her in the eyes of the Valkyries. It would mean facing down the Wild Hunt, seeing the hound that used to be Venge destroyed—but she could do that to save Runa. She had to.

She looked back at her aunt, hoping the tears she felt at the corners of her eyes weren't showing. "I'm with you."

Chapter 19

Venge prowled around the ErlKing's camp. The kennel appeared to be the only permanent building, and Venge suspected one used infrequently. Most of the time the hunt would be on the move…traveling through the nine worlds, hunting, gathering souls.

And, with the Valkyries back on his trail, the ErlKing wouldn't be able to stay in one place too long. Besides, movement was good. Venge had been journeying since his release from Lusse's kennels. He had no reason to stay in one place, no ties, no one who cared about him… loved him.

Love. He stopped. His eyes darted side to side. There was something there…in the back of his mind.

Across the clearing, a hellhound snarled at another pack member who had passed too close. The second attacked the first and they tumbled across the ground like a swirling wind. Venge soared across the space and landed next to them. Flying had already become natural to him—more so than shimmering now. With a snap of his jaws, he turned on the hellhounds. They quickly separated, each slinking away, heads and tails lowered.

The pack was ready and growing restless. But the hunt was coming. The ErlKing was preparing his horse now. Within hours he would give the hellhounds their first scent and they would take to the sky.

Venge could think of nothing else.

Although it was barely noon, the sky was growing dark. Geysa pulled her jacket around her body and glanced at her aunt. "There's a storm coming."

Jora's gaze shot to the sky. "Maybe, or maybe it's something else."

A chill passed over Geysa's skin. "The hunt?" she asked.

But her aunt had already stood, leaving Geysa alone on the bar's front step. "I need to gather the others and ready the horses," Jora said.

Her eyes staring forward, Geysa gave a short nod. She heard her aunt turn, her boot swiveling in the gravel. "Jora?" Geysa asked.

Her aunt paused.

"Will you fly as a falcon?"

Her aunt stiffened. They hadn't talked about Jora's ability to shift yet, about why and how she had kept it a secret so long.

Seconds ticked by. Finally, Geysa turned to study her aunt. She stood with her arms crossed over her chest, her attention back on the sky. "Not unless I have to."

"Is it painful?" Geysa asked.

Jora glanced at her, surprise in her eyes. "No, not at

all—it's freeing, wonderful. The most wonderful feeling in the world."

"Then why…?"

"It's too wonderful. If I give myself to the falcon side too often, I'll get lost in it. I'm afraid one day I'll forget how to shift back. Or I just won't."

Geysa stared at her aunt with new understanding. Jora feared losing herself to her falcon side, just as Geysa had feared losing herself by loving Venge.

Her aunt gave her one last sad glance, then strode down the street toward the fenced area where the other Valkyries were practicing and their horses waited.

Geysa watched her aunt until she disappeared between two buildings. Geysa squeezed her eyes shut. Tears still managed to edge past her lids and down her cheeks.

Why did they have to choose?

It was growing darker. Geysa ran her hands up and down her arms, wondering where her aunt and the others were. Tired of being alone, she stood and started down the deserted street.

The wind whistled through the spaces between the buildings, hit an old can and sent it rattling down the road. Geysa's eyes darted toward the discarded trash. But it was just a can…garbage left by the hellhounds. Nothing to be anxious over.

The wind was strong now and the temperature was dropping—at least ten degrees in the few minutes since Jora had left. The wind caught Geysa's jacket, jerking it open. She gasped as the cold air cut through the thin T-shirt she wore underneath. She grabbed the edges of her coat and pulled it back around her, clamped her arms around her body—holding it closed.

Where was Jora? The thought pounding in her head, Geysa picked up her pace. Her aunt was right—whatever was coming, it was far from a simple storm.

Venge circled the waiting hellhounds, occasionally bumping one back into line or snapping a warning. The ErlKing approached, the horn in one hand, a strip of material in the other.

The scent…who would it be? Venge frowned. There was someone he hoped it would be…someone he wanted dead…the name wouldn't congeal.

The ErlKing stepped closer, held out the cloth for his alpha—for Venge.

Venge pressed his nose against the material and inhaled, let the scent go deep inside him—memorized every nuance of it. Once he held it within himself, there'd be nowhere the chosen prey could hide. Venge and his pack would be able to track him anywhere—on any world.

Honey and grass floated down to his lungs. Venge felt his lips begin to curl in pleasure. He knew this scent. Liked this scent. His neck stretched, pushing his nose more deeply into the cloth. A peace began to settle over him. His eyelids dropped and he inhaled again. This scent was calming him, seducing him.

He jerked back, a frown lowering his brows. What was happening? He was the alpha. This was the scent of his next victim. The smell should be invigorating—adding to his anticipation, not… He shook his head and stared at the cloth in the ErlKing's hand. Had the cloth belonged to the person he had planned to kill?

Concentrating, he returned his nose to the material and inhaled again. Familiar…so familiar.

"Alpha, are you ready?" The ErlKing spoke in his head.

Venge pulled his face away from the material. The ErlKing needed him; the hunt couldn't start without him. Still...he glanced back at the strip of white cloth.

"Alpha." A warning this time. Venge felt the cutting edge of the ErlKing's voice like the snap of whip against his skin.

He glanced at his pack. They waited, their eyes glazed but their bodies rigid—ready.

The hunt. The hunt. The chant started again.

He looked back at the ErlKing and lifted his head in agreement. He was ready.

The ErlKing held the cloth out again, but Venge turned away—trotted to the head of the line of hellhounds.

He needed no reminder of the scent. It was burned into his memory. Now, to find its owner.

"Geysa." Geysa could hear her aunt's voice calling her, but faintly. It had grown so dark, Geysa could barely see her own hand, and the wind so strong she could barely stand.

Then she felt someone beside her. A hand wrapped around her arm. "Take this." Something smooth and cold was shoved into her grip. As soon as the object made contact with her skin, Geysa opened her fingers and tried to drop it. A cold wire of power slithered around her wrist, up her arm. She shook her hand trying to dislodge whatever the item was, but another hand was wrapped around hers, holding her own closed.

"It's a knife. It's your only hope. The hunt...it's been called for *you*," Sigurd's voice yelled in her ear. In her desperation to separate herself from the object he'd forced into her hand, it took a few seconds for his words to register.

"No," she yelled back, shock hitting her like a bucket of cold water in the chest. He had to be wrong. Even as lost as Venge was, he wouldn't target her...would he?

"The storm. It's only around you. Look." Sigurd pulled her face against his chest, used his arm to shield her eyes from the wind.

She blinked, her eyes tearing from the bitter air blowing into her face, but with the small protection Sigurd offered, she could see what he was referring to. As she had walked down the street, the darkness where she had been had left. At the very edge of the town, there was sun now. It glared back at her—the truth unavoidable.

"This blade can save you. It's the one your mother used," Sigurd yelled again.

"But how…?"

"Your sister saw it, in her stones—that you're the target. Your aunt tried to get to you, but the wind was too strong. She gave it to me to bring to you."

"But you…?"

"Can shimmer. Besides, the hunt isn't designed to repel hellhounds." As he spoke, Geysa felt another presence nearby. Venge's father, Risk, pressed a hand against her back.

"We'll stay with you, help you fight, but you have to wield the knife. The magic only works when held by the hunt's prey."

"What does it…?"

Again, Sigurd guessed her question. "It will kill a hound of the hunt. You have to use it—on Venge."

Geysa turned in his arms. Her back to the wind, she stared at the two hellhounds.

Risk placed a hand on her shoulder, his face grim. "It's the only way."

Geysa wanted to scream at them, to run, to hide—from them, from her aunt, from everything. But all she could do was stand there rooted to the ground, her mind spinning, unable to compute what was being said.

She couldn't kill Venge. Hellhound or not. Alpha of the Wild Hunt or not. He was still Venge, wasn't he?

"When he gets here, he won't be the male you remember." Risk's low voice was somehow making its way past the wind that now shrieked like a banshee around them. Taunting them. Laughing at them—at her.

"Don't think about it—just do it. You'll be surprised what you can do when death is staring at you." Sigurd squeezed her hand, pressed her fingers against the knife's cold hilt.

Geysa swallowed hard, her throat dry and raw.

"Remember your mother." Sigurd's voice was little more than a whisper, but it pierced Geysa's soul. *Her mother.* The trip through the woods. The hounds behind them—catching them. Screams. Geysa clawing at a tree's bark, struggling to get up as Runa shoved her from below.

The sound of a knife slicing through the air—her mother cursing, yelling for Runa to get up the tree, too. Then she and her sister staring down as her mother plunged the blade into first one hellhound and then another, until she wobbled on her feet.

The ErlKing had arrived then, his dark horse swooping from above; he'd grabbed her mother around the waist as she spun, her gaze searching the trees. Geysa and Runa had huddled there, watching.

How could she have forgotten this? Forgotten the stricken pale face of her mother as she was pulled from them. The horror on her mother's face changing to cold determination as the last hound caught Geysa and Runa's scent and lunged upward toward their hiding place. A whistle had cut through the night as her mother threw the only weapon she had—killing the final hound, saving her daughters. But giving up her own life in return.

Geysa stared at the knife in her hand. Could this

weapon have killed the ErlKing if her mother had used it on him instead of aiming it at the hound that threatened Geysa and her sister? Could Geysa get close enough to the ErlKing tonight to try it herself? Would she have to kill Venge to find out?

The last echoed through her head. Would she have to kill Venge? Could she?

The wind drove against Venge—so cold and sharp, he could barely keep his eyes open. But he didn't need sight to fulfill his mission tonight. The scent the ErlKing had shared with him tugged at him, pulled him along as surely as a rope lashed around his neck.

Behind him, the other hellhounds followed and, farther back, the ErlKing was on his horse. They were silent now. Despite legends of hounds baying in chase—they flew in silence. Their calls would come later—when their prey was trapped, as they lunged at their victim's throat. And after, as they celebrated their kill—a warning and a promise to others.

The hunt was back, and they wanted all to know, but not yet. Now, stealth was a necessity.

Venge flew on, the scent growing stronger, his pulse hammering through his veins. "Here," he yelled into the minds of the rest of the pack. They curled into formation behind him. Below them a deserted town appeared—a light spot in the surrounding forest of evergreens.

As they grew closer, a shadow fell across the town. Venge circled once. The other hellhounds followed close behind—so close he could feel their breath, smell their anticipation. This was it, the moment they had dreamed of. The hunt was back and they were at its lead.

The ErlKing appeared in the distance. He raised the hand holding his horn, raised it to his lips.

The peal slithered across the sky, through Venge's body. He shivered as the sound liquefied, mixed into his very soul.

With a nod of his head, he shot a last command to his pack. "The first kill is mine." Then he dove, heading to the tan strip of road below and the prey he knew was waiting—for him.

"They're coming." Sigurd loosened his grip on Geysa's hand. "I can hear the horn." He stepped back, still within her reach if she lunged at him, but not so close she felt crowded. He was leaving her room—to wield the knife, to kill Venge.

She bit her lip until she almost cried out in pain. Her heart pounded. She wanted to scream at Sigurd, make him admit this wasn't real, that she wasn't facing a choice that could end in Venge being dead.

"You or him—and he's already gone." Sigurd's voice somehow made it across the few feet that separated them. "Don't let the ErlKing win."

The ErlKing. He had taken Geysa's mother, tried to take her sister. If Geysa gave up, he'd come back for Runa, surely. But if Geysa killed Venge, it would slow him down—give the Valkyries a chance to stop the ErlKing completely.

For the first time her fingers wrapped around the knife of their own volition. The leather hilt warmed in her hand. She moved the blade back and forth, testing its balance.

She could do this. She had to do this. Not just for the Valkyries or even her mother. She had to do this for everyone who had lost family to the hunt, and everyone who might lose someone in the future.

She tilted her face to the sky, saw the silvery forms of the spectral hounds circling above.

It was up to her.

* * *

Venge landed in the middle of the gravel road. The wind whirled around him. He felt the other hounds come to a rest behind him, but he ignored them. This was his kill; he'd claimed it and they wouldn't interfere.

He raised his nose to sniff the air. Dust, pine and various smells he associated with humans traveled on the wind toward him—but they were all faint, overwhelmed by the scent he held in his memory. The one given to him by the ErlKing.

His prey. She was here.

He padded forward, his head swinging slightly side to side—scanning. He had nothing to fear; he was the alpha of the hunt. But still, he was wary.

The wind increased and the sky darkened—so much so that he couldn't see. He could feel the wind, smell the scents it carried, but even his hellhound sight couldn't break through the blackness that shrouded the space around him.

He narrowed his eyes, let the scent pull him deeper into the darkness. He could smell her, feel her now, too, but she wasn't alone. He sensed others nearby, breathing, polluting her smell with their own.

He growled. Other hellhounds—there was no disguising their sooty scent. He needed to see so he could pinpoint her location, target his leap to her. He closed his eyes and concentrated on the thought, the desire—he felt a fire begin low inside him then flicker to life.

His lids flew open and he knew something had changed. A new skill—a gift from the hunt. He could see her. Not as he might have seen her before, but with a new sight— one that showed only her shape, the heat of her body, the thumping movement of her heart in her chest.

He smiled, inhaled again. Then sighed. She was his,

waiting for him to take her. Concentrating on the in and out movement of her heart, he leaped.

Soon it would beat no more.

Chapter 20

Both hands wrapped around the knife's hilt, Geysa waited. The hunt was here and moving closer. The world around her was cast in darkness; she could see nothing, not even her own hands gripping the knife and trembling in front of her.

Seconds passed. The temperature continued to drop—as though a door to the Arctic had opened and a stiff breeze was blowing through it, directly on her. Something was approaching; she couldn't see who or what, but her body had tightened with tension.

"Venge?" she murmured.

No response.

"Venge?" Then she saw him…*it*. His eyes glowed green, instead of the red she'd come to expect from an angry hellhound. The space between them lightened, like a spotlight just on the two of them. The eye of the storm, she realized—the spot where the hunt and its prey met.

Where she and Venge met.

He paced sideways, his glowing eyes focused on her. She swallowed. Her hands damp with sweat, she gripped the knife tighter, prayed she wouldn't drop it.

"Venge." She heard the yell from far away. Risk's voice, then Sigurd's. They were trying to draw Venge's attention, she realized, to give her a chance to attack before Venge attacked her. But their calls were distant and Venge didn't even glance their way as he continued to pace around her.

Geysa's heart pounded. Her breath escaped ragged and loud from her lips. Her eyes were wide and, as she stared at Venge, saw what he had become, she felt new tears freeze to her lashes.

Lost. He was lost. There was no sign of the man she loved. No recognition in his eyes, no compassion. Just a cold, calculating appraisal as he assessed her, decided how big a threat she presented.

Sigurd was right. There was nothing of Venge left.

She wasn't staring at her lover. She was staring at the alpha of the Wild Hunt.

Resolve hardened inside her. She had to kill him. She had no choice. A part of her regretted that her last memory would be of this beast and not the man she remembered.

But another part was relieved. This—she glared at the silvery animal still stalking around her, his glowing eyes hungry, eager—she could kill.

Venge circled his prey. Why he was waiting, he didn't know. Maybe he didn't want to rush, didn't want to leave the anticipation behind. Nothing, not even the kill, could be as exciting as this…seeing his victim with his new sight. Smelling her fear and indecision.

Something shimmered at him…something in his prey's hands. It burned with some kind of power. Something ancient and deadly.

His prey planned to kill him. His lip curled in disbelief. Let her try. Already her hands trembled so badly she could barely keep hold of the artifact—one move from him and she'd fall to her knees, paralyzed by what she knew was coming.

With a laugh, he pulled back. He was ready. Time to end the anticipation and fulfill his duty.

Geysa saw Venge flying toward her—he was little more than a wraith now. Nothing of the man was left…. Nothing. She forced the thought into her brain. Clung to it.

She could kill him.

Her hands trembling, the blade moving up and down, she took a step back and squared her stance. She held her eyes open wide and forced herself to stare at the spectral hound zooming toward her.

He was closer, so close she could see the expression in his glowing eyes—or lack of expression. No softness. No recognition. There wasn't even determination. Nothing. Absolutely nothing stared back at her. The ErlKing had won. He'd taken Venge.

Now all that was left was for Geysa to complete the act by plunging the knife into his chest.

She blinked, a small crack forming in the wall she'd built around her emotions. In the instant her eyes were closed, an image of Venge, the real Venge, appeared in her mind. The crevice quickly sprang open into an undeniable gap. Every bit of love and hope she'd harbored sprang forth. Disappointment at the life that was left her crashed around her.

Gods damn her. She couldn't do it. Let Venge kill her. Let the ErlKing take her soul to destroy as he had destroyed her mother's, but she couldn't take the life of someone she loved.

Not to save herself.

Tears fell from her cheeks onto her shirt. She blinked them away, then flung the knife to the ground and waited for Venge's attack.

Venge saw his prey waiting for him. She stood strong—stronger than he'd imagined—for a time, but then, as he'd guessed, she crumbled, tossing the knife to the ground. He expected her to run then, or at least bow down, curl into a ball as she awaited his attack, but she didn't. Instead she stood straighter, her tear-filled gray gaze catching his own.

Then he felt it—smelled it. Sorrow. Mourning. She was mourning…for him, for his loss. She—he shook his head, the realization hitting him hard—loved him.

Venge ground to a halt. She couldn't love him. No one loved him and she was his prey. She should fear him—loathe him. But—he stared at her again—there was no mistaking her emotion. She did love him, and—something clicked—he loved her, too. She was the only being for whom he had ever truly felt the emotion.

She was the only reason he believed love existed.

He stared down at himself, searched inside his brain. What had happened? What was he now? He knew the answer was simple—the alpha of the hunt. But at the same time, it wasn't simple at all. Somewhere he had lost something—something important. And now, faced with

Geysa's—the name came back to him—emotion, he knew it was something he valued. Something worth giving up everything for—hate, pride, his life.

He knew there was nothing he wouldn't lay at her feet. He knew he couldn't kill her. But he couldn't be with her, either. He was the alpha of the Wild Hunt. For her to survive, to have a chance, he had to die.

The knife she had dropped gleamed at him from the dirt. It had landed hilt down, tip up.

With one last glance at Geysa, he leaped and threw himself on tip of the blade.

"No." Geysa threw herself across the few feet that separated her from Venge—the blade of the knife she'd held glowing within him. *He'd thrown himself on it...why?* She reached out, her fingers clawing through fur so fine she could barely feel it tickle against her skin.

The knife—where was it? She reached under him, trying to flip him over to find where the blade had struck— or where he had struck the blade.

"Geysa." A strong hand grabbed her by the shoulder, tried to pull her free. She shook it off.

"The knife. Where did it go in?" She could tell she was yelling, but she didn't care.

"Geysa. Stop."

Two voices now, two pairs of masculine hands pulling at her. She jerked away, reached into her boot and pulled her own blade free. Spinning in a squat, she faced the two—Sigurd and Risk—her knife held out, ready.

"Help me or leave." She held their gazes for a second to make sure they realized the depth of her desperation, then plunged her knife into the dirt beside her and turned back to Venge.

"Is he breathing?" Sigurd kneeled next to her. Beside him, Risk did the same. She thought about screaming at them again, just to release her own frustration, but she saw their faces—the concern and the grim edge of reality hardening their jaws.

"I think so." She pressed her hand against Venge's side. She could feel the faint up-and-down movement of his chest...and something else.

"Sigurd?"

The hellhound beside her turned his head.

"Does he look different?"

Sigurd shook his head. "Maybe less ghostly, more solid, but I've heard…"

She frowned and grabbed Sigurd's arm. "What have you heard?"

Sigurd glanced at Risk, then at Venge. "That hounds of the hunt, if they're killed, they revert to their old forms first."

"So…" She swallowed. For a moment she'd had hope—thought the slight solidifying of Venge's body was a good sign. "So, this might mean he's…dying?"

Sigurd nodded. "The knife is deadly."

"But you said it had to be wielded by the hunt's target. I didn't use it." The words were hard, determined, as if just by uttering them she could force the gods to save Venge.

"You were the last hand to hold it."

"But…?"

Sigurd shrugged, his gaze on Venge. "I don't know, but this doesn't look good."

"Geysa?" A third voice broke through Geysa's panic.

She turned to see her aunt standing a few feet away, her feathered cape hanging from her shoulders.

"The hunt turned back. We lost them. Lost the horn."

Her voice was bitter, then she glanced at Venge. "You used the knife," she murmured.

"No, I didn't. I couldn't—" Geysa started, but Venge's body heaving beneath her hand stopped her. She jerked forward, started to press her chest against his side, but both Risk and Sigurd grabbed her by the upper arms, halting her.

"He's changing," Sigurd explained.

Round-eyed, Geysa watched. Venge's body shimmered, changing so quickly she could hardly note the shift from spectral hound to the man she had known and loved. Then he lay on the ground beside her, naked and pale, as if every drop of blood had been drained from his body. Her heart pattering in her chest, she leaned forward. The two hellhounds released her and she pressed her hand to Venge's chest. She was rewarded with the beat of his heart—but it was faint, too faint.

Her aunt called her, but Geysa refused to look up. She could feel those around her withdrawing—staring at her as if they held some knowledge she didn't. But they were wrong. She knew exactly what was happening. She'd flown over battlefields. She'd seen other Valkyries draw warriors' spirits from their broken bodies.

But that didn't mean she would allow it to happen now—to Venge.

"Pull out the knife," she ordered.

Sigurd glanced at her. "I don't think—"

"Do it," she said. She jerked her shirt over her head and balled it into a makeshift compress.

"Geysa…" Sigurd began.

She caught his gaze with her own and held it. "Hellhounds heal fast, right?"

"Not—"

"But he can't heal with the knife still in there, right?"

Sigurd just stared back at her.

Jora stepped forward, her sword slipping from its scabbard. "If he lives, will he still be bound by the hunt?"

Geysa jerked her dagger from the dirt where she'd shoved it earlier and pointed it at her aunt. "No."

Jora paused, disbelief flicking through her eyes.

Her voice softening, Geysa added, "Don't make me choose. Not again."

Jora stared at her niece, then the prostrate hellhound beside her. When she made no move to step closer, Geysa returned her dagger to the dirt and turned back to Venge, trying to shift his body so she could reach the knife stuck in his chest, to remove it herself.

Risk placed a reassuring hand on her arm, halting her struggles. "Here." He lifted Venge so his front was facing Geysa. With Venge's head cradled against his chest, Risk reached around and grasped the knife's handle. "Are you ready?" he asked.

Licking her lips, Geysa edged closer, then nodded.

Without pause, Risk pulled the knife from Venge's chest. As the metal slid from his body, Venge stiffened. Geysa ignored the movement. She couldn't think of what it might mean. Her jaw clenched, she shoved the balled material against Venge's wound and pressed until her bicep screamed from the effort.

Jora stepped forward and retrieved the knife from the ground where Risk had dropped it. Her gaze on Geysa, she wiped Venge's blood onto her pant leg, then slowly wrapped the knife in a cloth before dropping it into a leather case. When that was done, she knelt next to her niece.

"Do you love him?"

Her eyes locked onto Venge, Geysa gave a short nod.

"He's dying." Jora placed her hand over Geysa's, set it on Venge's heart. "You can feel it."

No. Geysa wouldn't listen to her. Venge wouldn't die. He wasn't meant to die—not here. Suddenly, Geysa knew it was true. Venge was meant to live. Her Norn half coming to life? Or only a hope so intense, it felt real?

"We can give him a place in Valhalla. I'll do that, for you." Jora wove her fingers in between Geysa's, pressed her fingertips to Venge's chest.

Valhalla. The reward for brave warriors. Despite her pain, Geysa almost laughed. What kind of reward was existing as a shadow? Having no memory of your past life? No desire to grow or change? No ability to connect with another person? To spend each day exactly as you spent the day before…eating, drinking, fighting? To spend eternity experiencing glory that didn't exist?

No reward at all—and one Venge didn't need because he was going to live. She pulled her hand from beneath her aunt's and started to tell her so, but Jora was closed off…couldn't hear what Geysa was saying.

Jora had opened her shields, linked with Venge, and was luring his soul from his body.

Geysa's gaze shot to Sigurd and Risk, but they stared back, unaware. Geysa wasn't sure what they were seeing, but she realized they didn't see her aunt stealing Venge's soul, claiming it for Valhalla. No one except the Valkyries and the fallen could see that.

But Venge wasn't fallen. Venge was meant to live.

"No." Geysa shoved her aunt, knocked her over. But Jora's connection didn't break. She began to float, her cape flapping behind her, her arms in front of her, ready to welcome Venge.

"No," Geysa yelled again, but she could feel Venge slipping, see his soul edging from his body.

Turning her back on her aunt, she flung herself onto Venge—as if she could force his spirit back into his body with the pressure of her own.

Still and pale, Venge lay beneath her. Cold. Was he growing cold?

Geysa screamed, picked up a handful of dirt and flung it at her aunt. Jora didn't waver.

Her knife. Geysa stared at it still sheathed in the earth. Without letting herself think, she leaned forward and wrapped her fingers around the handle.

Her necklace, her shield charm and her mother's, swung forward, knocking against her chin. Geysa froze—the tiny ornaments jerking her out of her panic, reminding her who she was, what she was. Her Norn half had finally shown itself, but she was also a Valkyrie. If a Valkyrie, her aunt, could draw Venge's soul out, why couldn't Geysa urge him to stay—to fight?

Dropping the knife, she wrapped her hand around the charms and kneeled until her forehead was flush with Venge's. Then she opened her shields and begged him to stay…to heal.

Venge was cold. He'd never been cold before—not like this. A painful cold that seemed to shear through his flesh, down to his bones. He wanted to shiver, but he couldn't. It was as if he had lost touch with his own body.

Then he heard a call, more beautiful than the horn that had lured him to this town, more beautiful than anything he could remember. Promises, of peace and joy…of simple things. Rest. The call, a voice of sorts, wanted him to rest.

He leaned up…or tried to. He had a sense of moving, but knew he wasn't, not really.

But part of him was edging forward, toward the call. The warmth was waiting for him, pulling at him. He wanted to go.

Then another call broke through the first…closer and familiar.

He paused, confused.

"Stay. Stay with me," the second voice pleaded. And tears, there were tears in this voice. Sadness and hope.

He wavered. Cold. It was so cold. The first voice kept calling, promising rest and warmth, but the new voice, the one he recognized, begged him to stay—to face the cold, to fight through pain.

He drifted up toward the first voice, then back down as the second called again. Cold and pain. Why should he face those, when life could be simpler—pleasant, restful?

"Don't leave me alone." Moisture fell on his cheeks— or the cheeks of the body he used to claim. Warm lips parted over his, breathed into his mouth.

And he could feel it—feel everything—the love, the determination…and the pain that awaited him if he chose this path.

Cold. Pain. Life…with Geysa.

With a shudder, he fell back into his body and sucked in a heavy breath.

Chapter 21

Geysa felt Venge move in her arms, his chest expanding with a loud breath as he broke the string of power Jora had hooked into his soul. Geysa smoothed her hands over his cheeks, wiping away the tears that streaked his face—her tears.

His eyes opened and he stared up at her. She held her breath, waiting. She'd never known of someone rejecting the call of a Valkyrie…or coming back to life when they'd been so close to death.

Who was inside the body she held in her arms? Venge? Or the beast who had almost killed her?

Then he smiled, and Geysa's lips tilted in return. She leaned down and pressed her mouth to his, gentle…afraid. But he ran his fingers through her hair and pinned her mouth to his, capturing her lips with a kiss so bold and strong she forgot how close he had been to death.

"I won't leave you," he murmured, his lips still brushing hers.

"Ever?" she asked.

"Ever," he said.

"He can't come to Valhalla. Not like this." Jora strode forward, her lips pulled to the side—disapproving, but in her eyes Geysa saw something…. Envy?

"I know," Geysa replied. She looked back down at Venge. "I think I found my wings."

Her aunt frowned, her face growing sad, but she gave a short nod. "Don't get lost in the wind." Then she turned and left.

Sigurd stepped into the dark bar. The Valkyries had left the day before, taking Runa, still as their prisoner, with them. Risk and Kelly had left before that, right after Runa had informed Risk he was to be a father within the hour. Leaving Sigurd alone to plan what came next in his life, in his quest to find the hellhounds once bound to Lusse and secure their freedom—from whatever powers that tried to bind them.

A door behind the bar creaked; Venge, his bag of weapons in his hand, stepped through.

Suddenly tired, Sigurd pulled out a chair and sat. "I thought you had left with the others."

"What others? The hellhounds who followed me to the hunt haven't returned, and those who didn't make the cut never came back here." Something flickered in Venge's eyes. Guilt?

"They made their own choices," Sigurd replied.

"Didn't we all?" Venge plopped the bag onto a table between them. "You were behind all the attacks on me, provided all the weapons, didn't you?"

"Yes." Sigurd wouldn't apologize. He'd had reasons for

what he had done, but he also understood Venge's need to search him out—to exact revenge.

Venge leaned down, place one palm flat next to his bag on the table. "I have something for you."

"Do you?" Sigurd didn't bother glancing at the bag. He'd misjudged Venge, thought loving the Valkyrie would soften him, let him forgive if not forget the past they shared.

It had been five years since Sigurd had truly battled the younger hellhound. Could he best him in a fight now? Did it matter? If Venge, who had found someone who loved him, couldn't let go of the past, how could Sigurd expect any of the hellhounds to move on, be free? Perhaps his entire mission was a waste of blood, sweat and effort.

With a silent sigh, he began to push himself up. The sound of metal clinking onto the table stopped him. Lying on the table, coiled into an innocent-looking pile, was a thick silver chain. Startled, Sigurd's gaze flew to Venge's neck. It was bare.

"The witch—?"

Venge pulled his hand from the bag. Wrapped around one finger was a thin metal wire. "Elvin," he replied. "I thought you might have a use for it."

Sigurd held out his hand. The wire wound from Venge's finger to Sigurd's almost as if it were alive and knew its ownership had been transferred.

"How…?" Sigurd studied the delicate thread of metal spiraling around his index finger.

"Just touch it to the chain, and it will do the rest." Venge picked up the chain he'd laid on the table and turned to leave.

"That simple?" Sigurd muttered.

Venge stopped, his eyes serious. "It's never that simple, is it?" Then he shimmered.

Sigurd sat for a moment, staring at the wire. Despite his

plans to free the other hellhounds in his pack, he'd given little thought to freeing himself, to removing the last claim Lusse had on him.

Holding a breath, he slowly lifted the wire and lightly tapped the chain around his neck. For a second nothing happened, then the wire came to life, slithering from his finger to the chain, wrapping around it and convulsing like a crazed boa constrictor. With a snap, one link, then a second, broke, and the chain tumbled from his neck into his lap.

Free. He was free.

Two weeks later...

"I shouldn't be here." Venge stared at the simple wooden door in front of them.

Geysa wrapped her hand around his arm and tugged him forward. "Too late. I already knocked."

"It's never too late." Venge began to shimmer. As he did, the door flew open.

Kelly stood on the other side, a white cloth tossed over her shoulder and a harried look in her eyes. "Why did you knock? He never sleeps. Don't knock." From behind her, a cry pierced the air. "Crap. He's awake again." She spun on the ball of her foot and tromped into the house.

Not waiting for Venge, Geysa hurried to catch the witch. Squaring his jaw, Venge followed.

Still moving forward, Kelly yelled over her shoulder. "Risk and Kara aren't here. Risk took her...somewhere. And, like an idiot, I agreed to watch my nephew." She stopped at a second door and paused to take a breath, her palm pressed against the wood. "I swear the hounds of the hunt have nothing on this kid," she muttered.

The cry sounded again. A shiver shook Kelly's frame.

"Shouldn't you—" Geysa began, but Kelly held up a hand.

"He's fine. Trust me, he'll be better if I'm calm when I go in there."

"We should go." Venge, grinding to a halt next to Geysa, grabbed her by the hand and prepared to shimmer.

Kelly spun. "No, you don't. You aren't leaving me here alone." Her eyes narrowed, she looked at Geysa. "You're a Valkyrie, right? Maybe you can do that shield thing, calm him down, get him to sleep."

Geysa blanched, but before she could reply, the crying stopped.

Kelly twisted back toward the door, then glanced at Venge and Geysa over her shoulder. "That's good, right? You don't think I should check on him, do you? Because if I do, he might wake up again, and, well…"

Silently, the door swung open. Framed in the doorway, a tiny bundle nestled in her arms, stood Kelly's twin. "Well, what?" she asked, but her lips curved into a smile as she glanced at the baby. "I told your daddy Aunt Kelly wasn't ready for a whole hour alone with you, Kristian."

"A whole hour." Risk walked up behind Kara. He stopped when his gaze hit Venge. Venge felt himself stiffen in response. He didn't belong here—shouldn't have let Geysa talk him into coming.

"At least I tried." Kelly shoved a handful of hair back from her face. "You run if he so much as wrinkles his nose."

Risk's face snapped toward his sister-in-law. "I do not run."

"So…" Kara stepped forward. "You—" she smiled at Venge "—must be Venge, and…" She switched her attention to Geysa. "Geysa?"

Venge froze. He wasn't used to social chitchat, didn't

know how to respond to the witch's encouraging question. He glanced at his father. Risk stared back at him, his emotions impossible to read or smell. Venge waited, the gift he'd brought his new, tiny half brother clenched in his fist.

The air thickened around them; everyone waited for someone else to make the first move. Finally, Geysa nudged Venge in the side. He jerked, then glanced down at her.

"Give them what you brought," she said, her eyes filled with support.

Venge frowned and shook his head. "No, it wasn't a good idea."

"What? Oh!" Kara reached out to touch the silver chain dangling from Venge's fist. "Is this...?" She glanced at her husband.

Risk stepped forward. "Lusse's chain. You removed it?"

The length of gleaming silver hung between the two hellhounds like a line neither was sure they could cross.

The chain felt unnaturally heavy, pulling at Venge's hand. He ignored the sensation, concentrated on saying what he'd come to say. "I'd had the tools for a while, but I hadn't—" his gaze shifted to his father "—been ready."

Risk nodded. "But now you are?"

Venge glanced from his father to Geysa, then the baby. A weight seemed to lift off of him. "I guess I am."

"Then that's the best present Kristian could ever get." Kara pulled the blanket away from the baby's face, and tilted him upright so he could see the silver chain swinging from Venge's fist. His eyes, huge in his tiny face, studied the swaying metal with unnatural solemnity.

Risk extended his hand and Venge released the links one by one, letting go of a little piece of his past as he did. As the chain spiraled onto his palm, Risk added, "The best present for all of us."

The moment extended, Venge and Risk both staring at the pile of chain.

Suddenly, Kelly stepped back, knocking into a baby swing and sending it clacking. Everyone jumped; the females let out relieved breaths, and Venge and Risk both looked around the room, avoiding eye contact with anyone.

As the swing slowed to a stop, Kelly jerked the cloth off her shoulder and twisted it in her hands. "I should get back to the bar. You all need…" Her glance darted around the group. "I should go."

Remembering Geysa's gift, Venge squeezed her arm. The Valkyrie who had given him so much, saved him from himself, held up a shaking "wait a minute" finger, then began working nervously at the tie of the silken bag she had carried with her. Finally the cords loosened and Geysa reached her hand inside. With reverent care she pulled a glowing orb from the sack. Instantly the room filled with warm light.

"What is it?" Kara asked, her voice low.

Geysa licked her lips, the crack in her voice giving away her nervousness. "Kristian's destiny. I can't guarantee that it's all good, but it feels like it is, doesn't it?" She glanced at Venge; he gave her arm another squeeze for assurance and nodded for her to go on.

Geysa turned back to Kara. "My sister's the Norn. At least we always thought of her that way, and me…well, she was supposed to bring this to Kristian, but she's still being held by the Valkyries. And she asked me to bring it in her place. Is that all right?"

Venge could feel Geysa's unease, the pain she would feel if Risk or Kara denied her gift.

Kara took a step closer. "Why don't you ask Kristian?" Her eyes glimmering, Geysa held the shining orb over the baby. His huge eyes latched onto the ball and his body stilled. Then, slowly, with no apparent guidance from Geysa, the orb rolled off her hand and tumbled onto the waiting child.

Everyone gasped and Venge moved instinctively to stop the ball from striking the infant, but, as soon as the orb reached Kristian, it flattened, conforming to the shape of his body, and just as quickly, it was gone, seeming to slip through his pores. For a few seconds, the baby didn't move, then with a loud sigh, he smiled and his body glowed from within.

"Oh." Kara ran a hand down her son's face as if assuring herself he was intact. Then she grabbed Geysa with one arm and pulled her into a hug. "Thank you. We may not know exactly what his destiny is, but at least now we know he has one—and with this family it has to be for big things."

Glancing around the group and feeling the love contained in the small space, Venge had to agree.

* * * * *

SCOTTISH BORDERS COUNCIL

LIBRARY &

INFORMATION SERVICES

*Mills & Boon® Intrigue brings you
a sneak preview of…*

Delores Fossen's Expecting Trouble

*Special agent Cal Rico lives by the rules. He would
never get involved with someone he has sworn to
protect, which is why it comes as a shock that Texas
heiress Jenna Laniere would name him as the father of
her baby. With an assassin hot on Jenna's trail, though,
and Cal falling hard for both mother and daughter, he
faces his most important
assignment yet.*

Don't miss the thrilling third story in the new
TEXAS PATERNITY: BOOTS AND BOOTIES
*mini-series, available next month from
Mills & Boon® Intrigue.*

Expecting Trouble
by
Delores Fossen

A deafening blast shook the rickety hotel and stopped
Jenna cold.

With her heart in her throat, Jenna raced to the
window and looked down at the street below. Or rather
what was left of the street, a gaping hole. Someone had
set shops on fire. Black coils of smoke rose, smearing
the late afternoon sky.

"Ohmygod," Jenna mumbled.

There was no chance a taxi could get to her now to
take her to the airport. And worse were rebel soldiers,
at least a dozen of them dressed in dark green uniforms.
She'd heard about them on the news and knew they had
caused havoc in Monte de Leon. That's why by now
she'd hoped to be out of the hotel, and the small South
American country. She hadn't succeeded because she'd
been waiting on a taxi for eight hours.

One of the soldiers looked up at her and took aim
with his scoped rifle. Choking back a scream, Jenna
dropped to the floor just as the bullet slammed through
the window.

She scurried across the threadbare rug and into the bathroom. It smelled of mold, rust and other odors she didn't want to identify, and Jenna wasn't surprised to see roaches race across the cracked tile. It was a far cry from the nearby Tolivar estate where she'd spent the past two days. Of course, there'd been insects of a different kind there.

Paul Tolivar.

Staying close to the wall, Jenna pulled off one of her red heels so she could use it as a weapon and climbed into the bathtub to wait for whatever was about to happen.

She didn't have to wait long.

There was a scraping noise just outside the window. She pulled in her breath and waited. Praying. She hadn't even made it to the please-get-me-out-of-this part when she heard a crash of glass and the thud of someone landing on the floor.

"I'm Special Agent Cal Rico," a man called out. "U.S. International Security Agency. I'm here to rescue you."

A rescue? Or maybe this was a trick by one of the rebels to draw her out. Jenna heard him take a step closer, and that single step caused her pulse to pound in her ears.

"I know you're here," he continued, his voice calm. "I pinpointed you with thermal equipment."

The first thing she saw was her visitor's handgun. It was lethal-looking. As was his face. Lean, strong. He had an equally strong jaw. Olive skin that hinted at either Hispanic or Italian DNA. Mahogany-brown hair and sizzling steel-blue eyes that were narrowed and focused.

He was over six feet tall and wore all black, with various weapons and equipment strapped onto his chest, waist and thighs. He looked like the answer to her un-finished prayer.

Or a P.S. to her nightmare.

"We need to move now," he insisted.

Jenna didn't question that, but she still wasn't sure what she intended to do. Yes, she was afraid, but she wasn't stupid. "Can I trust you?"

Amusement leapt through his eyes. His reaction was brief, lasting barely a second before he nodded. And that was apparently all the reassurance he intended to give her. He latched on to her arm and hauled her from the tub. He allowed her just enough time to put back on her shoe before he maneuvered her out of the bathroom and toward the door to her hotel room.

"Extraction in progress, Hollywood," he whispered into a black thumb-size communicator on the collar of his shirt. "ETA for rendezvous is six minutes."

Six minutes. Not long at all. Jenna latched on to that info like a lifeline. If this lethal-looking James Bond could deliver what he promised, she'd be safe soon. Of course, with all those rebel soldiers outside, that was a big *if.*

Cal Rico paused at the door, listening, and eased it open. After a split-second glance down the hall, he got them out of the room and down a flight of stairs that took them to the back entrance on the bottom floor. Again, he looked out, but he must not have liked what he saw. He put his finger to his lips, telling her to stay quiet.

Outside, Jenna could still hear the battery of gunfire

and the footsteps of the rebels. They seemed to be moving right past the hotel. She was in the middle of a battle zone.

How much her life had changed in two days. This should have been a weekend trip to Paul's Monte de Leon estate. A prelude to taking their relationship from friendship to something more. Instead, it'd become a terrifying ordeal she might not survive.

Jenna tried not to let fear take hold of her, but adrenaline was screaming for her to run. To do something. *Anything*. It was a powerful, overwhelming sensation. Fight or flight. Even if either of those options could get her killed.

Cal Rico touched his fingers to her lips. "Your teeth are chattering," he mouthed.

No surprise there. She didn't have a lot of coping mechanisms for dealing with this level of stress. Who did? Well, other than the guy next to her.

"Try doing some math," he whispered. "Or recite the Gettysburg Address. It'll help keep you calm."

Jenna didn't quite buy that. Still, she tried.

He moved back slightly. But not before she caught his scent. Sweat mixed with deodorant soap and the faint smell of the leather from his combat boots. It was far more pleasant than it should have been.

Stunned and annoyed with her reaction, Jenna cursed herself. Here she was, close to dying, only hours out of a really bad relationship, and her body was already reminding her that Agent Cal Rico smelled pleasant. Heaven help her. She was obviously a candidate for therapy.

"I'll do everything within my power to get you out of here," he whispered. "That's a promise."

Jenna stared at him, trying to figure out if he was lying. No sign of that. Just pure undiluted confidence. And much to her surprise, she believed him. It was probably a reaction to the testosterone fantasy he was weaving around her. But she latched on to his promise.

"All clear," he said before they started to move again.

They hurried out the door and into the alley that divided the hotel from another building. Cal never even paused. He broke into a run and made sure she kept up with him. He made a beeline for a deserted cantina. They ducked inside, and he pulled her to the floor.

"We're at the rendezvous point," he said into his communicator. "How soon before you can pick up Ms. Laniere?" A few seconds passed before he relayed to her, "A half hour."

That was an eternity with the battle raging only yards away. "We'll be safe here?" Jenna tried not to make it sound like a question.

"Safe enough, considering."

"How did you even know I was in that hotel?"

Cal shifted his position so he could keep watch out the window. "Intel report."

"There was an intelligence report about me?" But she didn't wait for him to answer. "Who are you? Not your name. I got that. But why are you here?"

He shrugged as if the answer were obvious. "I'm a special agent with International Security Agency—the ISA. I've been monitoring you since you arrived in Monte de Leon."

Still not understanding, she shook her head. "Why?"

"Because of your boyfriend, Paul Tolivar. He is bad news. A criminal under investigation."

Judas Priest. This was about Paul. Who else?

"My ex-boyfriend," she corrected. "And I wish I'd known he was bad news before I flew down here."

Maybe it was because she was staring craters into him, but Agent Rico finally looked at her. Their gazes met. And held.

"I don't suppose someone could have told me he was under investigation?" she demanded.

He was about to shrug again, but she held tight to his shoulder. "We couldn't risk telling you because you might have told Paul."

Special Agent Rico might have added more, if there hadn't been an earsplitting explosion just up the street. It sent an angry spray of dirt and glass right at them. He reacted fast. He shoved her to the floor, and covered her body with his. Protecting her.

They waited. He was on top of her, with his rock-solid abs right against her stomach and one of his legs wedged between hers. Other parts of them were aligned as well.

His chest against her breasts. Squishing them.

The man was solid everywhere. Probably not an ounce of body fat. She'd never really considered that an asset, but she did now. Maybe all that strength would get them out of this alive.

© Delores Fossen 2009

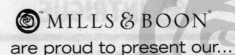

MILLS & BOON

are proud to present our...

Book of the Month

Pure Princess, Bartered Bride
by Caitlin Crews
from Mills & Boon® Modern™

Luc Garnier has secured the ultimate prize –
Princess Gabrielle – a pearl beyond measure.
But will Luc be able to break through her
defences to make this not just a marriage
on paper, but of the flesh?

Mills & Boon® Modern™
Available 15th January

Something to say about our
Book of the Month?
Tell us what you think!
millsandboon.co.uk/community

INTRIGUE

Coming next month

2-IN-1 ANTHOLOGY

EXPECTING TROUBLE by Delores Fossen

Special agent Cal lives by the rules. He would never get
involved with someone he has sworn to protect. That is, until
heiress Jenna names him as the father of her baby!

PRINCE CHARMING FOR 1 NIGHT by Nina Bruhns

Lawyer Conner needs down-on-her-luck dancer Vera as bait
to catch a thief. But could a crash course in social graces
turn Vera into the woman of his dreams?

2-IN-1 ANTHOLOGY

NATURAL-BORN PROTECTOR by Carla Cassidy

Melody has returned to her home town following her sister's
murder. Tough single dad Hank is determined to keep
Melody safe – as her bodyguard *and so much more...*

SAVED BY THE MONARCH by Dana Marton

Judi once refused an arranged marriage to sexy prince Miklos.
Yet when the pair are kidnapped, he is determined to save
her life and win her heart in the bargain!

SINGLE TITLE

VANISHED by Maureen Child

Nocturne™

After his destined mate abandoned him Rogan had no use
for desire. When mortal Allison inspires his passion he's
bewildered. Could she be his *real* true love?

On sale 19th February 2010

Available at WHSmith, Tesco, ASDA, Eason and all good bookshops.
For full Mills & Boon range including eBooks visit
www.millsandboon.co.uk

0210/46b

INTRIGUE

Coming next month

2-IN-1 ANTHOLOGY

THE COLONEL'S WIDOW? by Mallory Kane

Two years ago Air Force officer Rook faked his own death to protect his beloved wife Irina from terrorists. Now he's back and determined to regain her trust – and her love.

CAVANAUGH PRIDE by Marie Ferrarella

When Julianna is sent to help hunt a killer, detective Frank can't deny his attraction towards her. But will professional Julianna let passion come before the case?

SINGLE TITLE

SECOND CHANCE COWBOY
by BJ Daniels

Cowboy Hank is determined to find Arlene's missing daughter and soon they are both discovering that it's never too late to fall in love!

SINGLE TITLE

SENTINELS: JAGUAR NIGHT
by Doranna Durgin
Nocturne™

Shapeshifter Dolan needs to stop a deadly manuscript getting into the wrong hands. But wild loner Meghan has the book. Can he win her over to his cause and his heart?

On sale 5th March 2010

Available at WHSmith, Tesco, ASDA, Eason and all good bookshops.
For full Mills & Boon range including eBooks visit
www.millsandboon.co.uk

2 FREE BOOKS
AND A SURPRISE GIFT

We would like to take this opportunity to thank you for reading this Mills & Boon® book by offering you the chance to take TWO more specially selected books from the Intrigue series absolutely FREE! We're also making this offer to introduce you to the benefits of the Mills & Boon® Book Club™—

- **FREE home delivery**
- **FREE gifts and competitions**
- **FREE monthly Newsletter**
- **Exclusive Mills & Boon Book Club offers**
- **Books available before they're in the shops**

Accepting these FREE books and gift places you under no obligation to buy, you may cancel at any time, even after receiving your free books. Simply complete your details below and return the entire page to the address below. You don't even need a stamp!

YES Please send me 2 free Intrigue books and a surprise gift. I understand that unless you hear from me, I will receive 5 superb new stories every month, including two 2-in-1 books priced at £4.99 each and a single book priced at £3.19, postage and packing free. I am under no obligation to purchase any books and may cancel my subscription at any time. The free books and gift will be mine to keep in any case.

Ms/Mrs/Miss/Mr _____ Initials _____

Surname _____

Address _____

_____

_____ Postcode _____

Send this whole page to: Mills & Boon Book Club, Free Book Offer, FREEPOST NAT 10298, Richmond, TW9 1BR

Offer valid in UK only and is not available to current Mills & Boon Book Club subscribers to this series. Overseas and Eire please write for details.. We reserve the right to refuse an application and applicants must be aged 18 years or over. Only one application per household. Terms and prices subject to change without notice. Offer expires 30th April 2010. As a result of this application, you may receive offers from Harlequin Mills & Boon and other carefully selected companies. If you would prefer not to share in this opportunity please write to The Data Manager, PO Box 676, Richmond, TW9 1WU.

Mills & Boon® is a registered trademark owned by Harlequin Mills & Boon Limited.
The Mills & Boon® Book Club™ is being used as a trademark.